KU-516-337

THE RITUAL BATH

Violence has erupted in the yeshiva. Not the usual unpleasant anti-semitic vandalism – but rape. This Orthodox Jewish community is isolated and highly suspicious of outsiders, Peter Decker knows that investigating this case won't be easy. He's right.

Attractive young widow Rina Lazarus tries to guide him through the religious practices of the community and help him build a case.

Rina and Decker try to fight their growing attraction for one another as time runs out in their search for the attacker who is putting the yeshiva community at risk.

530662   *F

KELLERMAN, F.

THE RITUAL BATH

About the author

Faye Kellerman is not only a gifted storyteller but a dentist, an expert fencer, a musician who plays four instruments, a guitar-maker – and the mother of three young children. She is married to psychologist/author Jonathan Kellerman, and they live in Los Angeles. Her second novel SACRED AND PROFANE continues the adventures of Rina Lazarus and Peter Decker.

THE RITUAL BATH

Faye Kellerman

CORONET BOOKS
Hodder and Stoughton

530662

Copyright © 1986 by Faye Kellerman

The characters and situations in this book are entirely imaginary and bear no relation to any real person or actual happening.

First published in Great Britain in 1987 by William Collins Sons & Co Ltd

Coronet Crime edition 1989

This book is sold subject to the condition that it shall not, by way of trade or otherwise, be lent, re-sold, hired out or otherwise circulated without the publisher's prior consent in any form of binding or cover other than that in which it is published and without a similar condition including this condition being imposed on the subsequent purchaser.

No part of this publication may be reproduced or transmitted in any form or by any means, electronically or mechanically, including photocopying, recording in any information storage or retrieval system, without either the prior permission in writing from the publisher or a licence, permitting restricted copying. In the United Kingdom such licences are issued by the Copyright Licensing Agency, 33–34 Alfred Place, London WC1E 7DP.

British Library C.I.P.

Kellerman, Faye
   The ritual bath.
   I. Title
   813'.54[F]

ISBN 0-340-48767-4

Printed and bound in Great Britain for Hodder and Stoughton Paperbacks, a division of Hodder and Stoughton Ltd., Mill Road, Dunton Green, Sevenoaks, Kent TN13 2YA (Editorial Office: 47 Bedford Square, London WC1B 3DP) by Cox & Wyman Limited, Reading, Berks. Photoset by Centracet

For Jonathan. Ani l'dodi v'dodi li.
And for the munchkins: Jesse, Rachel, and Ilana.

1

"The key to a *good* potato kugel is good potatoes," Sarah Libba shouted over the noise of the blow dryer. "The key to a *great* potato kugel is the amount of oil. You have to use just enough oil to make the batter moist, plus a little excess to leak out around the cake pan and fry the edges to make the whole thing nice and crisp without being too greasy."

Rina nodded and folded a towel. If anyone would know how to cook a potato kugel, it was Sarah Libba. The woman could roast a shoe and turn it into a delicacy. But tonight Rina was too fatigued to listen with a full ear. It was already close to ten o'clock, and she still had to clean the mikvah, then grade thirty papers.

It had been a busy evening because of the bride. A lot of to-do, hand-holding, and explaining. The young girl had been very nervous, but who wouldn't be about marriage? Rivki was barely seventeen with little knowledge of the world around her. Sheltered and exquisitely shy, she'd gotten engaged to Baruch after three dates. But Rina thought it was a good match. Baruch was a good student and kind and very *patient*. He'd never once lost his temper while teaching Shmuel how to ride a two-wheeler. He'd be calm yet encouraging, Rina decided, and it wouldn't be long before Rivki knew the ropes just like the rest of them.

Sarah shut off the dryer, and the motor belched a final wheeze. Fluffing up her close-cropped hair, she sighed and placed a wig atop her head. The nylon tresses were ebony and long, falling past Sarah Libba's slender shoulders. She was a pretty woman with wide brown eyes that lit up a round, friendly face. And short, not more than five feet, with a slim figure that belied the fact that she'd borne four children. Meticulous in dress and habit, she worked methodically, combing and styling the artificial black strands.

"Here," Rina said. "Let me help you with the back."

Sarah smiled. "Know what inspired me to buy this *shaytel*?"

Rina shook her head.

'*Your* hair, Rina," said Sarah. "It's getting so long."

"I know. Chana's already mentioned it to me."

"Are you going to cut it?"

"Probably."

"Not too short I hope."

Rina shrugged. Her hair was one of her best features. Her mother had raised a commotion when she'd announced her plans to cover it after marriage. Of all the religious obligations that Rina had decided to take on, the covering of her hair was the one that displeased her mother the most. But she forged ahead over her mother's protests, clipped her hair short, and hid it under a wig or scarf. Now, of course, the point was moot.

Working quickly and with self-assurance, Rina turned the wig into a fashionable style. Sarah Libba craned her neck to see the back in the mirror, then smiled.

"It's lovely," she said patting Rina's hand.

"I've got a lot to work with," said Rina. "It's a good *shaytel*."

"It should be," Sarah said. "It cost nearly three hundred dollars, and that's for only twenty percent human hair."

"You'd never know."

The other woman frowned.

"Don't cut your hair short, Rina, despite what Chana tells you. She has a load of advice for everyone but herself. We had the family over for Shabbos and her kids

2

were monsters. They broke Chaim's Transformer, and do you think she offered a word of apology?'

"Nothing, huh?"

"Nothing! The boys are *vilde chayas*, and the girls aren't much better. For someone who runs everyone else's life, she sure doesn't do too well with her own."

Rina said nothing. She wasn't much of a gossip, not only because of the strict prohibitions against it, but because she found it personally distasteful. She preferred to keep her opinions to herself.

Sarah didn't prolong the one-way conversation. She stood up, walked over to the full-length mirror, and preened.

"This time alone is my only respite," she said. "It makes me feel human again."

Rina nodded sympathetically.

"The kids will probably all be up when I get home," the tiny woman sighed. "And Zvi is learning late tonight . . . I think I'll walk home very slowly. Enjoy the fresh air."

"That's a good idea," Rina said, smiling.

Sarah trudged to the door, turned the knob, straightened her stance, and left.

Alone at last, Rina stood up, stretched, and glanced at her watch again. Her own boys were still at the Computer Club. Steve would walk them home to a waiting babysitter so there was no need to rush. She could take her time. Removing her shoes, she rubbed her feet, slipped them into knitted socks and shuffled along the gleaming white tile. Loaded down with a bucket full of soapy water, a handful of rags, and a pail of supplies, she entered the hallway leading to the two bathrooms.

The first one had been used by Sarah Libba, who'd left it neat and orderly. The towels and sheet were compulsively folded upon the tiled counter, the bath mat draped over the rim of the bathtub, and care had been taken to remove the hairs from the comb and brush.

Rina quickly went to work, scrubbing the floor, tub, wash basin, and shower. She refilled the soap containers, the Q-tips holder, the cotton ball dispenser, recapped the toothpaste, and placed the comb in a vial of disinfectant. After giving the counter tops a thorough going-over, she left the room, taking the garbage and the dirty laundry with her.

The second bathroom was in complete disarray, but within a short period of time, it was as spotless as the first.

She dumped the garbage down a chute that emptied into a bin outside and loaded the towels, sheets, and washcloths into a large utility washer in the closet. Now for the mikvot themselves.

The main mikvah – the women's – was a sunken Roman bath four feet deep and seven feet square, covered with sparkling, deep blue tile. To aid the women in climbing down the eight steps, a hand rail had been installed. Religious law prescribed that the water in the bath emanate from a natural source – rain, snow, ice – but the crystalline pool was heated for comfort.

What a beautiful mikvah, Rina thought, so unlike the one she'd used in an emergency six years ago. They'd been visiting Yitzchak's parents in Brooklyn. It had been winter-time and blizzard warnings were out. The closet mikvah was nothing more than a hole of filthy, freezing water, but she'd held her breath and forced herself to dunk anyway. She'd felt contaminated when she got home. Though bathing wasn't permissible after the ritual immersion, Yitzchak had looked the other way when she soaked her chilled bones in steaming water to clean off the scummy residue left on her skin.

The wives of the men at the yeshiva had been very vocal about constructing a clean mikvah – one that would make a woman proud to observe the laws of family purity. And they'd gotten their way. The tile used for the mikvah and bathroom counter tops was handpicked and imported from Italy. As an extra touch, a beauty area was added, complete with two vanity tables fully equipped with dryers, combs, brushes, curling irons, and make-up mirrors. An architect was hired, the construction progressed rapidly, and now the yeshiva had a mikvah to call its own. No longer would the women have to travel hours to do the mitzvah of *Taharat Hamishpacha* – spiritual cleansing through dunking in the ritual bath.

Rina mopped the excess water off the floor, then turned off the heat and lights. She padded down the hall-way, took out a key and went inside the men's mikvah. It was comparatively unadorned, layered with plain white tile. The men had refused to heat or filter the water, but the Rosh Yeshiva was very insistent that they keep the place clean. Though she didn't have to, she mopped the floor as a courtesy.

When that was done, she relocked the door and finished off by cleaning the last pool – a small basin for dunking cooking and eating utensils made out of metal. A frying pan lay at the bottom. Ruthie Zipperstein must have left it when she had dunked her cookware. Rina would drop it off on her way home.

She dried her hands, then went back to the reception room and sat down in an old overstuffed chair. Taking out a stack of papers, she began to grade them to the low hum of the washing machine. She'd gone through half the pile when the cycle finished. As she got up to load the dryer she heard a shriek that startled her.

Cats, she thought. The grounds of the yeshiva were inundated with them. Scrawny felines that made horrible human-like cries, scaring her sons in the middle of the night. She slammed the door to the dryer and was about to turn on the motor when she heard the shriek again. Walking over to the door, she leaned her ear against the soft pine. She could hear something rustling in the brush, but that wasn't unusual, either. The yeshiva was situated in a rural area and surrounded by forest. The tall trees sheltered a variety of scurrying animals – jackrabbits, deer, squirrels, snakes, lizards, an occasional coyote, and of course, the cats. Still, she began to get spooked.

5

Turning the knob, Rina opened the door partway and peered into the blackness. A stream of hot air hit her in the face. The sky was star-studded but moonless. She heard nothing at first, then against a background chorus of chirping crickets, the sound of muffled panting. She opened the door a little wider, and a beam of indoor light streaked across the dry, dusty ground.

"Hello?" she called out tentatively.

Silence.

"Is anyone out there?" she tried again.

Out of the corner of her eye, she caught sight of a fleeing figure that disappeared into the thickly wooded hillside. A large animal, she thought at first, but then realized the figure had been upright.

She stood motionless for a brief moment and listened. Did she hear the panting again or was her overactive imagination at work? Shrugging, she was about to close the door when she was seized by panic. On the ground in front of her lay Sarah's wig, the black tresses tangled and matted.

"Sarah?' she yelled.

The only response was the panting.

She picked up the wig and examined it with shaking hands. Then, very cautiously, she ventured toward the surrounding thickets, moving closer and closer to the sound.

"Sarah, are you out there?" she shouted.

The panting grew louder.

The noise seemed to rise from a bowl-like depression in the heavily wooded area. She went in for a closr look and gasped in horror.

Sarah Libba was sprawled on the ground, caked with dirt. Her dress had been ripped into ribbons. Her small face was wet with ooze that ran down her cheeks and over her naked breast, her legs bare except for the underpants wrapped around her ankles and the sandals on her feet. Sarah's eyes bulged and convulsed in their sockets, her

6

breaths rapid and shallow. She was on the brink of hyperventilation.

Rina stumbled, caught her balance, then slowly bent down. Sarah cowered, retreating from her approach like a wounded animal. Kneeling down to eye level, Rina saw the fresh bruises on her face.

Sarah balled her hand into a fist and began to pound her breast forcefully. Her eyes entreated the heavens, and she moved her lips in silent supplication. Rina took the woman's arm and brought her to her feet.

For a small woman, Sarah was surprisingly heavy, and supporting her weight caused Rina to buckle. But somehow she managed to lead the bleating figure inch by inch back into the safe confines of the mikvah. Once inside, she had Sarah lie down. Gently removing the rent clothes, Rina wrapped her bruised and lacerated body in a freshly laundered sheet.

Rina's first call was to Sarah Libba's house. She left a message with the babysitter to find Sarah's husband, Zvi, in the study hall and tell him to come to the mikvah immediately. After that she phoned the Rosh Yeshiva. He, of course, was learning also, so she left the same message. Finally, she called the police.

2

Decker picked up the phone, and his mouth fell open as he scratched out the details in a small notebook. He knew the day just *had* to end up as lousy as it started out. First, it was Jan nagging him for more child support, then the entire day was wasted pursuing a dead-end lead on the Foothill rapist because of that call from the flaky broad. Now, as if things weren't bad enough, a rape at Jewtown.

Jesus, he thought, looking at the piles of paperwork on his desk. The weather gets hot, and the locals take to the streets. Plus, to beat the heat, the women dress scantier and scantier till some weirdo gets it in his head that "they're all asking for it anyway." God, he was sick of this detail. He'd considered transferring back to Homicide, tired of seeing rape survivors hung up to dry by a fucked-up – and misnamed – justice system. At least with Homicide the victims never had to face the perpetrators.

But a rape in Jewtown? Few locals, including himself, had ever set foot in the place. The grounds were gated and walled off, and the Jews kept themselves to themselves, rarely venturing into town except to shop at Safeway or maybe get a car fixed. They were different, but they never caused any trouble. Decker wished he had a city full of 'em. He wondered how God's chosen were going to deal with a rape and didn't look forward to getting the answer.

He glanced around and found Marge Dunn at the coffee pot. Walking over to the most popular spot in the room, he touched her lightly on the shoulder.

"I need you, babe."

She turned around, holding a steaming mug of coffee. Her big-boned frame made people think she was a lot older than her twenty-seven years, but that was okay with her. She liked the respect her height and weight brought her. Her face, in contrast, was soft – large bovine eyes and silky wisps of blond hair. She was an enviable combination of toughness and femininity.

"For you, Peter my love, anything."

"It's a dandy. A rape just went down at Jewtown."

Marge put her cup down. "You're kidding."

"No such luck.' Decker frowned, then chewed on his mustache. "Let's move it."

"Pete, why don't you let Hollander take the call?" She wiped a bead of sweat from her forehead. "We're already working overtime with the Foothill thing, and he's just come off vacation."

"I'd love to pass this one over to him, but he's at Dodger Stadium now."

"So beep the lazy butt."

"I don't believe in interrupting a ball game."

"How about interrupting a woman with a fresh cup of coffee?"

"Let's go."

Decker started for the door. Marge grabbed her purse and followed reluctantly. It was the usual pattern: he hot-dogging it, and she trying to slow down the big redhead. One thing about Peter, Marge thought, he was a good cop, smart and dedicated. But it worked against him. The brass constantly saddled him with all the rotten cases.

Together they left the station – a dilapidated stucco building, once white, now washed with grayish grime – and walked to the brightly lit parking lot. Flipping Marge the keys to a faded bronze '79 Plymouth, Decker scrunched into the passenger side and pushed the bench seat back to the maximum. Like a fucking sardine, he thought as his shin grazed the undersurface of the dash-board. One day the Department would have unmarkeds

9

that accommodated someone over six feet. When I'm ready to retire.

He rolled down the window. Jesus, it was hot. Decker could already feel moist circles under his armpits and rivulets of sweat running down his neck and back. He hiked up his shirt sleeves and leaned a thick, freckled arm out the window.

"Scorcher," Marge said. "Must be hell with your metabolism."

"I always know when we're about to get a heat wave," Decker moaned. "The air-conditioning goes out in the car a week before."

"A rape in Jewtown," Marge muttered. "I've always thought of the place as sacrosanct. Sort of like a convent. Who'd rape a nun?"

"Who'd rape, period?" Decker said.

"Good point."

Marge started the engine and eyed him. "You look exceptionally bad tonight, Peter."

"Thanks for the compliment."

Marge peeled rubber. "I sure hope this isn't the first in a string of Jew rapes."

Decker exhaled audibly, thinking the same thing. Some people had lots of animosity toward the Jews. Their place had been hit several times by vandals, but there hadn't been any violence against the people themselves. Not until tonight.

"Let's take it one step at a time, Marge. Maybe there'll be a logical explanation for the whole thing."

"I doubt it, Peter," she said. "There never is." She drove quickly and competently. "How're your horses?"

"I just got a pinto filly," he said, smiling. "A real cutie."

"How many are you up to now?"

"Lillian makes six."

"You must shovel lots of shit, Peter."

"True, but unlike the urban version, it's biodegradable." He lit a cigarette. "How's old Clarence?"

"Speaking of shit," Marge grumbled.

10

"Oh?"

"He forgot to tell me about the wife, the two kids, and the dog."

"The louse."

"Stop laughing. That's exactly what he was. As far as I'm concerned he's dead and buried. You're not up to date, Pete. My newest is Ernst. He's a concert violinist for the Glendale Philhamonic. We've played some nice flute-violin duets. When I get good enough, I'll invite you and the lucky date of your choice to a recital."

"I'd like that." He smiled at the image of the big woman playing such a delicate instrument. A cello would have seemed more in character. Not that she had any talent. The guy must really be hot for Marge, he thought, to put up with her playing, which Decker had always likened to a horny parrot's mating call. He couldn't understand how she could continue with music if her ears heard the same thing that his did. The only logical conclusion was that she was deaf and had maintained the secret all these years by artful lip reading.

Marge turned onto the 210 East, and the Plymouth grunted as it picked up speed.

Decker dragged on his cigarette, looked out the window, and surveyed his turf. Los Angeles conjured up all sorts of images, he thought: the tinsel and glitter of the movie industry, the lapping waves and beach bunnies of Malibu, decadent dope parties and extravagant shopping sprees in Beverly Hills. What it didn't conjure up was the terrain through which they were riding.

The area encompassing Foothill Division was the city's neglected child. It lacked the glamour of West L.A., the ethnicity of the east side, the funk of Venice beach, the suburban complacency of the Valley.

What it did have was lots of crime.

Bordering and surrounding other cities, each with a separate police department, Foothill's domain could best be described as a mixture of small, depressed towns segregated from each other by mountains and scrub.

11

Some of the pocket communities housed lower-class whites, biker gangs, and displaced cowboys, others were ghettos for blacks and migrant Hispanics, but most had a common denominator – poverty. People scratching by, people not getting by at all. Even Jewtown. These people weren't the wealthy Jews portrayed by the media. It was possible that the yeshiva held a secret cache of diamonds, but you'd never know it by looking at its inhabitants. They dressed cheaply, buying most of their clothes at Target or Zody's, and drove broken-down cars like the rest of the locals.

The station was twenty freeway minutes away from the yeshiva – a quick ride along a serpentine strip of road cut into the San Gabriel mountains. In the dark, the hillside lurked over the asphalt, casting giant shadows. The air in the canyon was hot and stagnant, but as the Plymouth sped along, a cool jet stream churned through the open windows.

"I'm glad you were available," Decker said. "You do a hell of an interview."

"Sensitivity, Peter. That's why I work so well with the kids in Juvey. Being a victim of life myself, I know how to talk to people who have been thoroughly fucked up. Like you, for instance."

Decker smiled and crushed the cigarette butt in the overflowing ash tray. "Is that an example of your sensitivity?"

"At its finest." Marge's face grew stern. "I'm not looking forward to this. The Jews don't relate well to outsiders."

"No, they don't," he agreed. "But rape survivors experience lots of common feelings. Maybe that'll supersede the xenophobic inclinations."

"Yes sir, Professor," said Marge, saluting. She pulled onto a winding turn-off ramp marked *Deep Canyon Thoroughfare, Deep Canyon*. The "thoroughfare" was a two-lane road blemished with dips and bumps. The

12

unmarked car bounced along for a mile, until the street turned into a newly paved four-lane stretch.

They cruised slowly for another mile, inspecting the street with cops' wariness. Scores of local kids were hanging out in front of the 7-Eleven, sitting on the hoods of souped-up cars while smoking and drinking. Their raucous laughter and curses sounded intermittently above ghetto-blasters wailing in the hot night air. While the teenagers filled themselves with Slurpees and Coke, their elders tanked up on Jim Beam or Old Grand Dad at the Goodtimes Tavern. The place was doing a bang-up business judging from the number of cars parked in the lot.

In front of the Adult Love bookstore, a group of bikers congregated, decked out in leather and metal. The ass-kickers leaned lazily against their gleaming choppers and stared at the unmarked as it drove by.

As they headed north the activity began to thin. They passed a scrap metal dealership, a building supply wholesaler, a discount supermarket, and a caravan of churches. Poor people were always attracted to God, Decker mused. The area was a natural for a yeshiva – except for the anti-Semitism.

The street narrowed and worked its way into the hillside, the landscape changing abruptly from urban to rural. Heavy thickets of brush and trees flanked the Plymouth, occasionally scraping its sides as it meandered through the mountains. Two miles farther was another turn-off, then the property line of Yeshivat Ohavei Torah.

Marge pulled the car onto a dirt clearing and parked. Decker stepped outside, took a deep breath, and stretched. The dry air singed his throat.

"Gate should be open," Marge said. "The place is all walled in, but they always leave the gate open."

"They've been vandalized at least twice and you can't get them to put a lock on the damn gate." Decker shook the wire fence. "This is just a psychological barrier, anyway. Wouldn't stop a serious intruder."

13

He pushed open the gate and walked inside. "Let's get on with it."

The grounds of the yeshiva were well tended but sparsely planted. A huge, flat expanse of lawn was surrounded by low brush and several flat-roofed buildings. Across the lawn, directly in their field of vision, was the largest – a two-story cube of cement. To its right were a stucco annex off the main building, a nest of tiny tract homes, and a gravel lot speckled with cars, to its left, two smaller bungalow-like structures. Behind the houses and buildings were dense woodlands rising to barren, mountainous terrain.

Decker gave the area a quick once-over. The rapist could have entered the grounds anywhere and exited into the backlands. They'd never be able to find him. Unless, of course, he was someone from the inside.

The two detectives walked on a dimly lit path that ran the length of the lawn.

"Where are we going, Peter?"

Decker looked around and saw two figures approaching. They were dressed in black pants, white long-sleeved shirts, and black hats. They must be dying in the heat, he thought. As they grew closer, he saw that both of the men were young – barely out of their teens – and thin, with short beards and glasses. They walked in a peculiar manner, clasping their hands behind their backs instead of swinging them naturally at their sides.

"Excuse me," Decker said, taking out his shield.

One of the men, the taller of the two, squinted and read the badge. "Yes, Detective? Is anything wrong?"

"Can you please direct us to the bathhouse?" Decker asked.

Both of the boys broke into laughter.

"I think you're in the wrong place," the shorter one said, smiling.

"Try Hollywood," the taller one suggested.

Decker was annoyed. "We received a report that an incident took place here, at the bathhouse."

14

"An incident?" said the short one in a grave voice. "You mean a criminal incident?"

"Do you think they mean the mikvah?" the taller one asked his friend, then turned to Decker: "You mean the mikvah?"

"Maybe you should direct us to this mikvah," Marge said.

"You can't go there now," the tall one said to Decker. "It's only open to women at this time of night."

The short one prodded him. "The *incident* obviously has to do with the mikvah." He looked at Decker and asked, "Was anyone hurt?"

"Stop asking them questions and answer theirs," his friend scolded, then said to Decker: "The mikvah is that little building in the corner."

"Thank you," Marge answered, walking away.

"I hope it's nothing serious," the big one added.

Decker gave them a smile, but not a reassuring one.

They walked a few steps, then Marge said, "Notice how they looked at me?"

"They didn't."

"That's what I'm saying."

They'd arrived before the black-and-whites.

Marge knocked on the door and a young dark-haired woman opened it, allowing them to enter after a flash of badges. Immediately, the murmuring that had filled the room died. The detectives were greeted with icy, suspicious stares from four kerchief-headed women crammed into the reception area. In the corner, an elderly bearded man who looked like a rabbi was whispering into the ear of a younger man who was rapidly rocking back and forth.

The young woman motioned them outside.

"I'm Rina Lazarus, the one who called the police," she said. "The women inside were here earlier tonight. We've called a meeting to find out if anyone heard or saw anything unusual on their way home. Unfortunately, no one did."

15

"What happened?" Decker asked.

She hesitated and looked around. "A woman was raped."

"Where is she?" Marge asked.

"With one of the women in a dressing room. She's about to take a bath – "

"She can't do that until she's been examined," said Marge sharply.

"I know," Rina said. "The officer I spoke to over the phone mentioned that, but I don't know if she's going to be willing to have herself examined."

Marge eyed Decker, then said: "I'll talk to her." Turning to Rina, she asked: "What's her name?"

"Sarah Libba Adler."

"Miss or Mrs?"

"Mrs."

"Is she dressed?" asked Marge.

"I'm not sure. Her husband brought her a change of clothes, but I don't know if she put them on yet. You'll have to knock on the door to the bathroom and ask."

"Where are the original clothes?" Decker asked.

"In a paper sack to the left of the bathhouse door. They're nothing more than shreds, but I thought you might want them."

"We do," Marge said. She slapped Peter on the back and disappeared inside.

Rina wasn't comfortable being alone with a man, even a detective, and suggested they go back inside. That was fine with Decker since the mikvah was air-conditioned. Then seeing two uniforms coming toward the building, Decker motioned them over. He excused himself for a moment, then brought the policemen back to Rina.

"Ma'am, do you know where the rape took place?" Decker asked.

"Over there." She pointed to an area two hundred feet to the right of the entrance to the bathhouse.

"Could you show us the exact spot so we don't accidentally trample on evidence?" asked Decker.

16

She led them to the depression in the brush.

"I don't know if he actually" – she paused to catch her breath – "if he actually raped her here, but this is where I found her."

"You found the victim?"

She nodded.

"Was she conscious at the time?"

"Yes. *Baruch Hashem*."

"Pardon?"

"Nothing. Mrs Adler was conscious."

"That's fine," Decker said. He faced the uniforms. "Cordon off this area and call the lab boys. Then poke around and see what you can come up with."

He turned back to Rina.

"I'd like to ask you a few questions."

"Can we go back inside the bathhouse?"

"Certainly."

Rina led him back into the building and to a quiet corner. He was a big man, she thought, with strong features and, despite the fair skin and ginger hair, dark penetrating eyes. He looked intimidating yet competent, a man who'd know how to hunt an animal like a rapist. Although she knew size had nothing to do with apprehending a criminal, she was still glad he was big.

"You told me your name, but I didn't catch it," said Decker.

"Rina Lazarus," she answered, then quickly added, "Mrs."

Decker smiled to himself.

"Exactly what happened, Mrs Lazarus?" he asked.

"I was grading papers right there" – Rina pointed to the armchair – "and I heard a scream. I went outside and saw something take off into the woods. Then, I found her wig lying on the ground and knew something was wrong . . ." Her voice trailed off, and she shuddered.

"You saw something fleeing into the brush?" he asked, slipping out a pocket pad.

She nodded.

17

"Where?"

"From the spot I showed you . . . Maybe a little farther down to the right."

"Did you see *something* or *someone?*"

"I'm not sure. It happened so fast." Rina sighed. "I'm sorry."

"That's okay. You're doing fine. Let's try taking it from the beginning. You're inside this mikvah . . . What's a mikvah, by the way? Like a health club?"

"It's a ritual bathhouse. Women come here to dunk for spiritual purification."

"Like a baptism?"

Rina nodded. It was close enough.

"Okay, you were inside and you heard a scream outside. What did you do?"

"I opened the door and looked outside. I heard panting."

"Panting?"

She nodded. "Next thing I knew something fled into the bushes." Her eyes lit up. "I think it was a person because it was upright."

"Could you describe any details at all?"

"No. It was nearly pitch black, and his clothing was dark. I only saw him for a second."

"Tall, short, fat, thin, muscular?"

"Average."

"Did the figure look shorter or taller than me?"

"Offhand, I'd say shorter than you" – she looked up at him – "but you're very tall, so I guess that isn't saying a lot." `

"But you think the figure was human."

She nodded.

"Could you tell if it was male or female?"

"No."

Decker began to scrawl some notes on the pad, then looked up: "Okay. After the figure disappeared, what did you do?"

Rina's eyes darted about. Several of the women were

staring at her, Chana in particular. Rina looked back at Decker and lowered her voice. "I saw Mrs Alder's wig. Then I found her in the bushes. Her clothes had been ripped off and she'd been . . ." Her eyes welled up with tears.

Decker liked this one. She had an intangible presence – a quiet elegance. And she didn't cover her hair with a kerchief like the others, allowing him a view of her thick, black mane. There was something classic about her face – the oval shape, creamy skin, full, soft mouth, startling blue eyes. Doll her up and she'd blend nicely into high society.

"It must have been quite a shock," he said, offering her a tissue.

She took it and wiped her cheeks. "To say the least. All of us are stunned. We're so closely identified with one another, and now we feel so vulnerable. It could have been anyone of us, especially me. I happened to run a little late tonight. She was attacked at the time I usually go home."

"Do you live on the grounds?"

"Of course."

"How do you usually get home?"

"I walk. It takes me five minutes."

"And no one has ever approached you?"

"Nobody, Detective. *Nobody*. We're isolated out here. I guess that makes us perfect victims for some lunatic, but it never occurred to us before. The mikvah door isn't even locked."

"You've been hit by vandals – "

"Mostly kids. Both we and the police know who they are. They're a nuisance, something we wish we didn't have to deal with, but we've never thought of them as . . . as rapists."

Decker thought a moment, then resumed the questioning.

"There's no lock on the door?"

"That's right."

19

"You mean women regularly come here to dunk in holy water in an unlocked building?"

She shrugged sheepishly.

"As I said, we've never thought about it."

"Do you have any security patrol on the grounds?"

Rina shook her head.

"This place is an anachronism, Mrs Lazarus. You're sitting ducks. It's amazing you've lasted this long without an assault. Call a locksmith tomorrow, and get a dead bolt on the door. And discuss with your neighbors the possibility of getting a wired fence and gate. Anyone can break through the one you have now and escape into the forest."

"It wouldn't work because on the Sabbath – " She stopped herself. He wouldn't understand.

Decker looked at her, expecting to hear more. Instead she cast a flurry of glances around the room.

A pretty one, he thought, but very jumpy. Then again, she was stressed. He wouldn't mind talking to her again in a couple of days if the occasion presented itself.

"Is that all?" Rina asked.

"Just about, for the moment. How do you spell your name, Mrs Lazarus?"

"R-i-n-a L-a-z-a-r-u-s."

"Age?"

"Twenty-six."

"Address?"

"Twenty-two Road C."

Marge interrupted their interview. Decker knew from the disheartened look on her face that it hadn't gone well.

"I got nowhere, Pete. She refuses to go in for the exam, and says she doesn't remember anything. She spent almost the entire time praying." She turned to Rina. "I'm not saying there's anything wrong with praying, but it won't help us find the man who raped her."

"Maybe she thinks it will," Rina said defensively.

Marge grimaced and turned to Decker.

"She still hasn't bathed, but the longer she waits – "

20

"The woman has been traumatized," Rina snapped. "You can't expect her to make split-second decisions."

Marge said nothing. Rape cases, especially ones with recalcitrant witnesses, got to her, but she was too good a cop to lose her cool. She took a deep breath and blew it out forcefully. Decker liked her control. And he knew that if Marge couldn't bring out this woman, no one in the division could. They needed help from the inside.

"Mrs Lazarus, you've been very helpful. And you seem like a very reasonable woman. You know we need Mrs Adler's cooperation if we want to catch this animal." Decker paused to let his words sink in. "If you were in our shoes, how'd you go about gaining it?"

Rina looked to her left and into Chana's scrutinizing eyes. She knew she'd spent too much time gabbing to the police.

"I can't give you any advice," she whispered. "But if I were you, I wouldn't bother trying to enlist Mrs Adler's help directly. I'd talk to that man in the corner."

"Is he the rabbi?" Decker asked.

Rina nodded. "He's the head rabbi – the *Rosh Yeshiva*, the director of this place. There are a lot of rabbis here. The man he's talking to is Mrs Adler's husband. Be patient and you might have some luck. I've got to go now."

Decker flipped out a business card and handed it to her. "If you happen to think of anything else, or hear anything interesting, that's my number."

Rina slipped it in her skirt pocket.

"How are you going to get home?" Marge asked.

"The women will walk with me."

"Would you like me to accompany you?" Marge asked. Part of the offer, Decker knew, was genuine concern for the women's safety; the other was an attempt to get a little more insight into the yeshiva.

"Thank you very much, but we'll be okay. Please be easy with Sarah. She's a lovely person, and a wonderful wife and mother."

21

3

"Shall we pay a visit to the man of the cloth?" asked Marge.

Decker tapped his foot. "I think the best way to go about this is a division of labor. You wait with Mrs Adler and make sure she doesn't wash away evidence, and I'll have a whirl with the rabbi."

Marge hadn't paid all those dues to be a babysitter, but she didn't protest the arrangement. She knew Pete had a better chance of getting somewhere if the two men spoke alone and reminded herself that Decker wasn't a sexist pig like some of the others.

"How are the uniforms doing in the bushes?" she asked.

"Might be a good idea if you found out."

Scouring the brush sounded more appealing to Marge than staring at a fanatical rape survivor. She'd pay a quick visit to the lady, then try her luck outside.

After Marge left, Decker eyed the husband and the rabbi. They hadn't moved since the detective entered the room half an hour ago. The younger man was still rocking, and the rabbi's mouth was still up against his ear.

He walked over to them. If they were aware of his presence, they gave no physical indication. But Decker was a patient man. He'd bide his time instead of storm-trooping it. It would take longer but was more likely to produce results. Which is what the job was all about.

Besides, it wasn't as if he had anything to rush home to. He'd fed and groomed the horses and left Ginger some hamburger earlier in the evening. Next to his daughter, the animals and the ranch were the loves of his life. There was no place like home in the daylight: the glow of the sun-drenched living room, the air pungent with the tangy smell of citrus from the groves, exercising the horses, working up a sweat. After the time he spent dealing with human slime, it made him feel clean.

But the nights he found lonely. He knew some women, and that helped, but the relief was short-lived. More and more he found himself coming back to the station after the sun went down. Such had been the case tonight.

Decker parked himself in the overstuffed armchair, the one that the Lazarus woman had sat in while she graded papers. So she was a teacher. Made sense. She dressed like a schoolmarm – collar buttoned up to the chin, long-sleeved blouse and below-the-knee A-line skirt. Of course, so did all the other women in the place. Even primmer.

But there was something about her that was different – more secular. Maybe it was her long, loose hair. He tried to imagine her out of the yeshiva context and dressed in more contemporary fashion. Tight pants and a clingy sweater. Then he shifted gears and visualized her in a string bikini, that thick black hair hanging down a smooth, slender back, skin deeply bronzed, her ass slightly falling out of the panty bottoms as she waded in the water. He'd bet she had a nice ass under all that camouflage.

He reveled in his fantasies, then snapped himself out of it. She was religious and *married*. Shit. When he'd been married, it had seemed as if the whole world was single, and now that he was single, all the desirables had been snatched up.

Why was he always one step behind, in work as well as romance? Like with the Foothill rapist. Just when Decker thought he'd figured out his next move, the asshole would elude him with a change of technique. He wondered if this case was his handiwork. Unlikely, since the Foothill rapes had always taken place in Sylmar, far west of this area. But you never knew: The prick was clever with twists and turns.

24

He glanced back to the rabbi, who was still talking. What was he saying to the husband? Life goes on? You'll survive, she did? Decker felt a great deal of empathy for the young man. He could sense the rage, the frustration and helplessness. ("I wasn't there to prevent this.") Buddy, if it's any consolation, there are plenty of others who have felt the same way you do. Decker had spoken to hundreds of them.

Marge returned from talking with Mrs Adler, gave him a thumbs up sign, and went outside. Good. The lady still hadn't bathed.

Finally Decker caught the rabbi's eye, and the old man gave him a cordial nod. The detective knew he was going to have his chance soon and was determined not to come away empty-handed.

Ten minutes later, the rabbi got up and so did Decker. The husband walked away without a word.

The rabbi was a tall man, not as tall as Decker, but at least six one. Decker put him in his early seventies. Much of his face was covered with a long salt-and-pepper beard, and what wasn't hidden by hair was a road-map of creases. His eyes were dark brown, clear and alert, the brows white and furry. For a man his age he was straight-backed, slender, and a fastidious dresser. His black pants were razor-pressed, his white shirt starched stiff, and the black Prince Albert coat carefully tailored. Crowning his head was a black felt homburg. It all added up to a stately demeanor. Regal, like an archbishop.

"Thank you for bearing with me," the rabbi said, offering him a firm, dry hand. "Terrible, terrible thing."

The old man's voice was crisp and slightly accented.

"How's he holding up?"

"Zvi?"

"He's the husband, isn't he?"

The rabbi nodded. "He's in shock, almost as bad as his wife. Numb."

Decker said nothing, suddenly feeling tired. He was sick of crud.

"What can I do for you?" the old man asked.

"Please sit down, Rabbi." Decker offered him the armchair.

"Thank you, but I prefer to stand. I sit all day."

"That's fine."

"Would it bother you if I smoked?" the rabbi said.

"On the contrary, it sounds like a fine idea." Decker took out a pack and offered one to him.

The rabbi shook his head. "Those aren't cigarettes. The tobacco leaves have been sprayed, watered down, processed, and diluted by a filter." He pulled out a silver case, opened it, and showed him a dozen hand-rolled cigarettes. "Try a real smoke."

Decker lit the rabbi's, then took one for himself and lit up.

Both of them inhaled in silence.

"Nu, so how does it taste?" the rabbi asked.

"It's wonderful tobacco."

"My own special blend. Turkish with just a hint of Latakia." The rabbi blew out a haze of smoke. "Now, how can I be of service?"

Decker ran his fingers through his hair. "We're having a bit of a compliance problem here, Rabbi. Mrs Adler isn't willing to have herself examined for criminal evidence."

"Internally?"

"Internally and externally. She's not willing to have her bodily injuries photographed either. Although it's much easier with pictures, we *could* get by with detailed notes. But we really need the internal."

The rabbi stared at him impassively.

"Since you're the head of this place, I was hoping you could persuade her to help us out."

"I suppose you could demand legally that she come in for the exam," the rabbi said.

"I was hoping it wouldn't come to that. The poor woman has already gone through enough."

"You're a wise boy, Detective. You don't mind me

26

calling you boy, do you? I call all my *bochrim* – my pupils – boys. At my age everyone around me looks like a boy."

Decker smiled.

"I didn't catch your name, Detective."

"Decker. Peter Decker." He handed the rabbi a card.

"Decker," the rabbi mouthed to himself. "I am Rav Aaron Schulman."

"Honored, Rabbi Schulman."

The old man let out a cough.

"Mrs Adler is a free agent. Despite what the local residents think, this place isn't a cult and I'm not a guru. People are free to come and go on their own. More important, people are free to think on their own."

He began to pace. "I can't go up to her and say, 'Sarah Libba, cooperate with this man.' That's not my function. But if you want some advice, I can give you some."

The Rosh Yeshiva's voice had taken on a sing-song cadence.

"Please, Rabbi."

"If you want to get her to cooperate, you're going to have to understand a little about her before this ordeal. Psychologically and sociologically. The women here have their own doctor, in Sherman Oaks I believe. A female named Dr Birnbaum. Phyllis Birnbaum. I don't think Sarah Libba's frightened about the exam per se, but she's not going to allow herself to be touched by a man, especially after what happened."

Schulman sucked hard on the cigarette, causing the tip to glow bright orange.

"So if I were you, instead of wasting my time trying to talk her into something, I'd call up my captain and see if the Department can't work something out – an exception – allowing Dr Birnbaum to act as a medical examiner this once. No doubt there will be bureaucratic problems. But if you want it to get done, it will get done, my boy. Correct?"

Decker smiled and nodded assent.

"After Dr Birnbaum has been approved by the officials,

27

I'd call her up and request her help. She's a conscientious woman, and I'm sure she'll cooperate. Then, I'd have your female partner approach Sarah Libba and say the exam will be with Dr Birnbaum, the same one who delivered two of your four lovely children. And if you feel it's necessary, you may say that Rav Schulman says it's permissible halachically – according to the rules of Judaism – to be examined."

The old man was a sharpie. Decker liked him. But not as much as the Lazarus girl.

Marge and the two uniforms walked in.

"*Nada*, Pete," she said. "I came up dry."

"Didn't expect anything really." Decker made introductions, then turned to the patrolmen – two linebackers. The one named Hunter seemed to be in his middle twenties. The senior partner, Ramirez, was shorter and looked ten years older.

"Find any tracks or hear anything?" Decker asked.

"There are plenty of tracks," Hunter said. "Deer, rabbit, coyote, lots of cats. But nothing that looks human."

"Thanks anyway."

"We'll file a report of what we found," Ramirez said, then amended it. "Or rather, didn't find. It'll be ready by tomorrow."

"Okay."

After they left, Decker turned to Marge. "I've got to make a call to headquarters and try to arrange a deal. You've got to call a Dr Phyllis Birnbaum in Sherman Oaks, explain what went on here, and ask her if she'd be willing to open up her office and do a forensic internal on Mrs Adler now."

Marge looked skeptical.

"I know it's irregular, but it seems to be the only thing we've got." Decker turned to Rav Schulman. "Do you think Mrs Adler would object to a county doctor working side by side with Dr Birnbaum?"

"If the doctor was a man she'd object. I'd try and keep

it as natural as possible. Even then, Mrs Adler still might not agree."

Decker reached for a cigarette, but the rabbi was too quick for him, offering him one of the homemades. He took it eagerly.

"Marge, see if you can get Mrs Adler to agree to see Dr Birnbaum. I'll call Morrison." He faced the rabbi. "That's the station's captain. He's a good guy, eminently reasonable."

The rabbi spoke up.

"If you'll excuse me, I must be getting back to my duties. On Thursdays I give a midnight lecture to the advanced students. Feel free to use the phone in the mikvah."

"Thanks for your cooperation, Rabbi. And please call me if you have questions or suspicions."

Decker held out his hand and the rabbi took it, pumping it several times with surprising strength.

"This is our home, Detective Decker. At least until we all make it to the Holy Land. We were not intimidated by vandals. We will not be intimidated by rapists, thieves, or murderers. If the police can't adequately protect us, we will use our own means."

"The police are on your side, Rabbi," said Marge. "Unfortunately, with budget cuts, there's not a whole lot of us to go around."

"Rabbi Schulman," Decker said, "I've already suggested a dead bolt on this door to Mrs Lazarus. And I also mentioned building a safer fence and gate. But frankly, there are a few misinformed people out there who have something against you people. It mightn't be the worst idea to obtain a security guard for the place."

The rabbi nodded. "Especially for Mrs Lazarus's safety. She has to walk home from here every night. I was never worried until now."

"Maybe her husband can pick her up," Marge suggested.

"She's a widow." The rabbi thought out loud: "I could

29

have one of the *bochrim* walk her, but she's a religious woman and might object to walking home alone with a man. And I'm too old to offer much protection."

"There are female security guards," Marge said.

"Perhaps I am being overly optimistic, but I'm hoping that this is an isolated incident and it won't come to that. But if somehting proves me wrong, rest assured that we will do whatever is necessary to protect ourselves. In the meantime, I will call up Rina Miriam and work something out individually with her."

The rabbi patted Decker on the shoulder.

"I must go to my pupils. Find this monster, Detective." He nodded good-bye to Marge and left.

"I don't know about this case," Marge said when they were alone.

Decker shrugged. "I'd better call the station."

"You think this is going to be an isolated incident?"

He hesitated a moment, then said, "No. He got away with it once. I'll lay odds he'll try again."

"That Lazarus woman is a perfect target."

"You'd better believe it."

"You might want to call the poor widow and tell her," Marge said, grinning. "All in the name of civic interest, of course."

"Of course. What kind of cop would I be if I settled for less?"

"Forget it, Pete. She won't walk with a guy, let alone do anything you'd be interested in."

He smiled, then his face turned serious. "If the Adler woman doesn't open up, you know what we've got? Nothing. No evidence or M.O., ergo no suspect. A big, cold zilch."

He thought a moment.

"Let me run this by you, Margie. We're assuming she's not talking because she's traumatized and religious. Maybe she's hiding something."

"Think it's one of the yeshiva men?"

"Or a local punk who has her terrorized. Remember a

30

year ago when they were extorting money out of some of the students here."

She shrugged.

"I didn't pick up any of those vibes, Pete. She didn't seem to be holding back." Marge pounded her fist into an open palm. "Damn it, she seemed like a nice woman. Even though her lips were zipped, you could tell she was a nice woman."

"We'd better get a move on. I'll use the radio to call headquarters, and you can use the phone here to call this Dr Birnbaum. Hope she knows what she's doing. Then you'll have to get it okayed with Mrs Adler. Let's see some of that first-rate sensitivity in action."

"Another long night," Marge groaned. "But aren't they all when you're working in muck?"

4

Rina gave up on sleep. She'd attempted it, but no rest had come. Only distorted holograms of the ghastly event.

Then came the phone call from the detective. Sarah Libba could be persuaded to have herself examined by Dr Birnbaum, but only if she could reimmerse in the mikvah afterward. Being the mikvah lady, could Rina please help out?

Of course she'd help out. Even if it meant waiting up the rest of the night, trembling with fear, jumping at the slightest sound.

She got up from the couch and made herself another cup of tea in the kitchen. With no air-conditioning and all the windows closed, the house had become a furnace. Her clothes were soaked with sweat. Her *tichel* – the head covering she wore in the presence of outsiders – was hot and itchy against her scalp. But she couldn't shake the chills.

She glanced at her watch. It was close to two A.M. How much longer would it take? At least she'd used most of the waiting time wisely by cooking for Shabbos. The room smelled wonderful.

The timer on the stove went off. The bell startled her, causing her heart to pump wildly. She brought her hand to her breast, then went over to the oven and took out the noodle kugel. Despite all her anxiety, the food had turned out perfectly – chicken juicy, roasted to a golden brown, six braided challahs, full and fluffy and topped generously with poppy seeds, the soup brimming with fresh vegetables. She was expecting company for the

Friday evening meal. The Kriegers and their three kids, plus two of her tenth-grade students. With her two boys and herself that made ten altogether. By tomorrow, she hoped she'd be calm enough to pull off the role of gracious hostess.

The doorbell rang and she bolted up. Looking through the peep hole, she saw the two detectives. She opened the door and invited them inside.

The living room was tiny. Most of the floor space was taken up by the sofa, coffee table, an armchair, and bookcases overflowing with volumes of Hebrew books. The walls were covered with artwork on Jewish themes and family photographs. Though the place was neat, Decker felt cramped and claustrophobic – Gulliver in the land of Lilliput. He loosened his tie and stood at the threshold of the open door.

"Something smells great," Marge commented.

"Thank you," answered Rina, nervously. "I had to do something with myself."

"We appreciate your cooperation, Mrs Lazarus," said Decker. He noticed that she'd covered her hair.

"If Sarah Libba was willing to help, how could I say no?"

"It's late. We'd better get on with it," he said. "One of us will stay here to watch your kids. The other will walk you over."

She knew he was giving her the choice, and it wasn't an easy one. According to the halacha, Decker should be the one to stay and the woman should walk with her. But Rina knew that should her kids wake up they'd be more terrified by a strange man than a strange woman.

She made her decision and felt it necessary to explain why.

"Do you mind if I open up a window?" Marge asked.

"No, no. I'm sorry about the heat. But after what happened, I was afraid to keep them open."

"It's probably a good idea for the time being to keep

33

them closed at night." Decker held the door open for her. "Let's get going."

Rina stepped outside and basked in the fresh air. The night had cooled a bit. No moon was out, but starlight filtered through the thick branches of the eucalyptus and pines. A lone nightingale sang its aria to the spangled heavens, the crickets provided the chorus. She tried not to look at the detective, but her eyes kept drifting toward his face. He finally caught her glance and smiled. She quickly lowered her gaze and kept it fixed on the ground. Their footsteps seemed abnormally loud. Finally, she spoke just to ease her anxiety.

"I take it Rav Schulman was helpful?"

"Invaluable." Decker noticed she was walking a good ten feet away from him.

"He's a brilliant man," she said.

"I can believe that."

"He's a lawyer as well as a rabbi, you know."

"No, I didn't." Decker slowed his pace slightly. "Where'd he go to law school?"

"First in Europe. Then he graduated from Columbia. That's in New York."

Decker smiled. "Yes, I know."

Rina felt embarrassed. "Yes, I'm sure you do know. I'm sorry."

"Don't apologize. You didn't do anything wrong."

"I – I'm very upset."

"You have good reason to be."

She didn't answer, feeling she'd talked too much.

They walked a few more steps, then Decker spoke: "Well, the rabbi and I have something in common. I was a lawyer once. I even practiced for a whole six months."

"That's interesting," she said politely.

She doesn't give a damn about you, asshole, so cut the bullshit and do your job.

Decker said nothing.

The silence became tangible.

34

"Why did you give it up?" she asked to break it, and immediately added, "I don't mean to get personal."

"No problem. I became a cop."

"Isn't it usually the other way around?"

Now she was sounding intrusive – as big a yenta as Chana. Why was she running off like this with a total stranger . . .

He let out a small laugh. "Yes, it usually is."

They walked the rest of the way without speaking.

Sarah Libba was with a policewoman in the backseat of a patrol car. In the front sat the partner – a beefy man with a pencil-line mustache. In the background was radio noise: clipped calls and static. The female officer helped Sarah Libba out of the car, then Rina took her arm and led her inside the mikvah. Decker dismissed the uniforms, saying he'd take it from here.

Rina flicked on the lights.

"It will take about forty-five minutes, Detective," she said.

"Do what's necessary."

Rina took her into the bathroom, went to the tub, and turned the hot water spigot full blast. They waited together and watched the steaming water pour into the bath. Rina felt awkward. She suddenly realized how people must have felt during the *shiva,* her mourning period for Yitzchak. She'd talked a lot during those seven days, possessed with an overpowering sensation to speak about him and his death. Some people had been extremely uncomfortable as she rambled on about a dead man. But others were relieved that the burden of conversation had been lifted from their shoulders. What would Sarah Libba want now?

She felt she must say something.

"I'm sorry, Sarah."

The other woman looked at her with tears in her eyes. "I'm truly lucky," she said softly. "I thank *Hashem* that I'm alive. I would be a fool to think otherwise."

35

The two of them embraced, then sobbed.

"Of all the people who could have found me, I was glad it was you," she whispered, still hugging Rina desperately. "You understand pain and know how to deal with it. I don't think someone else would have been as calm."

"I'm glad I was helpful to you."

Sarah Libba broke away. "You were."

"Was the exam bad?"

"No, it was like a regular exam."

"That's good."

Sarah tried a smile, but her face crumpled. Rina took her in her arms again.

"You're safe now," she cooed and rocked her. "It's all over."

"It will never be over," the other woman wailed.

"You're safe."

Sarah cried for a while, then reluctantly broke away. "I'm all right, Rina. I'd like to be left alone. I'll call you when I'm done."

"I'll go heat the mikvah and wait for you. Just come out when you're ready."

Forty minutes later, Sarah came out of the adjoining door, wrapped in a white sheet. Her hair was dripping wet but free of tangles, and on her feet were paper sandals. She took off the slippers, stepped onto the bathmat, and dropped the sheet to reveal her naked body.

Rina immediately saw the ugly bruises on her chest, buttocks, and left thigh – deep red and raised, as if the milky skin had erupted in anger. She was seized with sadness.

Though she didn't have to, Rina went through all the rituals, just like the first time. She checked the nails on Sarah's small fingers and toes to make sure they'd been recently clipped and were spotlessly clean, and examined the soles of her feet for specks of dirt. Examining the soft arms gently, she found them gouged and raked.

"You know," Sarah said, her voice breaking, "I don't

36

even know if I can use the mikvah with all these fresh scrapes."

Rina softly moved her fingers over the damaged flesh. "They didn't soak off the half hour you were in the bath. They don't come off easily. I think you can go in with them."

She knew that the brief halachic debate was symbolic, as was the redunking itself. Despite the fact that she'd been raped, Sarah Libba was permitted to have sex with her husband. Her first dip had purified her.

But that wasn't the relevant issue at all. Sarah wanted to start over; she needed to undo what had been done.

Rina scrutinized Sarah Libba's back, chest, and arms for loose hairs that might have adhered accidentally to the skin. There were none. She moved on to the routine questions. Had Sarah brushed her teeth? Had she gone to the bathroom? Removed all foreign objects from her body including rings, earrings, dentures, and contact lenses? Sarah answered yes mechanically, and Rina gave her permission to immerse herself.

Sarah walked down the eight steps until the water covered her breasts. At Rina's nod, she dunked into the water with her eyes and mouth open. When the water covered the top of her head, she popped out and Rina announced that the dip was kosher. Sarah repeated the dunking two more times, then looked up.

Rina handed her a wash cloth that Sarah placed on her head. After reciting the prayer out loud, Sarah uttered a few more words to herself and gave the cloth back. She dunked four more times, each one affirmed as kosher, then began her ascent out of the pool. Rina extended her arms and held the sheet open, completely concealing herself from Sarah's field of vision. When emerging from the mikvah, a woman was honored with complete privacy.

After Sarah reentered the dressing room, Rina cleaned up and shut off the mikvah heater and the lights. Then she had no choice but to wait with Decker in the reception room.

"All done?" he asked.

"We're just waiting for her to dress."

"How's she doing?"

"I'm not sure. Compared to what?"

"Well, is she talking at all?"

"She's talking. But not about the . . . the incident, if that's what you mean."

"Do you think she might be willing to talk to us sometime later?"

"That's up to her," Rina answered.

Decker didn't pursue the conversation.

"I'm not being deliberately evasive, Detective. I just don't know."

"I understand. And I don't want to put you on the spot. But frankly, without something more concrete, there's no way we're going to catch this guy."

Rina stood up, walked over to the linen closet, and busied herself with rearranging the already neatly folded towels and sheets. A minute later Sarah Libba appeared. Her head was covered with a kerchief – her new *shaytel* had been confiscated for evidence along with her torn clothing.

Decker rose and held the door open for the women. Rina turned off the waiting room lights, and the three of them walked in silence across the grounds to the residential area, the women in front, he following.

When they reached Sarah's house, Decker knocked on the door and Zvi answered. He was still dressed in street clothes – white shirt, black slacks, black oxfords and yarmulke. His long, thin face was grim and stoic behind a thick pelt of light brown beard. After helping his wife in, he stepped outside.

"Thank you," he said politely to Rina.

"If she needs anything, Zvi, call."

"I will," he said softly, then focused on Decker. "Are you the detective in charge?"

"Yes, I am." He gave the young man his card.

Zvi looked at it and placed it in his breast pocket.

"Detective Decker, you find this *thing*," he spat out. You look high and low, and find this *thing*. And when you do, you don't arrest him or put him in jail. You just bring him here and leave me alone with him for an hour. That way justice will be done."

Decker let the words hang in the air for a moment.

"I'm going to need your wife's help, Mr Adler, if I'm going to find him."

Zvi didn't seem to hear. He stared into space, finally looked back at Decker. "Just find him and bring him here." He turned abruptly and walked inside.

Rina knew Sarah wouldn't talk. The case wasn't going to go anywhere. She looked at the detective. He knew it too, and she sensed his frustration. They began to walk.

"It's been a long night," Rina said.

"Yes, it has."

"Do you get a lot of long nights?"

"Lately."

"You're the detective on the Foothill rapist, aren't you?"

Decker nodded.

"It didn't dawn on me before, but now I recall seeing your name in the newspaper." Rina started to shake. "That nurse who was beaten up, how's she doing?"

"She's on the mend."

"That's good." Rina swallowed a dry gulp. "Do you think there's any connection between this and the other Foothill rapes?"

"Mrs Lazarus, at this point I honestly don't know."

There was so much she now wanted to ask him, but knew she couldn't. They continued walking, and he stopped suddenly, a few feet from her door.

"You want to help? This is how you can help," Decker said. "First, get a good, solid dead bolt on the mikvah door in the morning. Second, be very careful, even a little paranoid, for the next couple of weeks. Third, you might try to talk Mrs Adler into giving us a statement of some

39

kind. If she can't talk to me, maybe you can convince her to talk to Detective Dunn."

"I'll do what I can."

"Thanks." Decker brought out his pad and a pencil. He scribbled a number on it and gave the slip of paper to Rina. "This is my home number. I don't want you walking alone at night unless there's some sort of security patrol on the premises. If you can't get anyone to walk with you, call me. I'm only fifteen minutes away. I'd much rather take a few minutes of my personal time to assure your safety, than to have to come on official business. All right?"

"I'll be careful," she said.

"Look, I'm not telling you how to worship. The rabbi said you're a widow, that you don't like to walk alone with a man. But in my book, religion comes second to personal safety. I'm sure he can give you dispensation."

Rina said nothing.

Decker knew he was wasting his breath. She wasn't listening. Goddam Hollander and his fucking ball game! Decker didn't want to be here. He didn't want this case. It was going to dead end, and he'd have another unsolved rape on his hands.

But that was just part of it. Some force was sucking him into this place. He *knew* he'd be returning here in a professional capacity. And that worried him.

5

Rina sat at her desk in the stuffy basement classroom and looked out at a sea of bobbing yarmulkes. Heads down, her students were busy scratching away at the test. She'd thought the exam would be challenging, but the kids seemed to be whipping through the pages in record time. It was getting harder and harder to challenge them, she realized with delight. It was a pleasure to teach such a bright group of kids. Her only major complaint about the job was the poor facilities. In the summer the room became a sauna, and the two large floor fans did little to mitigate the heat.

Her eyes returned to the open pages of the *Chumash*. She'd finished studying the *parsha* – the biblical portion of the week – and was on the *haftorah*. Sunday was the new moon, so the reading would be the story of the friendship between David and Jonathan. It was one of Rina's favorites – a tale of unswerving love and trust. She'd never had a relationship like that with anyone, including Yitzchak. Theirs had contained some of those elements, but Yitzchak's first and true love had been the Torah.

The rabbis had regarded his brilliant mind as a gift from God. He was their prize pupil, one of the few young men who was a real *talmid chacham*. They'd showered him with attention, but it had never gone to his head. He wasn't interested in adulation, just in the acquisition of knowledge.

Rina had been astonished by Yitzchak's intellect when they first met. He was a living, breathing genius, and she was willing to put up with his idiosyncracies for the privilege of being around him. He'd turned out to be a warm-hearted man and a good father, but their relationship had always been a bit distant.

It was cruelly ironic that his brilliant brain cells eventually led to his demise.

Rina felt melancholia nibbling at her gut. She looked up from the text, and her eyes landed on the sandy-haired boy in the corner. His expression hadn't changed since he'd entered the room. Usually one of the quickest thinkers, today he gazed at the chalkboard as if it contained some magic words of comfort. Yossie looked just like his father, Zvi, and his face bore the painful, numb expression that his father's had last night. Rina was sure they hadn't told him, but he knew. Oldest children always knew when something wasn't right.

A few of the best students had handed in their exams. Rina would grade them, but really didn't have to bother. She knew they'd be perfect. Soon the rest of the boys followed, until Yossie was the only one left. He continued to stare blankly, not even moving when Rina was standing right next to him. She looked down at his papers and found them untouched.

"Yossie," she said gently.

The glassy hazel eyes inched their way upward.

"Yossie, you're having an off day."

He nodded.

"Take the test home. I trust you. Finish the exam when you're in better spirits."

"Thank you," he whispered.

He got up, stuffed the papers in his overloaded briefcase, and left the room.

Rina was the last of the trio to enter the room. She had last-minute chores before Shabbos and hoped the faculty meeting wouldn't take too long.

Three times a semester she and the two other secular teachers got together to discuss the curriculum. She was

42

the head of the math department – and its sole teacher. The men were the departments of humanities and physical sciences.

Matt Hawthorne taught history and English. He was a jovial man in his mid-twenties, a little on the short side, with a puckish face and dark curly hair. Quick with a joke, he got along extremely well with the rowdier boys.

"Want to close the door, Rina?" he asked her.

"I'd prefer to leave it open," she replied automatically.

Hawthorne had a gleam in his eye. "You don't want all the students to hear our trade secrets, do you?"

Rina sighed. It was an old story. Matt knew she left the door open for religious reasons, but insisted on teasing her about it anyway. Ordinarily she took it in good humor. Today she wasn't in the mood, and the expression on her face reflected it.

"What trade secrets?" asked Steven Gilbert, coming to her defense. "Leave the door open. It's hot enough in here without cutting off the little circulation we do have. Let's get on with business."

Of the two of them, Rina preferred Steve. They were both nice enough, but Steve was more subdued. He was older than Matt and her, in his middle thirties, balding and bespectacled, but with facial features that were still youthful. Like Matt, he was a public school teacher who moonlighted by teaching the yeshiva kids in the late afternoon, when the boys learned their secular studies.

They went through the meeting with choreographed efficiency.

"Shall we call it a day?" Rina asked when they were done.

"I've got nothing else to add," said Gilbert.

Matt looked down. His eye suddenly twitched. It was a nervous tic that Rina had noted before.

"What's the problem?" she asked.

"This has nothing to do with the curriculum, but I heard that something went on here last night."

Rina hesitated a moment.

43

"What'd you hear?"

"Did a rape take place at the mikvah last night?"

"Where'd you hear that?" Rina wanted to know.

"Campus rumors," Gilbert said. "Is it true?"

She nodded.

"That's horrible!" exclaimed Hawthorne. "They said it was Yossie Adler's mother."

"Let's drop the subject," Rina said. "Suffice it to say that everyone's alive and healthy."

"Well, that's good," Hawthorne said. "You know, you can't pick up a newspaper or turn on the news without hearing about the Foothill rapist. Then this happens – " Hawthorne stopped himself and looked at Rina through a fluttering left eyelid. "I'm doing a lot for your nerves, aren't I?"

"It's all right."

But her voice lacked conviction.

"Listen, Rina," said Gilbert calmly, "we know your being alone makes you especially vulnerable. If you need anything, feel free to give either one of us a call."

"Thank you," she replied. "If there's nothing else, I'm going to be off."

Hawthorne stood up and pulled out her çhair.

"My, you're chivalrous," Gilbert said, his tone cool.

"My mama taught me well, Stevie."

"Before I forget . . ." Gilbert searched through his briefcase and pulled out a few loose sheets of computer paper. "Take these home to your boys. They're the programs they developed yesterday in Computer Club. I ran them this morning."

"And they came out?" she asked, taking the papers.

"Of course they came out."

Rina swelled with parental pride.

"Kids are born brighter these days," she said. "But then again, they have better teachers."

Gilbert acknowledged the compliment with a nod and stood up. The three of them remained motionless for an awkward moment.

44

"I'm glad you're okay," Hawthorne said to Rina.

"Thanks for your concern."

"Do you want me to walk you home?" Gilbert asked.

"Thank you, but it's really not necessary. After all, one can be overly paranoid, right?"

When neither one responded, she smiled weakly and left.

Though the synagogue had no assigned seating, people tended to sit in the same spot. Rina's was in the front row of the balcony – the women's section.

She saw Zvi davening, making him out very clearly though she was peering through a diaphanous curtain that hung in front of the upper level. He was at the podium, leading the service, rocking back and forth as he moved his lips. To his right stood Yossie, looking lost, and his two younger brothers, poking each other mischievously.

Rina wasn't the only one looking at Zvi. All the women who had used the mikvah last night were gaping at him. The "incident" was the topic of whispered conversation in the balcony. Rina couldn't stand the gossip and specula-tion. Though they tried to engage her in conversation, she remained aloof.

She concentrated hard on the Hebrew text in front of her. Tonight, praying seemed especially significant, and she davened with renewed spirit. Truly, fate is in the hands of *Hashem*, she thought. But to help Him along, she'd take the detective's advice and be very careful. Usually after services she and her boys rushed home, allowing her to complete preparations for the Shabbos meal. But tonight she waited for her guests, and they all walked together.

The dinner came off without a hitch. The table was set with her finest silver, china, and table linens and spot-lighted in the warm glow of candlelight. The food was plentiful and superb. Everyone had a grand time singing and telling stories. Her children and the Kriegers' each had a chance to relate their amusing incidents of the week, then her students gave a short *dvar Torah* – a Talmudic lesson. They ended with grace after the meal and more singing.

The festivities lasted until midnight. By the time everyone left, her boys were overwrought with fatigue. Yaakov, the seven-year-old, was running around in circles singing at the top of his lungs. Shmuel, one year his senior, was break-dancing and singing an Uncle Moishy tune. Something about Gedalia Goomber not working on Shabbos Kodesh.

Rina kept her patience and calmed the boys down with a bedtime story and lots of kisses. She tucked them in, then headed for the kitchen. It was one-thirty by the time she'd finished cleaning up.

She crawled under the covers and immediately fell into a deep sleep.

In the wee hours of the morning she was awakened by a piercing scream. She shot up and ran to the boys' room. They were fast asleep. She rechecked all the locks on the doors but didn't dare peek out the window. Again, cries followed by scampering atop her roof.

The damn cats!

The house turned quiet – a suffocating quiet.

Rina trudged shakily back to bed. The adrenalin was surging throughout her body. Wide-eyed, she stared at the shadows on her wall until exhaustion overtook her.

6

"Eema, could you pin my *kipah*?" Shmuel asked.

Rina put down the paper and attached the big, black yarmulke to the soft, curly locks with four bobby pins. No matter how many she put in, the *kipah* would always fall off. Little boys, she thought, smiling.

"There you go, sweetie," she said, kissing his cheek. It was damp with salty perspiration and as soft as butter.

He thanked her and ran off to play G.I. Joe with his brother. Last she'd heard, the Joe team was beating COBRA, capturing and disposing of the evil forces with no mercy. Rina'd always felt that kids judged much more harshly than adults. If it were up to them, all criminals would receive the death penalty.

She reopened the paper, and the article jumped out at her. She wondered why she hadn't noticed it before. The Foothill rapist had struck again. Reading the article slowly, she saw Decker's name in the second paragraph.

She closed the paper and sipped her coffee. It had been nearly two weeks since the rape at the mikvah. The initial fright had abated, and life progressed as usual. The only differences were a dead bolt on the mikvah door and husbands walking their wives home after the ritual immersion.

But Rina was still worried. Oftentimes she'd walk home with the last woman to use the facilities, but that meant either coming in early to clean the mikvah from the previous night or finding someone to wait for her as she scrubbed the tiles. Recently she found herself getting careless, sinking back into the old bad habit of walking home alone. Several times she thought of calling the detective – sure she'd heard things outside – but hadn't wanted to bother him. Besides, nothing had ever materialized.

Now, seeing his name in print, she wondered about the progress of the case and wanted badly to call him. But the house was too tiny for privacy, and she didn't want her sons to overhear the conversation. She'd have to wait.

When it was time, she walked the kids to the yeshiva's day camp. Upon returning home she picked up the receiver and immediately put it down. Perhaps it wasn't the right time to call. With this new rape, he was probably up to his neck in work.

She fixed herself another cup of coffee and turned on the radio to a news station. It was a half-hour before the story came on. No details were given. Just another rape attributed to him. She flicked the dial to off and thought to herself: Wasn't she a citizen? Didn't she pay taxes to support a police force? She had even voted against the tax cut that would have reduced police and fire services. With newly summoned determination, she dialed his extension. Besides, she was sure he wouldn't be in.

To her shock he picked it up on the second ring.

"Decker," he answered.

She was momentarily speechless.

"Hello?" he said loudly.

"Uh – yes, this is Rina Lazarus. I don't know if you remember me – "

"Of course I do. What can I do for you, Mrs Lazarus?"

"You must be busy."

"Swamped."

She felt foolish for calling. "I was wondering how the mikvah case was coming along. I realize it's not as important as this Foothill rapist, but . . ."

She thought she heard him groan over the line. There was a pause.

"Frankly, Mrs Lazarus, we have no mikvah case. Mrs Adler never gave us any statement, so we have nothing to go on. The only way we're ever going to find the perpetrator is if we catch him doing something else and he admits the rape as a by-product of the confession."

Rina said nothing.

"Everything calm over there?" Decker asked.

"I hear a noise now and then. That's all."

"Someone walking you home at night?"

"Usually. We did get a lock on the door."

"That's good. Anything else I can do for you?"

"Not really." She hedged, then said: "Suppose Mrs Adler were to come in and give you a statement? Would that help reopen the case?"

"It would be a start."

"I'll see what I can do," she said.

"Do that."

7

Michael Hollander was fiftyish, bald, florid, and the proper weight for a man six inches taller. He, Marge, and Decker made up the juvey and sex detail for the division. They were referred to jokingly as The Three Musketeers – a title that Hollander had redubbed The Three Mouseketeers. He smoked a pipe, which was an inexcusable offense in such close quarters, but laughed off the complaints by demanding to know who'd be the squadroom's scapegoat if he became civilized. Discussion closed.

He entered the detective's quarters, poured himself his ninth cup of coffee of the day, and placed a meaty hand on Decker's shoulder.

Peter looked up from the phone, excused himself, and covered the mouthpiece with his palm.

"What?"

"A lady from Jewtown is outside."

Decker finished his call quickly and checked his watch. They were right on time. Then he remembered that Hollander had said *a lady*, not *ladies*. Damn it! The other one must have chickened out.

He got up from his desk, went out to the reception area, and saw Rina standing in the hallway behind the half door. She looked as good as he remembered, even better. Even though her hair was covered, tucked into a white knitted tam, she'd taken a little time to put on some make-up and jewelry. He liked that.

"Come on in," he said opening the latch and leading her to his desk.

Headquarters were not as she'd imagined.

She expected the place to be busy and crowded, but not so small. Metal utility desks and chairs were squashed against one another, taking up most of the floor space. What furniture wasn't metal was scarred, unfinished wood. A lone rust-bitten table in the corner housed a small computer. On the rear wall were wanted posters and floor-to-ceiling prefab shelves full of blue notebooks marked with various colored dots. To her left were two small rooms with the doors open and a map of the division taped carelessly on the wall. To her right were the coffee urn and its accompanying paraphernalia, more desks, and another map studded with multicolored pins. The place was minimally cooled by fans placed at strategic spots and blowing full force.

All the detectives were dressed in light-colored short-sleeved shirts, loosened ties, drab slacks, and scuffed shoes. Only their shoulder holsters suggested they were cops. Some of them were on the phone or doing desk work, others were conferring with one another; all of them looked preoccupied.

"Like the decor?" one of them shouted, a fat man smoking a pipe.

"Lovely," she said, smiling.

"Take a seat," Decker said, pulling up a chair that obstructed the aisle. His desktop was covered by piles of papers, a manual typewriter, and a black phone sporting a panel of flashing lights. "What happened to Mrs Adler?"

Rina lowered her voice. "She refused to come down."

"I can barely hear you."

"Can we use one of those rooms over there?"

"They're as hot as blazes. Great for sweating out confessions."

Rina said nothing and squirmed.

"I'll tell you what," he said, "I'll take my lunch break early. That way we can get a little privacy."

They got up to leave. The fat detective whistled.

* * *

"You have any food preferences?" Decker asked, starting the Plymouth.

"Detective Decker," she hesitated, "I can't eat in a restaurant because the food's not kosher. I brought my own lunch." She held up a paper bag.

Shit, he thought. Another Big Mac for lunch. "No problem. I'll just run by McDonalds and pick something up."

"I prepared lunch for Mrs Adler, so I have extra," she said timidly.

Decker smiled. "Okay."

"Is there someplace we can eat other than a car?" she asked uncomfortably.

"I think that can be arranged."

He drove to a bedraggled park. The grass had been burned yellow and the sandbox was nothing more than a pile of gray pebbles, but to one side was a large shady tree with umbrella-like branches and some warped wooden benches. A couple of naked Latino tots ran through a sprinkler jet that was attempting – without visible success – to revive a bed of dead marigolds. The toddlers' grandmother sat a few feet away, knitting as she watched them from the corner of one eye. Although there was plenty of empty seating in the shade, the old woman had elected to sit in the open sun with a bandana over her head, seemingly impervious to the heat. The temperature was well over a hundred, the air heavy with smog, but a slight breeze filtered through the lacy branches, providing some refuge.

Rina knew it wasn't right for her to be alone with this man, but she felt compelled to help. She wanted justice to be done and the monster locked up – for society's welfare and her own peace of mind.

They sat down and the old woman waved to Decker. He returned her greeting, and Rina opened the sack.

"I was in the mood for hamburgers," she said.

"Great. I love hamburgers."

"I made some cole slaw also."

"Great. I love cole slaw."

Rina laughed. "You're very agreeable."

"On certain occasions."

"I'm glad this is one of them." She unwrapped an oversized onion roll stuffed with a thick hunk of ground meat and gave it to him.

Decker regarded the sandwich. "This is a *hamburger*. It's amazing how quickly you forget what a real one looks like after eating fast foods for years." He took a chomp. The juices spilled out onto his mustache and chin.

"I brought extra napkins." She handed him a wad.

"It looks like I'll need 'em."

Rina unwrapped several beige cubes. "This is potato kugel."

"I like potatoes."

"It's best described as gelatinous hash browns – "

Decker laughed. "That sounds horrible."

"It tastes better than it sounds."

He bit into one of the squares and contemplated.

"You know what it tastes like?" Decker said. "It tastes like a latke. A big, thick latke."

That took her by surprise.

"That's exactly what it is."

"Not too bad for a goy, huh?"

She laughed.

"You've picked up an expression or two, Detective."

"Or three or four. My ex-wife was Jewish. But not like you," he qualified. "She and her parents were very Americanized. But her paternal grandparents stayed . . . ethnic. It was her grandmother who used to make me latkes."

"Were they good?"

"Dynamite."

Rina opened a thermos of orange juice and poured them each a cup.

"Thanks for sharing your lunch. It's been a while since I've had a home-cooked meal."

53

Rina lowered her head and said nothing. Decker noticed she hadn't unwrapped her sandwich.

"You're not eating?" he asked.

"Uh . . . In a minute."

She pulled out a paper cup from the sack and walked over to the sprinkler. She filled the cup up with water, poured it over each hand, then came back to the bench.

"You're very hygienic," Decker said, smiling. "I like that in a woman."

She smiled back but was silent. He wondered if he had offended her.

"That was a joke," he said.

She nodded, mumbled to herself and took a bite of her sandwich.

"I know," she finally said after she swallowed. "I couldn't answer you because I was in the middle of a blessing. You're not allowed to talk between hand washing and the breaking of bread."

Decker stared at her blankly.

"Never mind," she said quickly. "It isn't important."

He shrugged.

"You're a good cook."

"Thanks." She put down her sandwich. "Detective – "

"Why don't you call me Peter? People I like a lot less call me by my first name. Certainly you can."

"All right. You can call me Rina."

"Great. So we'll be Peter the Detective and Rina the Mikvah Lady."

"Sounds fine."

She turned serious.

"I couldn't talk Mrs Adler into coming down here. But she wants to help out."

"What's the game plan?"

"I managed to get her alone. She told me what happened in very explicit detail."

Decker stopped eating. "Unless it comes directly from her mouth it's not admissible as testimony."

"I understand that. If you catch someone that sounds

like this animal, she may even be willing to testify. But she doesn't want to have to expose herself prematurely."

"She wouldn't be exposing herself. She'd just be talking –'

"She just can't bring herself to talk about it to a total stranger, male or female. Your partner was very nice, but she doesn't trust her. And if you'd call Mrs Adler up and tell her that I just told you everything, she'd deny talking to me about it. We're very private people, Detective."

Decker thought for a moment. "So what do you have?"

She took a sip of juice. "This isn't easy."

"Take your time, Rina." He pulled out a note pad.

Despite herself she liked the way he said her name.

"Okay." She took a deep breath and let it out slowly. "Sarah . . . Mrs Adler had left the mikvah and walked a couple of feet when the person, attacker, whatever you call him . . ."

"Assailant."

"The assailant grabbed her from behind. She screamed and he punched her hard on the face. When she screamed again he stuffed something down her throat. A sock or a mitten, something furry. She remembers tasting the nap of the fabric. It nearly choked her."

"Did she see the man at all?"

"She said he was wearing a ski mask."

"Did he describe his clothing?"

"Just that it was dark."

"Go on."

"He ripped her dress and pulled at her hair. Sarah Libba was wearing a wig that night, as you well know, so it just came off, and for some reason, that made him furious. He hurled it away, and dragged her off and began to punch her again, all over her body."

"Did he say anything to her?"

"Not directly. But he muttered over and over, *'What a bitch, what a bitch.'*"

"What did his voice sound like?"

"Gravelly."

55

"Had she ever heard it before?"

"I didn't ask her that. I assumed she would have said something if she had."

"You can't assume anything. Anyway, go on, you're doing fine."

"Oh, I almost forgot. He told her he had a gun."

"Well, that's a pretty important detail."

"She wouldn't let me take notes. This is all from memory."

There was defensiveness in her voice. Decker realized he was coming across as critical and softened his tone.

"You're doing great. A-plus. Did he threaten to shoot her?"

"No. She distinctly said he didn't threaten to use it. He just said, 'I have a gun,' and she felt this cold thing against her temple."

"Okay."

"He finally stopped hitting her. He reached up her dress and pulled down her underwear . . . He . . . Excuse me."

"Take your time. Here." Decker poured her another cup of juice. "Take a gulp."

"Thank you." She took a sip. "This is very hard for me."

"I understand."

She sighed. "Let's see. He attempted to . . . tried to do it to her from behind. First the regular way, then sodomy, but he wasn't aroused."

"She saw his penis?"

"Uh, no, well, I don't know. She couldn't feel him penetrating her, I guess. She felt a little something anally, but nothing really physically painful."

Her account was consistant with the exam. It had revealed no sperm or seminal fluid in the vaginal mucosa and a few drops of seminal fluid in the anal region. Enough to get a serum typing, but not a really good one. But he didn't tell her that.

"Did she recall the man ejaculating?" Decker asked.

"She felt something warm and wet dribble down her leg."

Damn! If the doctor had looked a little farther down the victim's leg, she would have found a nice, big sperm sample. It was hell working with amateurs.

"Go on," he urged, suppressing his irritation.

"After he was done, he told her that he knew who she was, and if she talked, he'd kill her. He started to slap her, but then I came out. She's sure that scared him. Anyway, he took off as soon as he heard my voice."

"So the mysterious fleeing figure probably was the bastard."

She nodded and hugged herself.

"It gives me the chills just to think about it."

"Anything else?" he asked.

"Not that I can remember."

He stopped writing and put the note pad away.

"Detect – "

"Peter," he reminded her.

"Peter, does any of it sound like the Foothill rapist?"

There are certain similarities – the attempted anal penetration and the failure to achieve a full erection, but other things didn't fit. The ski mask for one. And Mrs Adler had been wearing sandals, not high-heeled shoes. But he wasn't about to commit himself one way or the other.

"Maybe, maybe not."

"Please don't be cryptic. Off the record."

"Off the record, maybe, maybe not."

She frowned.

"Listen," he said, "at this point it doesn't make a hell of a lot of difference, because we don't know much about the Foothill rapist either. Which leaves me sitting in a pile of shit, if you'll excuse my language."

"You must be under a lot of pressure."

"That's an understatement," he said lighting up a cigarette. "But I usually perform well when the heat's on." He smiled tightly. "Though I've got to admit, the barometer's been reading pretty high lately."

"So you're not close to finding him."

"Close doesn't mean a thing. Either you have him or you don't. Will you excuse me for a moment?"

She watched him walk over to the old lady, who was no longer alone. To her right stood a teenager – an emaciated Hispanic boy of about seventeen. A sickly pallor dulled a complexion that should have glowed bronze. He started backing away as the detective approached.

"Hey, I'm not doin' nothin', man!"

"Hey, Ramon, I didn't say you were doing anything," replied Decker, towering over the kid. "I just came over to be friendly."

"Hey, ain't I got a right to walk in a park?" The boy sniffed and wiped his nose on his sleeve. "I mean, hey, a park's a public place!"

"You've got rights. Sure, you've got rights. Everybody's got rights. I was just making sure that Mrs Sanchez gets her rights, too."

The grandmother gave him a warm smile.

Decker prodded a sunken chest with his index finger. "Why don't you beat it?"

"Hey, man, I'm goin', I'm goin'."

The detective watched him cross the street. When the boy had disappeared, he returned to the bench.

"Junkie," he said, sitting down. "They prey on people like the good little Señora: old women with children who can't give them chase. Sneak up, grab their purses, and they're a couple bucks richer with very little effort."

"What a world," Rina said. "Until now we'd always felt so insulated from all the outside problems."

"Unfortunately, you're not." He turned to face her. "You know what I'd really like?"

"What?"

"I'd really like to see you again."

Rina didn't reply.

58

"If you don't go out to eat, how about a couple of drinks, dancing?"

She felt sick.

"I don't think that's possible."

Decker's face was impassive.

"Well, we'd better be getting back," he said, standing up.

"It's nothing personal, Peter."

"Forget it."

"Honestly, it's not because I don't want to."

"Then why don't you do it?"

"It's impossible. You've seen the world I live in. You must understand."

She turned away. Decker stared at her profile and felt the frustration grow.

"What I'd like to understand is why you bothered coming down here in the first place? Feeding me lunch? Dragging me out of the station? Everything you told me could have been easily said over the phone. What the hell was I supposed to think?"

"I'm sorry. I thought you'd like getting out, escaping from all the tension. I was just trying to be nice."

"Well, you were very nice. Let's go."

"I've got to say grace after meals first."

Decker flipped his wrist and checked his watch.

"Go ahead."

She *bentched* rapidly in silence, but her eyes kept glancing at his face. The more she looked at him, the worse she felt.

"Please don't be mad," she said when she had finished her prayers.

"I'm not mad," he answered coldly. "Just disappointed. But I understand. I'm a goy, you're a Jew. Let's go."

He was driving exceptionally fast and still looked irritated, but she didn't say anything. He was right. She had given him the wrong impression, and now she felt stupid. It was a mistake for her to come down here. It was a mistake to leave the yeshiva.

He shot through the tail end of an amber light, and a black-and-white caught him.

"Shit," Decker said as he saw the flashing lights. "Who are those jokers? A couple of morons?" He swung the car over until he was side by side with the police car.

"Sorry, Pete," the policemen said. "My partner's a rookie and didn't recognize the car."

"Okay," Decker shouted back. "Hey, Doug, if you want to roust someone, I just saw Ramon Gomez, and he needed a fix badly. He was about to pull a 211 purse snatch on little old lady Sanchez."

"Where was he?" the officer asked.

"Arleta Park. I kicked him out, but he's probably hanging around."

"Will do."

The patrol car sped off.

Five minutes later they were standing in front of her old Volvo.

"I'm really sorry if I led you on."

Decker shook his head in self-disgust.

"People hear what they want to hear. I'm no exception. It was inappropriate for me – "

"Oh no, it wasn't. I mean, I'm not offended by anything you did."

"I'm glad." He smiled at her, and she seemed relieved. "Just take care of yourself. You still have my numbers?"

"They're pinned next to my home phone and the one in the mikvah."

"You're welcome to use them whenever you want."

"Thank you."

"I hope for your sake you don't *have* to."

8

Back at his desk, Decker reviewed the notes from his conversation with Rina, made a few corrections and additional comments, and angrily stuffed it all in the Adler Rape file.

He'd made a first-class ass out of himself. Jesus Christ! He was supposed to be investigating a rape case, not putting the make on a religious skirt twelve years his junior.

He picked up a pencil and twirled it absently.

Stop being so goddam hard on yourself, he chastised himself. Lighten up. But the pep talk didn't work. He felt sleazy and old.

His phone rang. Inhaling deeply, he stared at the blinking light, then picked up the receiver.

"Decker."

There was a loud whir on the other end.

"Hello?" said Decker.

"Hi," the voice responded. It was vaguely familiar. Female. Youthful sounding – possibly adolescent. She was shouting over the buzz.

"How can I help you, ma'am?" he asked tapping the pencil on the desk top.

"Are you the detective on the Foothill rape case?"

Decker sat up in his chair and pulled out a sheet of scrap paper.

"Yes, I am, Ms . . . ?"

"I was wondering about that last girl who was raped . . . You know, the librarian?"

"Yes," Decker said encouragingly. He could barely

hear her over the background drone. "Could you speak up, please?"

"What was her name? Ball or Bell . . . It was in the papers . . ."

"What about her?"

"Um, was she by any chance wearing black-and-white dress pumps?"

"Could be," Decker answered trying to contain his excitement. "That very well could be. I'll tell you what. Why don't you come down to the station, and the two of us can find out about it together, Ms . . . ?"

The line disconnected.

"Fuck," he said out loud. "Damn it!" He slammed down the receiver and quickly dialed communications.

"Arnie, it's Pete Decker."

"How's it going, Pete?"

"Just fine. Could you get me a location on my last incoming call? She hung up about a second ago."

"I'll see what I can do."

"Thanks."

Decker hung up.

Was she wearing two-tone pumps? You bet your sweet ass she was wearing two-tone pumps, and only the police were supposed to know it. The fact that that perp was a foot fetishist had been held back from the press. The lady knew something, and she'd slipped out of his hands.

Typical!

Fuck!

He knew he'd spoken to her before. She must have been one of the hundreds of anonymous tips that had floated through the station since the rapes began. But her voice stuck in his memory bank. He noted the date, time, and contents of the call, including the background noise, on a tip list and stuck it back in the file. A half-empty aspirin bottle lay on his desk. Opening it up, he popped two tablets in his mouth and washed them down with a cold sip of leftover coffee. He sat thinking. After a few minutes he got up, walked over to the central files and looked up the yeshiva vandalism episodes.

Nothing particularly illuminating. Broken windows, garbage strewn over the grounds, swastikas and obscene messages spray-painted on the walls: *Kikes, Cocksuckers, Baby Killers, Flesh Eaters, Christ Killers*. Maybe it should have bothered him more than it did, but he had passed it off as the same old stuff. Nothing new. Nothing that hadn't ever been said before. A few of the local punks were questioned, no arrests were made. Case closed. Kaput.

Decker put the file away, closed the drawer, and went back to his desk.

Anti-Semitism was nothing new to him. He'd grown up a good ole boy in Gainesville, where there was little direct contact with Jews but still a lot of prejudice. The locals regarded decadent Miami as a pinko watering hole for kikes, spics, and niggers. His first personal experience with a Jew came when he was fourteen. One of his buddies had been bumped off the first string of the local junior high football team by a Jew – a big strong boy who defied the stereotype. Later on in the day Decker and his friends ran into the Jew off campus. His buddy was pissed and baited the boy into a fight by calling him a Christ Killer. Decker did nothing as the two boys started duking it out, standing on the sidelines even when the rest of the gang jumped into the melee. It wasn't until he clearly saw that the Jewish boy was hopelessly outmuscled that he'd intervened and stopped the fighting. At fourteen, he was five ten, 170, with a developing pad of musculature that made grown men jealous. The boys listened to him, but weren't happy about it.

That evening at dinnertime he told his parents about the Jew and what had happened. After an initial silence, his father – a large, taciturn man with broad shoulders – spoke first. Gotta fight, he had said, when you're threatened. Gotta protect yourself, protect your family and country. But it's no damn good to fight someone just because of the way he was born. It's wrong, and it's stupid.

His mother's comment was more theological. The Lord Jesus turned the other cheek. Who are we to judge the infidels? Leave it to the hand of the Lord.

His little brother, Randy, six at the time, smiled and made designs in his mashed potatoes.

The discussion was dropped.

Decker's friends were cold to him for about a week, clearly angry at his befriending the Hebe. And the Jew wasn't any friendlier to him either, turning away whenever their paths crossed. Eventually things returned to normal and the fight was never mentioned by anyone again. But he had learned for a brief period what it was like to be a pariah.

Only his father had seemed to sense his alienation and tried, God bless him, to be more attentive. But Lyle Decker didn't talk much, and his idea of being therapeutic was having the two of them rebuild the garage together.

Not that Decker had minded the absence of man-to-man discussions. His father was a good person, a hard worker with a gentle soul. His mother had a tougher exterior, but she was also a good, solid person. There was always something sad about her. Decker suspected it had something to do with her not being able to conceive. He'd first learned of his adoption one day after school when he came home and found he had a new baby brother.

Where'd he come from, he'd asked his mother. *Same place you did,* she'd answered. *God.* Over the years he'd figured out the truth.

So much for sensitivity, he thought smiling. But it had been traumatic for him. He'd made a special effort to be open and communicative with his own daughter. It had been hard work, but it paid off. They had a warm, close relationship.

The phone rang.

"Decker."

"It's Arnie, Pete."

"Anything?"

"Local call from the Sylmar area."

"Nothing more specific?"

"Sorry. You want to come down here? Maybe we can work something out with Ma Bell."

"I probably will. Thanks."

"You bet."

Decker hung up.

Sylmar. Where most of the Foothill rapes had been taking place. Far from the mikvah, far from the Jews. There was probably no connection, but he'd read the files again just to be sure. He opened up a drawer and pulled out the Adler Rape folder. The lab reports showed the semen typing from the internal. The mikvah rapist was a secreter. The Foothill rapist had shown up as both a secreter and nonsecreter. But some of the women had had intercourse prior to their rape, confounding the results. Blood was found at the scene of the Adler woman's rape and on her clothing. All of it identified as hers. Fiber analysis of her clothes indicated foreign threads of yarn. Rina had told him that the attacker had been wearing a ski mask – probably knitted – and that something fuzzy had been crammed down Mrs Adler's throat. The fibers could have come from either or both. Nothing conclusive.

He threw the file back in the drawer and checked his watch. He had a court appearance to catch. An eleven-year-old had snatched the purse of a seventy-year-old grandma as she strolled her six-month-old grandson. The kid had been caught by a good Samaritan. First recorded offense. No major bodily injuries. They'd let him go with a stern lecture.

He got up and put on his jacket. Then he took out his notebook, scribbled "Call Dad" on his message page, and left.

Hawthorne caught Rina just as she was about to enter the classroom.

65

"What happened at the meeting with the cop?" he asked.

She stared at him in surprise.

"That bad, huh?"

"How did you know?" Rina asked.

"It's a small place here. Things get around."

Rina frowned.

"Actually, Sammy told me that you were meeting a policeman. I put two and two together. Find out anything about the rape?"

How in the world did Shmuel know? She'd have to be more careful around her sons in the future.

"Rina, did you hear me?"

"What?"

"The rape . . . Find out anything new?"

"No," she said, then turned to leave.

"Come on," Hawthorne coaxed. "Why else would you bother going down there?"

She hesitated.

"I remembered some more details. Matt, don't tell anyone about this conversation."

"My lips are sealed. What details?"

"Just details. They weren't even important. We've both got to go. We're going to be late."

"By the way, I picked something up for Sammy." Hawthorne reached in his pocket and pulled out a baseball card. "Da da! Fernando Valenzuela!"

Rina took the proffered card.

"Thanks, Matt. He'll be thrilled."

"Tell the little guy I'm still working on the few more that we've discussed."

"I will."

"You know, I'm free this Thursday night. If you'd like me to take him to a game, I wouldn't mind. He's been wanting to go for a long time."

"He has Computer Club."

"So let him skip a week. Steve won't mind. I know Sammy would have a ball."

"Not this week, Matt. Some other time."

Baring his teeth and mimicking Dracula, Hawthorne said, "Don't you trust me?"

Rina gave him a sick smile.

"We're late, Matt," she said.

Hawthorne held the door open for her.

"After you."

His courtliness rubbed her the wrong way. But she lowered her eyes: quietly said, "Thank you."

9

Something was going on outside the mikvah.

She'd been hearing things for days, now, and had grown sufficiently edgy to have Zvi Adler or some of the other *kollel* men walk her home.

Tonight the sounds seemed closer. The crackling of twigs, dull noises that could have been footsteps. It had been going on for the last ten minutes, but there was still a half hour's worth of work to do. She was sick of being frightened by shadows, terrorized by a phantom that lacked the courage to show its monstrous face in the daylight. She wanted this ogre captured and felt her fear turn to rage.

She grabbed up the phone receiver and called Foothill Division. Decker's extension rang twelve times before she finally gave up. She stared at his home number pinned on the wall. He'd said feel free to use it, but the pangs of anger had abated, and she was hesitant about intruding upon his privacy.

The footsteps outside returned, louder. She acted.

He picked it up on the third ring.

"Peter? It's Rina Lazarus."

"Are you calling to rescind your restraining order?" he joked.

"Peter, I'm at the mikvah. There's someone outside."

"Is everything locked?" His voice turned serious.

"Yes. The windows and doors are all bolted shut. But I'm scared stiff."

"Rina, it'll take me about fifteen minutes to get there.

68

If you really feel endangered, don't wait for me. Call up one of the yeshiva boys – "

"No, that's okay. I'm all right. Just get down here as soon as you can."

"Bye."

After hanging up, she forced herself to do the laundry. There was a light load tonight, but it took the same amount of time to wash a light load as a heavy one. The same amount of time *waiting*.

She slammed the washer lid shut and looked around for something that could be used for protection. Just in case. The only objects that looked remotely lethal were a blow dryer and a curling iron. She imagined using the iron on the intruder's genitals and felt better for a moment.

She paced aimlessly and heard a rattling at the door. Someone was trying to get in. Her heart began pounding wildly. She reached for the phone, but the sound disappeared. Gripping the receiver, she listened to the dial tone, then hung up.

Peter should be here any second. Don't panic. Stay cool. You can't always be dependent on someone else for protection. You have to use your own head.

Silence. Then the washer gurgled, and she jumped. She'd loaded the machine with too much soap, and the tub was frothing with bubbles. Damn it! The towels would probably have to be rinsed a third time.

Vowing to herself to retain control, she plopped into the armchair and picked up a sheaf of math papers. The numbers and symbols danced in front of her eyes, suddenly foreign. She didn't know what any of it meant. Just numbers and letters and funny Greek signs.

Calm. Stay calm. These were senior papers . . . This had to be calculus . . . She'd been teaching the seniors integrals. That Greek symbol was a summation sign. Slowly she relaxed, and the papers became comprehensible again. She picked up her red pen and began to grade.

A minute later she heard a loud, confident knock that

startled her and caused the pen to skid across the paper.
But she knew who it was.

"Who is it?" she asked, just to make sure.

"It's Peter, Rina. Open up."

She recognized the voice and opened the door.

"Am I glad to see you," she said spontaneously.

"Ditto," he smiled.

She blushed. "I didn't mean that as a – "

"I know you didn't. I'm just trying to lighten you up.
You look terrified."

"I am . . . I was. Did you look around outside?"

"Not yet. I'll be back in a few minutes."

"I'm coming with you."

He shook his head.

"Uh uh. If something's going on, you're much safer
inside."

"That's easy for you to say. You're not the one who
feels vulnerable, waiting alone and hearing noises."

"I'll be close by."

"You're not going to search in the bushes?"

"If need be, but – "

"I want to come with you, Peter."

"What will the neighbors say?" he grinned, moving
toward the door with long strides.

"*Pekuach nefesh*. The saving of a life takes precedence
over everything in Judaism." She looked upward. "For-
give me if I improvise a little."

"Come on. We're wasting time. Stay close," he said.

"That sounds fine to me."

They walked outside into a gust of warm air. Westerly
winds had cooled the valley but had also brought a plague
of gnats. Goddam bugs gnawed at your flesh, Decker
cursed to himself, slapping. Turning on a high-beam
flashlight, he swept it over the brush and the pathway.
Frowning, he began to walk slowly and deliberately
toward the woods. Rina kept slightly behind him and to
his left.

"See anything unusual?" she asked.

His ears perked up. "Hear that?"

She shook her head. "What is it?"

"I think you're right," he whispered. "Something's going on out here."

"Why?"

"Look here. Footprints leading to the forest. Sounds. Breathing. Not like any animal I know." He turned to Rina. "I don't want you out here with me. As a matter of fact, I wouldn't mind a back-up. Go back in the mikvah and call the police. When you get through say, 'Code Six.'"

"Walk back alone?"

"It's less noisy that way." He took out his gun. "I'll cover you. Who knows? Maybe we'll get lucky and flush out the son of a bitch."

"That sounds peachy," she said with an edge in her voice.

"All right," he said, "I'll walk you back. Let's not waste anymore time on it."

"No, I can handle myself. Just make sure I'm inside before you take off."

"Flash the lights twice when you've bolted the door."

"Be careful out there, Peter."

She started back and was almost at the door when she saw the figure coming. Before she had a chance to react, she heard Peter scream, "Police! Freeze!" Rina threw herself to the ground but could make out a silhouette swiveling toward Peter's voice and taking aim. She heard a burst of loud popping noises coming from all directions, then saw the figure make a dash for the woodlands.

"You okay?" shouted the detective, already moving.

"Yes!'

"Get the hell inside, and change the police call to a Code Three! I'm going after him." He was off.

She sprang to her feet, ran into the mikvah, and locked herself inside. She dialed the station and was amazed at her calmness in relating the story, going through the

71

motions mechanically. But once she got off the phone she began to shake uncontrollably. Minutes later she heard footsteps followed by more banging at the door.

She opened it.

There were a dozen policemen. Overhead, a helicopter rumbled like a giant locust, turning night to morning with its spotlight. She squinted and returned her gaze to the officers, looking for a familiar face. She found two: the big blonde, Marge, and the fat detective. They jogged toward her.

"Detective Decker's out there, somewhere in the hills," Rina said breathlessly to Marge. "I think the guy shot at him, but I don't think he got hit."

Marge, Hollander, and the uniforms conferred. The patrolmen scattered quickly into the brush, and Hollander went off to search the yeshiva grounds, leaving the two women alone.

"Want to go inside?" Marge asked.

"I'm fine. I'd feel a lot better if I knew Peter was okay."

"Peter?"

"Detective Decker."

Marge had to smile. "Yes. Detective Decker."

Rina looked up and laughed nervously. "I guess there was no need to explain who he was. I'm very jittery."

Marge threw her arm around the quivering woman. "You're holding up just fine. And don't worry about Peter. He knows what he's doing. You want to tell me what happened?"

As Rina related the events of the evening, students from the yeshiva began to converge upon the area. The boys stared wide-eyed at the squad cars and the circling 'copter and asked her what was going on. She turned away, weary of being the center of attention, just wanting to go home. She hoped to God the police would find this fiend and free her of the fear that was eating at her insides.

And she hoped nothing happened to Peter. Just let him

be okay. He was her responsibility, she felt, since she'd called him down in the first place.

Within minutes a sizable crowd had gathered and Marge was working hard to contain the mass to one area.

Chana, Ruthie, and Chaya came up to Rina. They had been attending a bible class that evening and on their way home were attracted to the tumult. What had happened? Rina tried to say as little as possible, but they kept pumping her. Why wouldn't they leave her alone and go home? They meant well, but her patience was gone, and she turned away. Finally, they shook their heads and gave up.

The helicopter kept whirling overhead, flooding the ground with a hot jet of white light. The minutes turned hopelessly long. Finally, she saw Peter emerge from the trees.

"*Baruch Hashem*," she said out loud, blessing God.

"Did they catch him?" Chana asked excitedly.

Rina looked at her, then at Decker. He was alone.

"No. I don't think they caught him yet."

"Then why the *Baruch Hashem?*"

Rina ignored her and walked over to Decker who led her to an isolated spot beyond the crowd. She felt Chana's eyes boring in on her. She was pleased when, a moment later, Marge and Hollander joined them. That made it took better.

"How are you holding up?" Pete asked her.

"I'm fine. Nobody shot at *me*. I'm glad you're all right."

Decker smiled at her. To the other detectives he said: "I lost the bastard. I saw him a couple of times, but I couldn't close in on him because he kept popping bullets at me. Asshole's a good shot. He came awfully close."

He lit a cigarette.

"Couldn't make a damn detail on him except he looked like he was shooting with his right hand. I'd put him at five eight to eleven with an average build. Dark clothing. And he was wearing a ski mask. That's it. So damn *dark* up there. The last time I saw him was about five hundred

73

feet behind the main building in the backlands. There're four uniforms up there right now. It's probably useless, but I told them to keep at it for another half hour. I'm going to poke around the grounds just in case the prick gets cute and decides to camp out overnight."

"I'll comb the buildings," Hollander said.

"Good idea."

A man was approaching them.

"The Adler woman's husand," said Marge. "Here goes nothing."

"Luck, Peter." Hollander saluted with his pipe and left.

"I'm sorry, Mr Adler," Decker said when Zvi was in hearing distance. "We're still looking."

Zvi's eyes were full of rage. "I want to help."

"There's nothing you can do, Mr Adler. It's in the hands of professionals."

"Professionals?" Zvi turned on Decker. "You can't find this *mamzer*, and you have the nerve to call yourself a professional? Is this what professionals do? Stand around and gab while he's still loose in the hills?"

"Detective Decker's been in the hills for over an hour, Zvi," Rina defended him. "That animal was shooting at him."

Zvi peeled off some rapid Hebrew at her. She fired some back. They stared at each other.

"Seems to me everybody's frustration is being misdirected," Decker said calmly. "It's the criminal's throat we want. Not each other's."

The Rosh Yeshiva walked over.

"What is going on here?" he asked tensely. "Nobody is telling me anything."

Decker filled him in on the details.

"And you called the police?" Schulman asked Rina.

"I called Detective Decker, actually."

The old man said nothing.

"She did the right thing," Decker said. "That's what I'm here for."

"Certainly not to catch bad guys," Zvi muttered.

Schulman barked something to Adler in Yiddish. The younger man looked down.

"There is a mob out there," Schulman said to Decker. "I'll do what I can to get the boys back in the classrooms and dormitories, but tell your men to ease up with the threats and pushing. A few of them are becoming abusive."

"I'll go back with you, Rabbi," Marge offered. "You talk to your boys, I'll talk to the police."

"I'd appreciate it."

Dunn and Schulman left the three of them alone.

"*At smaycha?*" Zvi said sarcastically to Rina.

"*Maspeek*, Zvi," she answered. She was almost in tears. "*Bevakasha.*"

Zvi sighed.

"I'm sorry, Rina." He looked at Decker. "I know this isn't your fault. I'm frustrated."

"It's okay. I understand," Decker answered. "I'm going to look around a little more. You'll stay with Mrs Lazarus?"

Adler nodded.

"You go home, Zvi," she said, wearily. "Tell my kids, I'm fine. I'll wait with the women."

"Detective?"

The three of them turned around and saw two patrolmen flanking a yeshiva student in his late twenties. The man was stooped and thin, with scanty, black, untrimmed whiskers that grew from a gaunt face. His black jacket was oversized and torn at the pockets, his white shirt wrinkled and tucked carelessly into patched black pants. The shoes on his feet were scuffed and caked with dirt. His eyes were dark and dull and swirled aimlessly in their sockets. On his head was a black homburg with the rim coming loose. His arms had been pinioned behind him and cuffed. He seemed as insubstantial as a scarecrow as the policemen shoved him along.

"Look what we found wandering in the bushes."

"Oh my God," Rina muttered.

"Read him his rights?" Decker asked.

"First thing," one of the policemen answered.

"Take him down to the station."

"Peter, that's not the rapist," Rina said.

He looked at her. "What do you mean?"

"That's Moshe. He's the groundskeeper."

"Well, he could also be a rapist."

"Moshe's harmless. He wouldn't hurt a fly."

"We'll find out how harmless he is, Rina."

"He's not the man you're looking for, Peter. Please. He's a waste of your time."

"Why? Because you know him? Because he's one of your own?"

Zvi mumbled something in Hebrew. Rina heard it and turned bright red. She was furious at both of the men, but fought to maintain control. "No, not because he's one of my own, but because I know he's not a rapist!"

"What should I do with him, Detective?" asked one of the patrolmen.

Moshe mumbled placidly, a slack smile on his lips.

"Wait a minute." Decker was angry and pulled Rina aside. "You called me here. Let me do my job."

"Peter, listen to me. Moshe's kept on by the yeshiva as an act of compassion. He's off-balance. He wanders around the grounds at night muttering to himself. Everyone in the place knows about him. He's cuckoo, Peter. But he's *harmless*. I swear to you, he's harmless."

"Unfortunately, your oath doesn't mean a thing, Rina. If the guy's a psycho, all the more reason to check him out. If he's innocent, there won't be any problem. I just want to ask him some questions." Decker sucked on his cigarette. "A woman was raped, I was shot at, I want some answers!"

"He won't have an alibi for the night of the rape. He spends every night roaming the hills. He won't know what you're talking about."

Zvi broke in. "Detective, may I say something?"

Decker gave him a hard stare. "What?"

"I know how this must look to you, but Mrs Lazarus is right. As much as I want to murder the *mamzer* who defiled my wife, I know with all my heart that it is not the man your policemen are holding. Moshe would be no more likely to rape than you or I. He's crazy, he's weird, but he's not a rapist. If you question him, he'll crack up. You could probably convince him he was the rapist, and he'd be fool enough to believe you."

"Peter, please," Rina pleaded. "If you arrest him, the people here will never trust the police again. That'll make us open targets."

"You know what you're asking me to *do*?" Decker said.

"Please," she begged.

"Okay," he said, mashing out his cigarette with his heel. "This is what I'm going to do. I'm going to release this weirdo into your custody, Mr Adler. But you people have got to explain to him what's going on and keep him away from the hills. Because if I get called down here again, and we go through another search and he's found on or about the area, he's going to be arrested. And I'm going to be very pissed at you all because I'll catch deep shit for letting him go in the first place."

Decker ordered the man released and stomped away. Zvi took Moshe aside immediately and began talking to him, patiently.

Fifteen minutes later, the search team called it quits. Within the half hour the mikvah area was quiet except for Decker, Rina, and a group of women who stayed steadfast at her side. The detective walked the group home, dropping them off one by one, until he was alone with Rina.

"I've got to pick up my kids," she said.

"Where are they?"

"I've been leaving them with Sarah Libba. I don't trust babysitters anymore."

"Pick them up."

"Zvi usually walks me home."

"So tonight I'll walk you home."

77

She said nothing.

Decker frowned.

"I'd be more than happy to leave right now, but I need to talk to you about this Moshe weirdo."

"It would be awkward if I let you inside my house, Peter."

"Then we'll talk here," he said testily, taking out his notebook.

"It would really be easier if we could let this go for the evening. I'd be happy to meet you somewhere and answer any questions you'd like."

He hesitated.

"Peter, I'm a nervous wreck."

He regarded her face. It was beautiful, but suffused with anxiety. Time to forget about being a cop and loosen the reins.

"Okay. I'll meet you at the station tomorrow at eleven sharp."

"Could we possibly postpone it until Monday? Tomorrow evening is our Sabbath, and I'm having company. I was planning to cook all day, since we're not allowed to cook once the sun goes down Friday night."

Decker said nothing.

"I could start cooking tonight, but it's so late – "

"No, no." Decker exhaled. "All right. Meet me Monday at the station."

She paused, then asked timidly:

"Could we meet at Arleta Park instead?"

She didn't want the guys at the station to get the wrong idea, he thought.

"Fine," he said brusquely. "I'll meet you at the park."

"Peter, thank you for coming down. Really, thanks for everything."

"It's my job, Rina."

"Thanks just the same."

He paused for a moment, then asked evenly:

"What did Zvi say to you?"

"He just bawled me out."

78

"What'd he mutter under his breath? That's what you get for trusting a goy?"

He was wounded. She almost reached out, but held back.

Softly she answered, "Something like that."

10

The Foothill rapist had dropped another turd tonight, and Hollander was pissed. The new rape meant more pressure from the brass and more of the media coverage that was turning the case and his detail into a circus. More important, it meant Decker and Marge were out on field work, leaving him stuck here to deal with the crazy Jews on a Sunday night, all in the name of public service. Shit!

The meeting, held in the community hall, was jammed with bodies and had been droning on for over an hour. The Jews didn't like anyone, but they had gotten sort of used to Decker. They considered him the head honcho and weren't overjoyed at dealing with a replacement. Hollander tried to answer their questions and assuage their anxiety, but he was getting tired. And he knew if he didn't make it home soon, Mary would be too sleepy for a roll in the hay. The only bright spot was the little black-haired gal Decker liked, sitting in the back row. She was a looker and didn't seem nearly as tight-assed as the others.

Rina sympathized with the fat detective. It was hard being center stage surrounded by hostile forces. Though he tried to ease the tension with humor, his off-the-cuff remarks came out flip and uncaring. Peter would have handled it better.

Zvi Adler was talking now. Sarah Libba had decided to show her face in public for the first time since the rape. She sat by his side, head down, hands folded tightly in her lap. Zvi was a difficult man, but Rina admired his unwavering support for his wife. He even had the guts to show his feelings for her *publicly* when she started to cry midway through the meeting. He had hugged her and kissed her on the cheek.

Zvi was putting Hollander on the spot again, and the detective was responding with bluster. Peter was sorely missed. He'd called her to tell her why he wouldn't be coming tonight and had asked her to keep mum about the newest rape. The knowledge, he'd felt, would raise the anxiety level and make the session harder on Hollander. But she felt sure the yeshiva people would suspect something from his absence.

Steve Gilbert and Matt Hawthorne entered the room and parked themselves next to her.

"What are you two doing here?" she asked.

"Personal invitation from Rabbi Schulman," said Hawthorne. "All will be explained."

"How are you doing, Rina?" Gilbert asked.

"Not too well."

"Where's your friend?"

"What friend?"

"The boys are saying you're pretty chummy with the red-haired detective," Hawthorne explained.

"What!"

"No need to get excited," said Gilbert. "What you do on your own free time is none of our business."

"He's not my pal. Unfortunately, we've been thrown together recently."

"Not so unfortunate for the good detective." Hawthorne grinned.

She ignored him.

"What's happened so far?" Gilbert asked.

"Nothing really. We're yelling at the poor man up there, and he's trying to defend himself. It's yeshiva twenty, detective zero."

Her face clouded.

"Everyone's scared, and for good reason."

"And yourself?" Gilbert asked.

"I'm petrified."

81

"Why don't you stop being the mikvah lady?" Hawthorne asked. "It's become a dangerous job for a lone woman."

"The yeshiva supports the boys and me. In exchange, I teach and run the mikvah."

"They wouldn't kick you out if you quit," Steve said.

"I'd feel like a moocher if I didn't contribute."

"Dedicated until the end." Steve shook his head.

She looked at him sharply, and he shrugged apologetically.

"Did Sammy ever thank you for the baseball cards, Matt?"

"He sure did. You should have let him come with me to the ball game Thursday evening. It would have been a lot safer there than it was here."

"The boys were perfectly safe," Gilbert said. "They were with me."

"Yes, I meant to thank you for walking them to Sarah Adler's after Computer Club," Rina said to him.

"No problem." Gilbert paused a moment. "Yossie Adler has been awfully quiet lately. Does he know what happened?"

"He must," Hawthorne replied. "He's thirteen and very bright."

"Did anyone say anything to him?" Gilbert asked, wiping his glasses with a tissue.

"No one that I know of," answered Rina. "Certainly his parents haven't said anything."

"We're being watched, comrades," whispered Hawthorne.

Rina turned and saw some of the women staring at her. She moved down a row.

I highly recommend this security company," said Hollander. "Many businesses and developments in the area have worked with them successfully. Their field of expertise is residential and ground patrol."

"What about the female guards?" someone asked.

"They're as well-trained as the men. And let me tell you people something: The women are *big* women. They wear firearms, and they know how to use them."

"I don't see why the yeshiva has to dole out extra money to do the job the police should be doing," someone else complained.

"Menachem, it's impossible for the police to be everywhere all the time," explained Rav Schulman. "On the other hand, Rabbi Marcus's skepticism is valid. The police did nothing about the vandalism. Why should this case be different?"

"Rabbi Schulman," Hollander sighed wearily. "We know the kids who're responsible, but unless we catch them in the act, it's impossible to prosecute."

"It's those punk kids." Ruthie Zipperstein grimaced. "They wear those Nazi arm bands and the leather pants. Anti-Semites, each and every one of them. I wouldn't be a bit surprised if they were behind what happened at the mikvah."

"They bother us when we do our marketing in town," Chana added.

"Did you file a complaint?" Hollander asked.

"What good would a complaint do against obscene language?" Chana shouted. "You can't control the vandals, you can't control them from raping, you're obviously not going to be able to control their mouths."

"If they are really harassing you – "

"Forget it," Ruthie said, disgusted. "I'm sorry I brought it up."

"Now I want to say something, Detective Hollander," the Rosh Yeshiva broke in. "First I think the police should show good faith and tell us the real reason for Detective Decker's absence."

Hollander chewed his pipe stem. What the hell? It would be on the eleven o'clock news.

"He's out investigating another Foothill rape."

"Is this madman the same one who attacked my wife?" Zvi demanded.

"I don't know, Mr Adler. You'll have to ask Detective Decker for the details."

Zvi turned to Rina. "Did you talk about this with him?"

She didn't know what to say, so she hedged. "I don't know any more than you do."

"Don't you have a hotline to the detective?" Chana said accusingly.

Why didn't they leave her alone . . .

"Anyone can call him," she snapped back. "You want to call him up and ask him questions, call him up."

"This is getting nowhere," the Rosh Yeshiva interjected. "I have a plan, and it's a good one. One, we hire a female security guard to watch the mikvah and walk the ladies home at night. Two, on Shabbos we will take extra precautions. I will not have this *rasha* violating our holy day of rest!"

The old man broke into a spasm of coughs. When the hacking subsided, he continued.

"I've just spoken with Steven and Matthew, and *Baruch Hashem*, they're *gutten neshamas*." He translated for Hollander: "Good souls. They want to help out and have volunteered to patrol Friday nights when we're in shul."

The audience turned to the teachers with grateful smiles, but Hollander was skeptical. He suspected everyone connected to the place, and the teachers were no exceptions. But he kept his opinions to himself and smiled approvingly.

"That's nice of you," Rina whispered.

"At least until Steve gets married," said Rabbi Schulman, smiling. "And that's going to be when, Steven?"

"Three months."

"So" – the old man clasped his hands – "we'll all work together. The police will do their job, and we will be especially vigilant. If it be the will of *Hashem*, justice will be served."

He turned to Hollander.

"We will fight back if we have to, Detective. Never again will we be lambs led to slaughter."

He looked as hard as an old Baptist preacher, thought Hollander. Gazing at the roomful of angry faces, the detective groaned inwardly. He could just see it. Some kid throws an egg at the gate and winds up in the hospital minus a pair of nuts.

"I understand your feeling of frustration, Rabbi, but please, if something comes up, I strongly urge you to leave it up to the police. It's dangerous to take the law into your own hands, and it could get you in a heap of trouble, legally.

The rabbi was not daunted. "That may be a chance we'll have to take," he said, firmly.

"Rina Miriam," the Rosh Yeshiva called out as she was about to leave.

She walked back to him.

"Yes, Rav Aaron."

"Rina Miriam," he said softly, "a yeshiva isn't the ideal atmosphere for a young widow with two children. Are you happy here?"

"I'm content. My boys have found a home here."

"Then I am glad we can do honor to Yitzchak, *alav hashalom*, by providing his family with a community."

"Thank you," she said.

But she knew there was more.

"We will always have a place for you and your boys, Rina Miriam. You have a very important role here. You teach, you lecture irreligious women on *Taharat Hamishpacha*. Many women now go to the mikvah because of you."

"That's good to hear."

"You and your children will always be welcome, but . . ." The old man's eyes became as hard as granite. "But there's no room for a goy."

She turned a deep crimson.

"I don't know what you mean."

"You're a very smart lady. You know what I mean."

"I don't know what kind of rumors you've heard – "

85

"I don't listen to rumors, Rina Miriam."

"Of course you don't." She looked at the floor.

"But, *Baruch Hashem*, my eyes still work, and I see things. Like the expression on your face last Thursday when you talked to the big detective. And the one on his face when he talked to you. He's a nice boy – rugged looking, hard working, well-mannered – a *mensch*. It's easy to get caught up, especially if you've been alone for a while."

"There is nothing between Detective Decker and me."

"I'm glad you've convinced your head of that. Now work on your heart."

11

Shit. She'd brought her kids.

Decker glanced at his watch. It was two past twelve. At least Rina was punctual. She was trudging toward him, weighted down by shopping bags while her two boys ran ahead and chased each other across the grass. He met her halfway, relieved her of the sacks, and escorted her to an empty bench.

She was goddam beautiful. No doubt about that. Even the long-sleeved shirt and dowdy skirt couldn't hide a curvacious body that brushed against the material as she walked. But it was her face – the combination of innocence and sensuality – that got to him. The yeshiva had her well hidden, isolated from the outside world. Otherwise there'd be no way she'd be walking around without ten guys following her, tongues lolling out like panting dogs. If she only knew . . . Then again, if she knew, he wouldn't stand a chance.

"You brought company," he said, making an attempt to hide his disappointment.

"My older boy came down with a scratchy throat last night that turned into croup. I took them both to the pediatrician for throat cultures, and we just got out. I didn't think you would mind."

"Not at all."

She called her kids, and they came plowing toward her full speed, managing, somehow, to stop short an inch from impact.

"Is this the policeman, Eema?" the smaller one asked.

"Yes. This is Detective Decker." She looked at Peter. "This is Sammy and this is Jake."

Decker extended an arm. "Pleased to meet you, boys."

They each took a turn at shaking his hand. At least she dressed the boys like normal kids, he thought. Baseball caps, shorts, T-shirts, and sneakers. Even if strings were sticking out from under the shirts.

"Do you have a gun?" Sammy asked.

"Shmuel, that isn't – "

"It's all right," Decker said with a smile. "Every boy I've ever met has asked me the same question." He turned to Sammy and tousled the black hair that stuck out from under the skullcap.

"Yes, I have a gun." He unsnapped the holster and lifted out the butt of the service revolver. After the boys had a peek, he nudged it back in and closed the flap.

"Is it real?" Jake asked.

"You bet."

"Did you ever shoot anyone?" asked Sammy with growing excitement.

"Did you ever *kill* anyone?" asked Jake with a gleam in his eye.

"Boys, I think that's enough with the questions. Why don't we eat lunch?"

"I'm not hungry," Sammy croaked.

"Throat's still sore, huh?" Rina asked.

"A little. I'll just take some juice."

"I'm not hungry, either," Jake said.

"Don't eat if you're not hungry." Rina took out a carton of cranberry juice.

"Well, I'm starved," Decker announced.

"Can I hold your gun?" Sammy asked.

"No," Decker said firmly. "But I'll tell you what. How about you boys giving me a few minutes to eat and talk to your mom in private? Then, I'll take you for a ride in my car."

"I don't see a police car," Jake said, dubiously.

"I drive that beat-up old brown thing parked over

there." Decker pointed to the Plymouth. "Doesn't look like much on the outside, does it?"

"Sure doesn't," the little boy agreed.

"If I was a criminal, I wouldn't be impressed," Sammy added.

Decker let go with a full laugh.

"I'll pass the information on to my watch commander. Anyway, it's stocked with a police radio and a gun rack."

"Does it have a siren?" Jake asked.

"Yes."

"How fast does it go?" inquired Sammy.

"Fast."

"Can you race it for us?"

Rina interrupted the interrogation.

"Boys, let the man eat."

"What d'you got, Eema?" Sammy asked.

"I thought you weren't hungry," said Rina.

Sammy parked himself next to Decker. "I changed my mind."

"Me, too," added Jake, taking the other side.

No matter how hard Rina tried, the boys couldn't contain themselves from asking questions. Decker finally told her to give it up. He didn't mind.

He related well to kids, she thought. In a short period of time he'd managed to get a good rapport with the boys. Too good . . .

After lunch, she instructed the kids to play by themselves. At first they protested their exile, but Decker reminded them of the excursion that awaited if they behaved, and they left without a fuss.

"Nice boys," he said.

"They are. They're usually not so nosy."

"They're inquisitive. It's healthy."

"They're excited at meeting a detective," she said, smiling.

He looked at her.

"Nice to know I can excite *somebody*."

She turned away.

89

He chuckled self-consciously. "That was a ridiculous thing to say."

She changed the subject.

"Do you want something else to eat?"

"No, I'm stuffed, thank you."

There was an uncomfortable silence. Rina broke it.

"How's the Foothill rapist – "

"Please! Don't bring up sore spots!"

"Sorry."

"I caught hell for not bringing in that Moshe character. There are mutterings that I'm partial." He shrugged. "I don't know. Maybe I am."

"I'm sorry if it got you in trouble. But, believe me, Peter, he's not the man you want."

"Who is he?"

She sighed. "His name is Moshe Feldman."

"What is he? Some stray that the rabbi took pity on?"

"No. A long time ago – actually not too long ago – he was a brilliant student. He was best friends with Yitzchak, my husband; they were *chavrusas* – learning partners. Moshe met his wife about the same time I met Yitzchak, and the four of us were inseparable. We even got married within a month of each other.

"Two months after Moshe's marriage, his wife announced that she didn't want to be religious and she didn't want to be married. I don't know what happened. No one would talk about it. She wrote to me a couple of times saying she had to find herself, but didn't go into specifics. Last I heard she was living with this rock and roll guitarist . . ."

Rina threw up her hands.

"Anyway, Moshe withdrew from people after that. Even Yitzchak. They no longer talked as friends, but they still learned together. Yitzy used to say that Moshe's mind was as sharp as ever, but he was blocked emotionally. When my husband died two years ago Moshe stopped learning formally. A month later he asked me to marry

90

him. I refused, and a week later he snapped. He's been like that ever since."

Her eyes moistened.

"I know, intellectually, that he was over the border before he proposed to me. He hadn't been in his right mind since his wife left him. But I couldn't help it. I felt it was my fault."

She looked at Decker.

"It was very important to me that you didn't arrest him. First, because he's not a rapist. Second, I called you down there. His arrest would have been my responsibility – "

"That's absurd, Rina – "

"I would have felt that I nailed his coffin. He was a wonderful person, Peter. A sweet man with a brilliant mind. In some ways he was much more attentive to me than Yitzchak. He would never do anything criminal, Peter. Just as you wouldn't. It's not in his make-up."

Decker said nothing.

"You're not convinced, are you?"

"No, not at all," he said. "If anything, you've given me more reason to suspect him. Rapists usually hold huge grudges against women. Nasty feelings that suddenly explode. Your friend sounds like a prime candidate for an explosion."

"He's not, Peter. You'll just have to trust me."

"I gave him his one break. Next time, I play by the book."

"I appreciate what you did." She started to pat his hand, but stopped herself.

"I don't bite," he said softly.

"I wish you did. It would make it a lot easier on me if you were crude and unappealing."

"Then it's a good thing you can't read my mind. A whole lot of crude thoughts are swimming around there."

She didn't say anything.

"Did I offend you?"

"Peter, I'm not some naive little Pollyanna who believes the whole world is cotton candy. Or an inhibited prude who thinks people should only make love in the dark with their clothes on. I'm *religious*. I realize that's a foreign concept to most people, especially in California, but that's what I am. I don't do certain things, not because I don't want to, but because I have religious values.

"I think it's wrong to have sex if you're not married. I don't think fire and brimstone will come pouring down if you do, but I think it's wrong. Why? Not on moral grounds – though a case could be made for that, too – but because it's immodest. *Tsnios* – bodily modesty – is important to us. That's why we dress the way we do, that's why married women cover their hair. Not to look unattractive – we like dressing up as much as the next person – but because we believe that the body is private and not some cheesy piece of artwork that's put on public display. We know our way of thinking is considered antiquated, as dated as an Edsel. But to me, it has meaning."

Decker was amazed at her intensity. "Well, it's a bit old-fashioned – "

"You know what a mikvah *really* symbolizes, Peter?" She became animated. "Spiritual cleansing. A renewal of the soul. For twelve days, starting from the first day of a woman's menses, she and her husband are forbidden to have sex. When the twelve days are up, if she hasn't bled for the last seven days, she immerses herself in the mikvah, and then they can resume marital relations, renew their physical bond. That means for at least twelve days every month a husband and wife are off-limits to each other. I bet that seems nuts to you, doesn't it?"

He smiled. "In a word, yes."

"And yet it seems so *normal* to me."

"Everybody's standard of normalcy differs, I guess." He looked at her. "But all Jews don't do this. I know my wife never did."

"Well, Torah Jews do. I did!" She paused, then said, "Now do you see why it's impossible for you and me to go out?"

92

"I'm starting to get the picture."

He laughed, and so did she.

"I can't believe that people actually . . . For twelve days, huh?"

She tucked ebony strands of loose hair back into her tam.

"You know, Peter, when you stop and think about it, the world's become perverse. You're an intelligent man and a good person. You have no problem in accepting that there are men who rape, men who have no impulse control. They see a woman, objectify her, and tear into her flesh as if she were a piece of meat. Yet, it's hard for you to fathom men who are the exact opposite, men who can control themselves and their drives. In fact, men who follow *Taharat Hamishpacha* – family purity – are the exact opposite of rapists. Yet, they're viewed as weirdos."

"You're talking about two extremes," said Decker. "There's plenty in between – lots of *normal* men, like myself, who'd find your customs very hard to deal with."

"That's exactly why we stick to our own kind."

He had no comeback, so he lit another cigarette and looked at the sky.

He still wanted her. The discussion had added hot blue fire to her eyes which only made her more appealing. She was passionate. He knew she'd be passionate in bed. But there was no choice other than to give up. Just concede defeat and forget about her. It would take a keg of dynamite to blast through her armor.

"I like you," he said sincerely. "I find you incredibly attractive and very nice to talk to. But I can see where a relationship between the two of us might run into some difficulty."

"I'm glad you understand," she smiled. "I hope this doesn't mean I can't call you if I hear something strange – "

"Of course not. One thing has nothing to do with the other. I'm still the cop assigned to the case. I could find you personally repulsive, and I'd still do my job."

"You're a good guy, Detective Decker."

"That's what they tell me." He stood up and watched her kids at play. They were waging a battle, using dried twigs and branches for guns and swords. For a brief instant he was transported back to his childhood – he and his friends playing cops, running through the glades during the hot, muggy summers, shooting at the bad guys. His friends had outgrown the games.

Decker thought of his own daughter. She was sixteen now, and a good kid. Neither Jan nor he had ever had an ounce of trouble with her, even during the worst parts of their divorce. He'd never felt he'd missed out by not having a son. But now as he observed her boys, and with forty less than two years away, he began to wonder.

12

The total was more than Rina had expected, eight dollars over budget, but she carried an extra ten in another part of her wallet for emergencies like this one. She handed the crisp bill to the checker, who snapped it in her hands.

"Fresh off the press," the woman said, placing it in the register.

Rina smiled, held out her hand for the change, then stuffed it in her purse hurriedly. Wheeling the shopping cart out of the market, she began the long walk back to her car. The lot was emptier now. When she'd arrived earlier in the morning, there hadn't been a space on the paved area. She'd had to park in a dirt extension full of broken glass and hope that her tread-bare tires would remain intact. The shopping cart was hard to push; a wheel was stuck, and it was loaded down with bags of groceries. She gave the thing a hard shove and something kicked in.

She couldn't understand how she'd run so afar from her budget. Maybe she was having more company for Shabbos than usual, or perhaps her boys and their friends were eating more. Certainly, her appetite had decreased ever since the mikvah incident. She'd lost four pounds, and her curves were beginning to angulate.

Stopping in back of her battered Volvo, she flipped open the trunk. It was full of junk: old sand toys that the boys hadn't used for years, newspapers that had yellowed with age, torn paper bags, and an empty juice bottle. She pushed the trash aside and began to load the groceries, but upon hearing sharp footsteps, stopped abruptly and looked up.

There were four of them – punk kids. Teenagers with greasy long hair, glassy eyes, and wise guy smirks. They were dressed similarly – jeans, black T-shirts emblazoned with images of Satan, scuffed up Wellington boots. The one who approached her was of medium height and build, with a weak chin and blond fuzz for facial hair. She had seen him before but had always avoided direct confrontation. Now he was giving her a lecherous smile that showed yellow buck teeth. His left arm sported a tattoo of a knife in a heart, and from his right ear dangled a gold hoop. He pulled out a cigarette and offered her one.

"No, thank you," she said quietly.

Her eyes scanned the area for signs of life. In the distance was a woman with two small children.

"Can I help you load those bags, *Miss?*" the kid said. "Miss Jewey. Miss *Kike*. Miss Kikey-ikey?"

The other three started to giggle. Rina attempted to ignore them and go about her business, but the punk encircled her arm with grease-stained fingers and yanked her away from the open trunk. Still gripping her tightly, he pulled off the kerchief she was wearing and let out a hoarse laugh. His breath was strong and stale.

"You're a cutey, little Miss Jew bitch. Those big blue eyes . . . Nice black kike hair . . . Where's your purse, honey?"

He took the bag off her shoulder, but released her arm.

"Let's see what you got in your goody bag," he chuckled. "Oh, boys, will you look at this?"

He pulled out her two dollars.

His comrades hooted with delight.

"I don't think a rich Jew bitch like you would mind makin' us a little loan, would you? Plenty of bread where this came from. Just gotta spread those nice legs for that rich fucker husband of yours and your purse magically fills up, don't it."

She gave him a hard, impassive stare.

He stuffed the bills in his pants pocket.

"Lookie here. What do we got? We got pictures. These two tykes your little ones?"

She said nothing.

"More little kike tykes." He clucked his tongue. "You fuckers are taking over the world, ain't you? First you take our money, now you move in our town and act like you own the place . . ."

He pulled the photos out of the plastic sheaths, tore them into pieces, ate one, and scattered the rest.

"She got any Jew dope in there, Cory?" One of them asked the leader.

"Nah, you don't want Jew dope. It'd make your nose hang down to your cock."

The punks howled.

"What else you got, honey? You got a pen. A nice one. Gold. Only expensive shit for you Hebee Jebees, huh?"

His eyes scrunched up and he moved his lips as he read the inscription.

"To Rina." He looked up at her. "With love from Yizjack?"

"You people have dumbshit names." He tossed it to one of his friends. "How fucking sweet! Little Jackshit gave you a *pen*!"

He searched further and pulled out a small pocket prayer book.

"What the fuck is this? Looks like a secret code to me. You some commie spy, rich bitch Hebe lady?"

He took out a knife and began slicing the pages. Rina's eyes became wet with fury.

One of the others peered into her shopping bag, pulled out a bottle of club soda and started shaking it rapidly.

"Hey, man, I'm kinda hot. Are you kinda hot, Cory?"

"Man, I'm real hot," he snickered. "I'm hot to trot with Jew baby."

"Hey, maybe this'll cool you off."

He unscrewed the top and let out a gush of carbonated water, drenching them all in the process. The boys doubled over in laughter, having so much fun that they decided to repeat the procedure. After they'd emptied all the bottles, they moved on to the other groceries. Cory, clearly the leader, threw each of his friends an egg.

"I'm hungry." He grinned. "How 'bout you, honey? You want some *scrambled* eggs?"

He cracked open the shell and emptied the contents in her trunk. The others elected to throw theirs against the car.

Cory belched out loud, filling the air with rancid fumes.

"Hey," he said, "I heard egg in the hair was real good for split ends."

He cracked an egg on her head. She stood there frozen and let the goop ooze down her face and neck. She wiped yoke from her eyes and waited for the next assault trying hard to retain *details* of what was happening.

"Don't take it personal, honey." He cracked an egg over his own head and the boys followed suit. "Is this what you people mean by an *egg*head?"

An older man strode up. He was in his middle fifties, but solidly built, and appeared to be in good shape.

"Why don't you boys beat it?" he said fiercely.

"Why don't you knock it off, you old fart, before you get your motherfucking skull bashed in?"

The man took a swing at the punk, but the boy easily ducked the punch. Rina tried to run away, but was grabbed by Cory. The other three pounced upon the man at the same time. She screamed and Cory cupped a dirty hand over her mouth.

"Don't waste him," Cory shouted, holding Rina tightly. He was incredibly strong. "Not yet anyway."

He leaned his back against the car and pulled Rina to his stomach, grinding his pelvis against her rear. Nausea surged through her gut. Two of the boys grabbed the man, pulled him upright and managed to restrain the writhing figure in their arms. He let go with a bellow, turning red as he struggled futilely in the boys' grips.

"You fucking asshole," the boy said as he landed a

punch on the man's nose. Immediately, out poured bright red blood.

Rina cried out again, and the boy stuffed a filthy headband in her mouth. She gasped and started to gag.

"You be a good little bitch, and I'll take it out."

He pulled out the piece of cloth. She spat and screamed again.

A moment later they all heard sirens.

"Cops!" Cory yelled.

Rina took advantage of his diverted attention and stomped hard on his instep. As he yelped in pain, she spun around and knee-dropped him. Cory recovered quickly, but not fast enough. Though his friends had managed to flee successfully, he found himself surrounded by patrol cars and cops. Overcome by panic, he pulled out a knife, grabbed Rina and brought the blade to her throat.

"Police officer! Freeze!" a cop shouted, pointing a gun. "Drop the knife! Drop it! Drop it! Drop the knife! Drop it!"

Cory knew he was finished. He felt his bladder relax and a warm stream trickled down his leg. He obeyed, and the steel fell onto the asphalt, bounced, and landed with a clunk.

"Hit the ground," the officer screamed at the top of his lungs. "Hit it! Hit the ground! Hit it! Hit it! Hit the ground!"

The boy fell to his knees, and three uniformed officers charged at once. They read him his rights while handcuffing him and kept the boy flat on the dirt, face down, as they conferred in a huddle.

Rina watched the whole thing in a daze. Though her heart was thumping against her chest and her breathing was shallow, she felt tranquilized. The images were fuzzy around the edges, lines and angles indistinct.

A policeman walked over to her, tapped her gently on the shoulder, and she jumped.

"Are you in need of medical attention, ma'am?"

99

She stared at him. His lips moved, his eyes blinked, his chest heaved, but he wasn't real. He was an automaton – an escapee from Disneyland.

"Huh?"

The robot repeated the question.

"I'm . . . I'm all right," she stammered.

She turned around and saw the man with the bloodied nose deep in conversation with another officer. The policeman-robot with whom she was talking was young. Very young. Twenty at the most. His badge had a number. His name tag said "Folstrom."

"Are you sure?" he asked.

"Yes, I'm fine," she said, trying to regain composure.

"Would you like to tell me what happened?"

The kid took out a pocket pad.

Not this again. Uh uh. No way. She wasn't going to talk to this kid. She was sick of talking. She was sick of the police.

"I want to go home," she announced.

"Ma'am, I realize that you've just experienced quite an ordeal, but we need to talk to you."

"I don't want to talk to you," she said forcefully.

"Ma'am, we need your cooperation – "

"The *hell* with my cooperation!" she screamed hysterically. "I cooperated enough with you people over the last month, and it hasn't helped with the noises outside, has it?"

The young officer looked at her quizzically.

"Forget it," she snapped.

An older man walked over to them. He had a hard chiseled face and cold blue eyes. His tag identified him as Walsh.

"How are you feeling, ma'am?" he asked her in a mild voice.

"I don't want to give a statement." Her voice had become shrill. "I want to go home. Do you mind? I've been through enough. I want to go home."

"Ma'am, why don't you rest here a moment or two?

100

Try to calm your nerves. Would you like something to drink?"

"No," she answered quietly. "I want to go home."

"What's your name, ma'am?"

"Rina Lazarus. You can get the exact spelling from Detective Decker."

"Peter Decker?" Walsh asked.

She nodded.

"You're a friend of his?"

"Yes."

Walsh took his junior partner aside. "Let's call Decker and make it easy on ourselves. He's working Juvey anyway. One more case won't kill him, and he'll be more likely to get something out of her than we will."

Folstrom looked angry but didn't say anything.

"Call up the station and find his unit number," Walsh said. "I think it's 16-552."

Folstrom complied but was steamed. Why didn't Walsh give him a chance with the lady? He could have gotten the information. He could have handled her.

Walsh went back to Rina. "We're calling up Detective Decker now. Would you like to wait and talk directly to him?"

She nodded wearily. "Can I sit in my car?"

"Go ahead. If you want anything, you might as well ask. You may be here for a while."

She touched the crown of her head.

"I'd like my kerchief back," she said.

"Did the kid use it in any way as a weapon against you? A gag, a whip, an object of strangulation – "

"He just pulled it off my head."

"When?" the officer asked.

Rina looked at him. "I'll tell Detective Decker. Can I have the kerchief?"

"What's that garbage in your hair now?"

"An egg."

"Boys do it?"

She nodded.

The policeman gave her a sympathetic look. "We may need the scarf as evidence. I'm sorry. Detective Decker should be here shortly."

They still had Cory spread-eagled on the ground when the Plymouth pulled up. Decker got out, glanced at the punk, waved to Walsh, and went over to the Volvo. He knocked on the windshield, and Rina got out of the car. She took one look at his face and tears started to flow.

The hell with religion, he thought. He threw an arm around her shoulder protectively, and she sobbed against his chest. He hugged her tightly and stroked the back of her head, noticing it was wet and sticky.

"You're all right, Rina," he soothed her. When she had calmed down, he asked: "Did they physically hurt you in any way?"

"I'm fine." She pulled away from him and wiped her eyes, amazed at how relieved she was to see him. "That one," she said, pointing to Cory, "pulled a knife on me. But I didn't get hurt."

Her hand drifted to her neck.

Decker's eyes clouded with fury.

"You've been through the wringer," he said with feeling.

"Peter, I'd like to go home. The boys will be back from camp in less than twenty minutes."

"Did you make a statement?"

She shook her head.

"Briefly tell me what happened. I'll get an official statement from you later. All right?"

She nodded and related the incident as quickly as she could.

"Rina, we're going to need the car and its contents for evidence. Eggs, empty bottles, the whole bit. This is going down as an assault with a deadly weapon and possibly an armed robbery, so I'd like photos and good detailed notes. I can have one of the patrolmen drive you home."

"That's fine." She hesitated, then asked: "Do you need a photo of the egg in my hair?"

"Goddam assholes," he muttered. "No, I saw it. I'll record it. Look, don't say anything about this to anyone at the yeshiva. At least keep it under wraps until I've talked to you officially. And it'll be a while before I'll make it over there. I'm swamped with work. It's the heat. Brings out all the roaches. And for some reason, this week they've all been juveniles. The three of us have pulled so much overtime, we're ready to camp out at the station."

He took a long drag and blew out a wisp of smoke.

"I'm sorry, Peter."

Her words rang in his ears, and he shook his head and laughed.

"Will you listen to me? *You've* been threatened with a knife, and I'm prattling on like some five-year-old brat. I'm the one who should be sorry."

She gave him a reassuring nod.

"I'll try to be at your place by nine," he said.

"I'll be at the mikvah by then."

"Tell you what. I'll pick you up there and walk you home."

She knew what the others were going to think, but too bad. She told him to be there around ten-fifteen.

"How's the new guard working out?" he asked.

"Fine." She laughed shakily. "At the rate I'm going, I think I'll hire her as my full-time bodyguard."

Decker smiled, but he was beginning to think that that might not be a bad idea. He loaded her into a police car, and she rode away, thankful the kids hadn't been there.

"Call a transport vehicle, Doug?" Decker asked Walsh.

"One should be here in about an hour. Must be a hell of a busy day." He turned to his partner, Folstrom. "Chris, you know Pete?"

"I don't think we've ever met." The young cop extended his hand.

103

Decker shook it and regarded the rookie. "You're the kid who tried to bust me for running a light," he said.

Folstrom smiled back, but his cheeks had turned pink.

"Don't worry about it." Decker grinned. "The only people who drive like that are assholes and cops. And sometimes it's mighty hard to tell the difference."

"The girl's from Jewtown?" Walsh asked.

Decker winced at the reference, which now seemed like a racial slur.

"Yeah."

"Was she involved in the rape case over there?"

"As a witness, not as the victim."

"You think there might be a connection?" Folstrom asked.

"Who knows?"

Decker related Rina's version of the incident to the officers. When he was done, he asked:

"You boys have any details to add?"

"Her side of the story jibes with the good Samaritan's," said Doug.

"Poor guy," said Folstrom. "He saw the boys rousting the girl and tried to help out. All he got for his efforts was a bloody nose."

"He's fucking lucky that is *all* he got," Walsh said.

"And the kid pulled a knife on her?" Decker asked.

Walsh nodded. "By the time our unit arrived, the other three punks had fled the scene, but this little prick had a knife at the girl's throat."

"Why didn't he split with the others?" Decker asked.

"Seems the little gal from Jewtown had the presence of mind to kick him in the balls. It held him back, delaying his escape time considerably."

Decker broke into full laughter. Good for Rina, he thought.

"She didn't tell you that?" Folstrom asked.

"Must have slipped her mind," Decker replied. He stared at the prone figure on the ground until he placed a name with the face. Cory Schmidt. A bad apple. He'd had a few minor dealings with the kid in the past – disturbing the peace, loitering, malicious mischief. The punk was preordained to fuck up big, and this time he had. He walked over to the boy and gently poked the kid's side with the tip of his shoe.

"Hey, Cory," Decker said. "What's happening? Looks like you pissed in your pants."

"Fuck off, Decker. I wanna lawyer."

"I am a lawyer."

"I mean a real lawyer. Not some goddam pig."

"You'll get a lawyer. You'll get a lawyer and your parents, too. We're going to make sure you're well protected. Then all of us are going to sit in a little tiny room that's hotter than hell and talk for a long time. Doesn't that sound like a shit load of fun, Cory? Almost as good as getting blasted on snowflake."

"Fuck you, dick."

Decker resisted a very strong urge to kick him and went back to Walsh.

"I have an appointment with the phone company right now," he said. "Some girl out there knows something about the Foothill rapes, and I'm going to catch her if she calls me again. Have Marge Dunn do the first relay without a lawyer and without the parents. See if we can wear the kid down. Break his confidence. Just delay the whole thing for an hour at the most. I don't want to trample on Miranda, just lightly step on its toes."

He took out a pocket-sized notebook and began to scribble furiously.

"I should be back around one. Make sure he has counsel by then, and try to get a parent down there. His parents are both unemployed alkies, so it may be hard to get them off their butts, but at least make an attempt to contact one of them. Don't let the little prick slip out of our hands until I've talked with him."

13

Lionel Richie was crooning on the portable cassette deck. Last night it had been the Pointer sisters, the week before, Smokey Robinson. It was nice to hear popular songs, Rina thought, mopping the mikvah floor. She liked the woman's taste in music, but not as much as she liked the woman. The six-foot, two-hundred-pound security guard not only made her feel well protected, but provided interesting company.

Florence Marley was thirty, with coffee-colored skin, a wide smile, a friendly disposition, and a slew of recipes. Good ones. Rina had tried out a few herself, making the appropriate substitutions to keep the dishes kosher. Food – the universal language. It nicely bridged the gap between the big black woman from Watts and the ladies of the yeshiva.

She finished the floors, glad that she'd made herself stick to her routines despite the shock of this morning's assault. Dragging a sloshing bucket, she went outside to the reception area.

"Let me help you with that, Rina," Florence offered.

The guard hefted the bucket as if it were a tin can, tossed the dirty water down the sink, and handed the pail back to Rina.

"There's really no need for you to stick around for me tonight, Florence," Rina said, checking the time. "Detective Decker should be here any minute."

"I'll wait," said the guard. "I'm not going to leave you alone in this place."

Rina knew it was useless to argue.

Florence twirled her nightstick and hiked up her beige uniform pants.

"I'm gonna have a look around outside," she said, patting her gun. "Be back in *five* minutes, Rina. You hear anything, remember I'm right outside."

Rina nodded. She bolted the door shut and gathered up the dirty linens. She was still jittery from this morning's incident, but at least things here had settled down. The security woman was a godsend. The noises had stopped the day of her arrival, the women had loosened up, and a sense of security had been restored. Florence was well worth her salary for the peace of mind she'd brought.

Her thoughts were interrupted by a loud shout. Rina's heart began to pound furiously. Muffled speech, foot-steps, then banging at the door.

"Open up, honey. It's Florence."

Quickly, Rina unbolted the door.

The black woman was standing in back of Decker.

"This woman almost took off my head," he said wryly.

"I was just doing my job, sir."

"I'm not faulting you, ma'am, just making a statement of fact." Decker entered the room and turned to face the guard. "I see a bright future for you with the LAPD."

Florence sputtered into laughter.

"Just as soon as I drop fifty pounds." She smacked her stomach and thumped Decker on the back. "Can I trust you alone with this little thing?"

"Ask the little thing," he answered.

Florence looked at Rina.

"He's all right, Flo."

"Okay, then I'm going to be taking off." She clicked off the tape deck, stowed it in an empty cabinet, and pounded Decker on the shoulder blades. "Nice meeting you."

"Same," he answered.

She left, chuckling to herself.

"The woman packs a mean wallop," Decker said mas-saging his back. "I'd pit her against any man in the precinct."

He stopped talking and appeared to be thinking.

"Maybe Fordebrand could give her a run for the money."

"Who's Fordebrand?"

"Homicide detective. He's shorter than I am by a couple of inches, but must outweigh me by at least sixty pounds of pure muscle. Naturally, his wife is this tiny little bird. Fordebrand also has phenomenally bad breath."

"He sounds lovely, Peter."

"It was a kick working with him."

"You worked Homicide?"

"Seven years."

"Why'd you transfer?"

"I thought it might be nice to work with the kids." He felt his shirt pocket for cigarettes and grimaced when he came up empty. "The kids I've worked with have been worse than the adults. Somehow, I've never had the wonderful experience you see on the boob tube. You know, cop befriends down-and-out kid. Conflict. Tough talk. Kid keeps messing up, but cop persists. The final scene shows the kid giving the valedictory at Harvard. His life has been rough, and he wouldn't have pulled through except for the one man who believed in him – the cop."

Decker shook his head.

"In real life, the kid who's as tough as nails on the outside is chromium-plated steel on the inside."

"You sound cynical."

"Not cynical. Realistic. I had my shot at parenting with my own kid. And she turned out terrific. But there are Cynthia Deckers and there are Cory Schmidts. Fact of life."

He smiled at her.

"You want to hear more, I can go on for hours."

"It's a little late."

"Yeah, yeah. Shut up, Peter."

"I didn't say that."

"Let's get the statement over with. You look like you could use some sleep."

Rina threw the towels in the dryer and started it. She'd fold them tomorrow. They headed for the door, but Decker stopped abruptly, suddenly alert.

"What's wrong?" Rina asked, alarmed.

Decker put his fingers to his lips and listened intently for a minute. Then noticing the frightened look on Rina's face, he felt like a jerk.

"Nothing's wrong," he said. "I'm listening to the dryer."

"The *dryer*?"

"For another case I'm working on."

"What case?"

"I'll tell you all about it after I make a collar."

"So don't worry my pretty little head about it," she answered dryly. But she was greatly relieved.

Decker smiled, placed his hands on her shoulders, and looked her in the eye.

"Do I look like a chauvinist pig?"

She nodded.

He burst into laughter. He wanted to do something impulsive and lighthearted – tickle her or throw her over his shoulder. And she'd show mock outrage and pummel his back. Then they'd wrestle to the floor, and finally, exhausted by their joust, they'd curl up and make love.

Fantasy.

He left his hands drop to his sides and walked over to the dryer. Big industrial type – a Speed Queen. He listened to its whir for another moment, then said,

"Okay, we can go now."

"Learn anything?"

He shrugged.

As they left, he gently slipped his arm over her shoulder, letting his fingers rest at the tip of her collarbone. She turned around, smiled, and pulled away.

As he'd thought – fantasy.

* * *

'What happened with Cory?" Rina asked as they walked across the grounds.

"He'll get off with a slap on the wrist. By the way, he ratted on his friends, so we've recovered your pen. Here it is."

She took it absently; she was aghast.

"That's the best they could do? A slap on the wrist? The kid held a knife to my throat."

"Fortunately, you sustained no bodily injuries. Plus, he's a juvenile with a basically clean sheet. And they plea bargained him down to the lesser charge of malicious mischief in exchange for the names of his friends. Old Cory's going to walk."

She buried her head in her hands.

"I can't believe this."

"Don't fret too much. It's just a matter of time before the kid messes up again. Eventually, he'll dig himself a grave."

Decker took a deep breath and let it out.

"Rina, I got him to admit the vandalism: breaking the temple windows, spray-painting the walls with swastikas, dumping the garbage on the lawn. When I questioned him about the rape, naturally he said he didn't know anything about it. And, of course, he doesn't remember what he was doing the night of the incident.

"Now Cory is a very skillful liar, so I'm going to check him out. But my own personal opinion is that he had nothing to do with it. An experienced rotten kid like Cory would have come up with a pat alibi immediately. The kid looked honestly puzzled."

He loosened his tie and unfastened the top shirt button. Goddam heat refused to break.

"But that's just a hunch, and hunches don't take the place of good old footwork. So I'll check it out."

She said nothing.

"If that kid ever comes within fifty feet of you, tell me, and so help me God, I'll see to it personally that he wishes he hadn't."

"I hope it won't come to that."

"Same here."

When they got to her house, she paused before opening the door.

"My parents are babysitting tonight. I told them about this morning. They were pretty upset."

"I don't blame them."

She hesitated, then placed the key in the doorknob and let Peter inside.

It was hard for Decker to imagine the sophisticated couple in front of him as Rina's parents. The mother was taller than her daughter and as lithe as a cattail. She looked around fifty; her face bore some wrinkles, the complexion was pale, but the features were fine and delicate. Her make-up job was meticulous, perfectly accenting her bright blue eyes and full lips without being gaudy. Her jet black hair was a nest of soft curls that framed an oval face. She wore a pale blue silk shirt, navy gabardine slacks, and lizard-skin shoes. Around her neck was a braided gold chain that held a heart-shaped diamond solitaire.

The father was shorter than his wife by about an inch, but his build was muscular. His eyes looked tired, with drooping lids, and his nose was full, with wide nostrils partially obscured by a thick gray mustache. He had a prominent chin bisected by a deep cleft and a thick thatch of gray hair that was crowned by a small, knitted yarmulke. He was dressed casually but expensively and smiled when the two of them entered the room.

"You were late," the woman said. Her accent reminded Decker of Zsa Zsa Gabor.

"I said I'd be here at ten-thirty, Mama," Rina answered "It's around ten-thirty."

"It's a quarter to eleven." She brought her hand to her breast. "I was starting to get worried."

She looked at Decker.

"Is this the policeman?" she asked.

"Yes. This is Detective Decker." Rina turned to Peter. "These are my parents, Mr and Mrs Elias."

"How do you do?" Decker said.

The woman looked at him and shook her head. "Horrible thing that happened to my daughter."

"It's a shame," Decker said.

"Terrible, terrible thing when you go to the store and you can't be safe."

"Mama, I'm fine."

"Why do you live here? It's not safe here, Ginny. You can't just think of yourself. You have to think of the boys, too."

Rina said nothing.

"Do you have children, Detective?" asked Mrs Elias.

"A daughter, ma'am."

"And if this were to happen to her, how would you feel?"

"Very angry, ma'am."

"That is how I feel. Very angry and very scared. She is a single woman, Detective."

"Mama, I'm all right."

The woman spoke to her in a foreign language.

"Mother, crime is everywhere."

"You know your mother, Regina," the man spoke up. "She is a worrier."

"Why don't you spend the weekend with us?" the mother asked. "You never bring the kids over anymore."

"They have camp – "

"First it was school, now it's camp," she sighed. "The kids need a summer, too. I never sent you kids to camp. You had so much school during the year, I didn't think it was good to have camp also. And you let them stay up too late, Ginny. They didn't go to bed until ten-fifteen. Young boys need sleep."

"They nap in the afternoon, Mama. They're not tired at nine."

"They're too big to nap."

113

"Mama, can we discuss this later? It's very late, and I still have to give the detective a statement."

The woman looked at Decker. "It's not a good area here, no?"

"We have our share of crime," he replied.

"It's safer in Beverly Hills, no?"

Rina was fighting to maintain control.

"As long as there are cars, Mama, no area will be free of crime. Beverly Hills has plenty of crime."

"Not teenage punks throwing eggs over the head." Mrs Elias turned again to Decker. "Beverly Hills is safer, no?"

"They have a lower crime rate, statistically, but unfortunately, things like this *can* happen anywhere."

"But it's less likely to happen in Beverly Hills, no?"

"Statistically, that's true."

"Mama, it's very late."

"Come this weekend. The boys had a wonderful time visiting with us. Come this weekend."

"I'll call you and let you know," Rina said.

The woman kissed her daughter's cheek. "It's only because I love you that I worry about you. Come this weekend."

"I'll see," Rina said, fighting back tears.

"We love you, Ginny," the old man said. "We love you, and we love the boys. We miss you, you're so far away from us."

"I appreciate your coming tonight."

"We could come more often if you lived closer," her mother broke in.

"Mama, please. It's really very late."

"Too late for a single woman to be working." The older woman turned to Decker. "Thank you for helping her. She said you were very kind. Tell her this is no place for a young woman with small children."

The man got up and kissed his daughter. He took his wife's arm and they left, whispering in Hungarian.

Rina's eyes were wet.

114

"Have a seat, Peter." Her voice cracked. "Would you like something to drink?"

"How about if I get you something?"

She buried her face in her hands and tried to prevent the onslaught of tears. "I'm sorry."

"Don't apologize."

"It's been a trying day."

"You don't have to do this now, Rina. Come down to the station tomorrow morning, and I'll get a statement from you then."

She looked up. Her cheeks were streaked. "No, I'm fine."

"It doesn't matter, Rina. The kid's probably out by now anyway. Do it tomorrow."

She sat down on the sofa, and he sat next to her.

"You know, living here hasn't been easy, Peter. This isn't an appropriate place for a woman in my position. This is a high school and college of Jewish studies for *boys*. The women here are the wives of the rabbis or wives of a special group of scholars studying in the *kollel*. That's what my husband used to do. He used to learn in the *kollel*. That was his job. I worked as a teacher so he could study. That's considered honorable. This place has no role for a single woman.

"I'm not afraid of living on my own. I don't live in the lap of luxury here, so struggling and working hard aren't things I'm afraid of. But I know as soon as I pack my bags and step off these grounds, I'm going to get swallowed up by that woman you just met."

She started to cry.

Decker knew it wasn't just her parents. It was this morning and the events of the past month. It was the culmination of everything. He'd seen it lots of times, victims at the breaking point. He put his arm around her heaving shoulders and, much to his surprise, she snuggled in closer.

"You want to know my opinion?" he said. "I think any

woman who can knee-drop her attacker couldn't be swallowed up by anybody."

She laughed weakly and leaned her head against his chest. She could hear his heartbeat; the slow, steady rhythm had a hypnotic, calming effect on her nerves. bringing her arm over his chest, she embraced him. She felt her own body being enfolded by his arms, his fingers playing against her spine. He removed the kerchief from her head, loosened a few hairpins, and a thick black wave of hair cascaded down her shoulders and back.

"How far do you want to take this?" he asked softly.

"Not very."

He cupped her chin, lifted her face, and locked eyes.

"Don't you find this frustrating?"

"Of course I find it frustrating. But sex isn't the quick and easy solution."

"You could have fooled me."

He kissed the top of her head and stroked her hair.

"If I get objective about the whole situation, I have to admit it's kind of nice. I feel like I'm back in high school. In the olden days, you used to have to beg for *everything*."

He grinned and put his palms together.

"Please, please, I swear I'll be gentle."

She slapped him playfully and pulled away.

Decker straightened up.

"Worked about as well on you as it did on the girls in high school."

"Maybe it's time to change your technique."

She cleared her throat and tried to sound casual.

"By the way, what did you think of my parents?"

"They seemed caring. *Very* protective. But, then, you were attacked this morning . . . They were much more modern than I'd have imagined. You didn't grow up yeshiva religious, did you?"

"We were modern Orthodox. Which is to say I grew up with a strong Jewish identity. My mother was far less strict with the rules than my father. That led to a lot of fights. So in keeping with Freudian psychology, my oldest brother – the *doctor* – married a girl much less religious than he, and I married a boy much more religious than I. We all marry our parents, don't we?"

Decker reflected. His former wife, his mother, his biological mother. Maybe it was programmed in the genes.

"On the other hand," she continued, "my middle brother – I'm the youngest – was a lost soul. My parents didn't know what to do with him, so he was shipped off to Israel. The Chasidim got to him, and now he's at a Satmar yeshiva, the most religious of the three of us."

"Two out of three ended up in a yeshiva. That's an interesting track record."

"Only my brother's Chasidish. That's the kind of Jew they depict in *The Chosen* and *Fiddler on the Roof*, the ones with the long black coats and the mink hats. This yeshiva is Misnagid, a totally different philosophy from the Chasidic yeshivas. You want to see a man emit smoke from his nostrils, call Rav Aaron a Chasid."

"Is that the ultimate ethnic put-down?"

"For Rav Aaron. Misnagdim and Chasidim are like the Hatfields and the McCoys. Never the twain shall meet." She thought. "It's not that bad, but the Chasidim think the Misnagdim lack human emotion, and the Misnagdim think the Chasidim are a bunch of ignoramuses.

"Rav Aaron was born in a small village but went to yeshiva in Minsk – a major city in Lithuania. He's a Litvak through and through, and Litvaks pride themselves on being very urbane and intellectual. That's why he had a field day with Yitzchak. Rav Aaron couldn't get over my husband's raw gray matter, his ability to learn and retain all that was taught to him. His ability to *reason*.

"Chasidism, on the other hand, gained popularity in the small villages. Its followers, back then, were generally less knowledgeable about Torah and the outside world. So the Chasidim appeased their constituency by saying Judaism is primarily in the heart, not in the brain."

She looked at him.

117

"To you and the rest of the world, we must look like a bunch of crazy Jews."

His face grew serious.

"Rina, I wish you wouldn't lump me and billions of other people into one gigantic category. I'm more than just a gentile."

She touched his cheek, but quickly pulled her hand away.

"Of course you are. I'm sorry. I get chauvinistic. I'm very proud to be a Jew."

"I can see that."

"You know, your daughter is considered Jewish, don't you?"

"Yes. And she considers herself Jewish. About five years ago she liked what she saw in the religion, and that was fine with me. She made up her own mind. No one crammed it down her throat."

He saw the look on her face and knew he said the wrong thing.

"I didn't mean it to come out that way."

"It's okay," she said coolly. "I'm ready to give a statement."

"Don't sulk. I think it's great that she's Jewish. Some of my best friends are Jewish."

She laughed.

"It's nice to see you smile."

"Yes, I do that every once in a while."

She folded her hands in her lap.

"I'm really not a fanatic, Peter. There are other yeshivas far more restrictive. We've got radios, the *kollel* families have TVs, we can subscribe to secular newspapers and magazines. Some of the yeshiva boys are enrolled at UCLA and Cal Tech. We're considered comparatively liberal."

Decker said nothing.

"One of the men from here even had the audacity to take me to the movies."

"You don't see movies?" Decker asked.

"It's considered *nahrishkeit* – foolishness. I think the one we saw was with Steve Martin."

"How did you like it?"

"The movie was okay, but the boy I was with . . ." Rina rolled her eyes. "What a weirdo! He wouldn't dare touch me, of course, but he threw me a lot of lecherous looks. It was when I first started dating, a year after Yitzy died. I was eager to go out. A couple of rotten dates and I went back into hibernation."

"What was so weird about him?"

"He asked me too many personal questions. Things like did I still go to the mikvah even though I was a widow? Or was I going to stop wearing my wedding ring? Or uncover my hair. I kept my hair covered for a long time afterward. Now I only cover it when I leave the yeshiva. Or if I know I'm going to see an outsider . . . or you . . ."

"What else did he ask you?" Decker prodded.

"Did I ever eat nonkosher food? Did I ever smoke dope? Those questions may not sound so strange to you, but they're highly irregular coming from a yeshiva *bocher*."

"Go on."

"That was all, really."

"Guy's still here?"

"Yeah, he's married now. Learns in the *kollel*. I think his wife straightened him out a bit."

"What's his name?"

She looked at him, suspiciously. "He's not the rapist."

"I didn't say he was. I just asked for his name."

She didn't answer, and Decker dropped it.

"So your dates just didn't work out, huh?"

"Disasters. I might have started dating too soon after."

"Or maybe you're just fishing in the wrong pond."

She sighed. "There are a lot of other Jewish communities. Bigger communities with lots of men. I'm just not ready to face the mating rituals again."

"You sound as if you could use someone close to home to help ease the transition."

She smiled. "And you're volunteering?"

"As a community service."

"You know, Decker, you would have made a great yeshiva *bocher*."

He broke up.

"No, I'm serious. You have all the external trappings. You're intelligent, curious, hardworking. You ask the right questions. You're even a *lawyer*. A yeshiva is like a Jewish law school with ethics and morals thrown in. Anyone who's ever studied both will tell you that Jewish law is much harder and more challenging than American law."

"I missed my calling, huh?"

"You laugh, but I can tell, Peter. If you'd been born Jewish and raised in an Orthodox environment, you would have been a fanatic."

Her words made him uncomfortable. He fidgeted.

"You don't have any cigarettes, do you?"

She shook her head.

"It's okay."

"Would you like some coffee or juice?"

"Just water."

She got up, and he let out a deep breath. Jesus, it was hot in here. Funny he should just notice it. She returned with a tall glass of iced water.

"Thanks." He drained the glass. "If you don't go to movies and don't eat out in restaurants, what do you do for fun?"

"What's that?" Rina said deadpan.

"Think back to when you were a baby and you used to smile, but everyone thought it was gas."

"Ah yes – it's coming back to me." She gave him a light poke. "We have fun."

"Doing what?"

"Shabbos is fun. I cook huge meals for Friday night and Saturday lunch until I'm ready to drop, and everyone stuffs themselves, leaving me to do the dishes." She laughed. "Seriously, I love Shabbos day. We go to services in the morning. Then, either I have people over for lunch or we'll be invited out. There's lots of talking, singing, learning, playing with the kids, eating, drinking . . . We don't use any electricity on the Sabbath. We don't even turn on a light, pick up a phone, or drive a car. Disconnecting from the outside world for one day is purifying, Peter. Like the plunge into the mikvah.

"I've done a lot of reflecting these past two years since Yitzchak died and found that I like being religious. There's purpose in it, and purpose in life is a rare treasure these days."

"Give me your hand," he said.

"What?"

"Don't worry, I'm not going to attack you. Yeah, even a lowly goy can control himself. I just want to hold your hand."

Surprisingly she complied.

"I like talking to you," he said. "Do you like talking to me?"

"You know I do."

"Find me trustworthy?"

"What are you leading up to?"

"Why don't we go out together? We can do something harmless like take a drive to the beach and talk. It would be really nice."

"I just can't do it."

"Why not? We won't tell anybody."

"It's not the external conflict. It's the internal one."

"So we'll just be buddies. Like Marge Dunn and me. Marge and I go out for drinks all the time. Everybody needs a good buddy."

She shook her head.

"Just one time. See how you like it."

"I can't, Peter. It wouldn't stop at one time, and you know it."

She was right. He might as well salvage what he could.

"Look, you went out with Goldberg, and you thought

121

he was a real weirdo. I'm not even a teensy bit weird, so how about your giving me as much consideration as old Goldberg?"

"Goldberg?"

"The weirdo who asked you all those questions."

"That was Shlomo Stein. Where'd you get the name Goldberg?"

"Shlomo Stein, huh?"

Rina glared at him, but didn't pull away. "That was really rotten."

"I was sincere about the invitation."

"I'll give you that statement now."

Decker grinned expansively. The evening wasn't a total loss.

14

Sammy gazed into space, knotted his fingers into a fist, and slammed it into the mitt. Rina checked the clock. He'd been gawking at the wall and punching the baseball glove repetitively for the last half hour, and there was still another fifty minutes to go before Peter showed up.

She'd tried talking to him, suggesting they play a game or learn some *Chumash* together, but he shrugged her off. Jacob, on the other hand, had spent the morning like every other Sunday morning – glued to the TV. He was excited about going to his first baseball game, but he was just as excited about the Jerry Lewis movie that came on at eleven. Jacob was so good-natured, so easy to please. Sammy was a sweet boy with a heart of gold, just much more serious by nature than his brother.

How could two boys with the same parents, born only a year apart, be so different?

She decided to bake. It was therapy for her, calming her nerves. Picking up the wooden spoon, she creamed the margarine with the sugar, mashing the yellow lumps into a smooth, sweet paste.

When Peter had first offered to take the boys to the Dodgers game, she'd refused. She didn't want them getting attached to him, and he said he understood – they were her kids, she knew what was best for them.

But guilt began to tug at her heartstrings. Every single morning after his prayers, Sammy would open the paper and pour over the sports section, studying it as diligently as he studied the scriptures. He'd memorized all the statistics, backward, forward, sideways. Name a Dodger, and he could tell you his life history. It just seemed cruel to deny him such a small pleasure. She'd been putting him off so long. So she asked him if he wanted to go to Sunday's game with Peter, and the boy's eyes livened with unabashed excitement. So she called Peter back.

She sifted in flour and cocoa powder, and stirred the batter vigorously.

"Eema?" Sammy called from the other room.

"What, honey?"

"What time is it?"

"Forty minutes to go."

Silence.

Then the dull thud of flesh hitting leather. She was sure his knuckles were red and raw by now.

Jake came in the kitchen.

"Whatcha making?"

"Cupcakes."

"Are they pareve?"

"Yes."

"Can we take them with us to the game?"

"That's why I'm making them," she said, pouring the batter into the paper liners.

"Can I lick the bowl?"

"One of you gets the bowl, the other the spoon. Work out the division between yourselves."

Jake pulled over a chair and watched her put the cupcake pan in the oven.

"Are you excited?" Rina asked him.

"Yeah."

"You like baseball, don't you?"

"Yeah."

"I hope the Dodgers win."

"Yeah. Can we buy a Coke there?"

Rina smiled. "I think that can be arranged."

"Thanks." He slid off the chair, went out to his brother, and returned a minute later. "Shmueli isn't hungry. Can I have the bowl and the spoon?"

Rina gave him the cookware coated with chocolate

batter. The little boy scooped up the bowl and utensils in his arms and returned to his television program. Just when the cupcakes had cooled sufficiently for packing, the doorbell rang. Sammy answered it.

Rina was taken aback by Peter's appearance. Her image of him until now had been that of a "professional detective" in a shirt, slacks, and tie. This afternoon he wore a white T-shirt, sloppy cut-off shorts and sneakers, and a baseball cap perched atop his thick patch of orange-red hair. He looked so all-American, so working class. So goyish. With him were two teenagers. The girl was attractive, but too gangly to be beautiful. She had her father's hair, cut short, big brown eyes, and an open, toothy smile. She was dressed in short shorts, a midriff tank top, and sandals. The boy was surfer blond and slightly taller than the girl, with meat on his bones. His dress was identical to the girl's. They had their arms looped around each other.

Immediately, Rina wondered if she hadn't erred in her judgment. Although she couldn't shelter her kids for-ever, perhaps it would have been wiser to expose them to the goyim at a less impressionable age. She had definite misgivings, but it was too late to back down now.

"Thanks for taking them," Rina said.

"My pleasure."

Something was bothering her, and Decker knew instantly what it was. Their dress was too secular. The kids were showing affection publicly. She was sorry she'd agreed to this, leaving her sons in the hands of a goy. He had almost told her about his adoption and origins that night. They had achieved a certain intimacy, and he'd wanted to be open with her. But something stopped him. Years of silence on the subject had put his lost identity in cold storage. To reveal himself to her would have opened a Pandora's box that he wasn't prepared to deal with. Not with a job to do, a rapist on the loose.

125

"This is my daughter, Cindy, and her boyfriend, Eric," Decker introduced. "Kids, this is Rina Lazarus and her sons, Sammy and Jake."

The teenagers smiled and tightened their grip on one another.

"What do you think?" Decker asked, cradling his daughter's face in his hands. "Isn't she beautiful?"

Rina smiled. "Gorgeous."

"*Dad!*" Cindy whispered, embarrassed.

"I do this to her every time." He grinned, then threw his arm around Sammy and touched the glove. 'You're coming prepared."

Sammy shrugged sheepishly.

"Ready?"

The boys nodded.

"Peter, this is their food." Rina handed him a double bag. "They can have Cokes or Seven-ups, but *nothing* else. No hot dogs, ice-cream, french fries, nachos, potato chips – "

"What if it has *hashgacha*?" Jake asked.

"Yonkie, I packed more than enough goodies for you guys." She turned back to Peter. "Only drinks. Here's a five dollar bill – "

"What are you giving me?" Decker laughed. "Even a cop can afford to buy a round of Cokes. And calm down. I'll bring 'em back in one piece. And they'll still be Jewish."

She took a deep breath and let it out.

"I trust you."

"Cynthia, why don't you and Eric walk the boys to the car. I want to talk to Rina for a minute."

"Sure," the girl answered. "Nice meeting you."

"Same here. Enjoy the game." Rina started to plant kisses on her sons. "Have a wonderful time, and listen to Detective Decker."

Sammy squirmed out from her grip and walked out the door with the teenagers. Jake stayed behind an extra moment to get another hug, then quickly caught up with the others.

"We hit paydirt with Shlomo Stein," Decker said when they were alone. "Guy's got a past. Indicted for two counts of possession of cocaine with intent to sell, one count of racketeering, and one count of assault with a deadly weapon. None of the charges stuck except the assault, and in that case, he beat the rap. Hired himself a hotshot lawyer named MacGregor Dayton. I've heard of the man. He was defending heavy-duty dealers back when I was still a boy in Florida. And they say he only got sharper over time."

He paused.

"In his secular days old Shlomo Stein was known as Scotty Stevens. I'd like to know what the hell he's doing here."

"Finding meaning, I guess."

"Yeah, well I'm cynical enough to think that major personality changes don't take place overnight."

"He's not the rapist, Peter."

"No, the guy is perfect now that he prays all the time."

"I didn't say that," she answered, defensively. "Granted, he's a weirdo. But he was in class with twenty other men at the time of the rape."

"How do you know?"

"I was one step ahead of you."

"What did you do, Rina?"

"I asked around – "

"Damn!" Decker interrupted. "Rina, you gave the guy a chance to set up an alibi."

"We are very protective of one another, but nobody here would cover up to protect a rapist. I asked a few trustworthy people – like Zvi. Now would Zvi protect a man who raped his wife?"

"Who the hell knows? I have trouble understanding this place's mentality."

"Peter, I'm not a character reference for Shlomo Stein. I'm just telling you that he didn't do it."

127

"Did you know about his former criminal activities at the time you went out with him?"

"Of course not! I wouldn't have gone out with him had I known. It wasn't until later that I found out he'd had some problems. Apparently, he was brought up Orthodox, strayed, and now has returned like the prodigal son, *lehavdil*. Rav Aaron let him stay after he found out, even though he wasn't happy about it. He doesn't want this place to be a refuge for weirdos and misfits. But a community can't turn its back on members who've made mistakes in the past."

"But you knew he had a record when I talked to you."

"No, I didn't." She looked down. "I knew he'd been in some sort of trouble. I thought it was drugs."

"Why didn't you mention it to me?"

"I knew you'd find out."

"But why didn't you tell me your suspicions?"

She said nothing.

"You'd rather protect your own, even if he's a criminal, than trust an outsider who happens to be a cop and, more important, a human being who's very concerned about your welfare."

"Peter, it's not that."

His eyes bore into her.

"I *do* trust you," she said, earnestly. "I didn't want to cast doubt on him just because he'd had a checkered past. I didn't know what he was. Let the investigation come from the officials. Let it come from you."

"I'm beginning to wonder about this place. I have a mind to conduct a complete investigation – "

"Peter, *this place* houses sixty families, two hundred college-age boys, and another one hundred high school kids. The boys graduate and leave, others take their places. Some kids come here mid-semester. There's a constant turnover of students, not to mention visiting rabbis and scholars who learn at the yeshiva for a year or so. With that many people coming and going, you're bound to come across a few oddballs."

128

"You've got a gangster and a psycho – "

"Moshe is harmless."

Decker said nothing.

"You must have had him checked out," Rina said.

"He's clean."

"Of course he's clean."

A beeper went off. Decker unhooked the portable radio from his belt loop and listened to a number being mumbled over a lot of static.

"I need to borrow your phone for a moment."

"Sure."

He made his call, gave a few instructions, and hung up the receiver.

"Anything important?" Rina asked.

"Not really. With this Foothill bastard on the loose, I like to be as accessible as possible."

"It must be hard on you."

"At least it saves on gas. I'm always taking the unmarked to be near the radio. I don't think I've driven my personal car in three months." He looked at his watch. "I have to go."

"Peter?"

"What?"

"Once you conned Shlomo's name out of me, I should have told you the rest. I'm sorry."

His expression softened, and he plopped his baseball cap atop her head. "Take care of yourself."

"Your daughter's lovely."

He gave her a wide smile.

"I'll tell her you said that."

Even though Rina showed up early for the Bible class, Ruthie Zipperstein and Chana Marcus were already there, deep in conversation. She liked the book they were studying – Samuel – for it described the excitement of the reign of King David. Not only was the book of Samuel interesting historically, but it provided magnificent insights into the frailties of human nature. David, the righteous Jew who did the unspeakable to obtain the woman he wanted. A leader, a learned man, a sinner, and humble servant of *Hashem*.

David was also a redhead.

She sat down and told the women where her boys were. She knew they'd find out anyway, so it might as well come from her mouth.

"Rina, I can't believe you let the boys go with him."

"It's just a baseball game, Ruthie."

"The high school boys were thinking about getting a group rate to a Dodgers game," Chana said. "Why didn't you wait and send the boys with them?"

"Chana, they've been talking about getting tickets for four months. The season is practically over. Plus, the seats Peter got – "

"Peter?" Chana asked.

"Detective Decker got box seats. Some commissioner gave them to him. I just couldn't put Shmueli off any longer."

"You're getting awfully friendly with him, don't you think?" Ruthie said.

"I don't have to justify my actions to anyone. *Hashem* knows what's in my heart."

The women made no attempt to hide their disapproval.

"Rina, I've got a cousin coming out from Baltimore," Chana said. "He's twenty-eight and a very nice boy. He reminds me of Yitzchak, except he's a little more fun-loving. He's already asked me about Universal Studios and Disneyland – "

"When's he coming out?" Rina asked.

"Chol Hamoed Sukkos."

She shrugged. "If he's nice, I'll go out with him. Where does he learn? *Ner Yisroel?*"

"He actually just got *smicha*. He's looking for a job. Maybe even here. We can always use a good Rav."

"Did you mention me?" Rina asked.

"In passing," Chana admitted.

"Did you tell him I had children?"

130

"Yes."

"And what did he say?"

"He didn't say anything. He said he'd like to meet you. I told him how pretty you are. Shimon has an eye for pretty women. So then I'll tell him to call you?"

"All right," Rina said unenthusiastically. She opened the *navi* and reread the passage in which David first saw Bathsheva. " . . . from the roof, he saw her bathing. And she was very beautiful to look upon."

She wasn't simply bathing, Rina knew. She was immersing herself in the mikvah.

Rina found him sitting underneath a sprawling elm. Directly behind the shade tree, filling the air with the pungent scent of menthol, was a grove of eucalyptus that tapered into the thick, woodland brush. The day sweltered under a blazing furnace of a sky. Briefly she thought about her boys at the game and sunstroke, but then dismissed worry from her mind. Peter had common sense.

Moshe had a prayer book on his lap, his eyes fixed on the page. He rocked back and forth on his haunches, muttering words that extolled the glory of the Lord. He was dressed as always: black coat, wrinkled white shirt, threadbare wool slacks, and a tattered black hat. Beads of sweat had coalesced on his forehead, but he seemed unbothered by the fire of the sun.

Rina sat down on a mound of leaves a foot away from him. He was neither happy nor upset by her presence. He was oblivious to it.

"Moshele," she said softly.

The man rocked back and forth.

"Moshele, I know you hear me. Please, answer me, Moishy."

His eyes trailed a path to her own. He nodded.

"How are you?" she asked.

"*Baruch Hashem*, I'm fine, thank you. Yes, very fine, thank you very much. I'm fine, *Baruch Hashem*."

"Moshe, did Zvi explain to you what went on that night?"

"Yes. Yes, he did. He explained everything. Yes he did."

"Did he explain to you how you had to stay out of the hills at night?"

"Yes, he did. Thank you very much. He did. He did."

"Moshe, it is very important that you listen to him. You can't go in the hills at night until the police catch the attacker. Otherwise, they're going to think you're the attacker."

"Yes, I understand. I understand what you are saying. Thank you very much. I understand."

"I've seen you in the hills at night, Moshe. Flo and I saw you two times last week. And I saw you on Shabbos when Steve Gilbert walked me home. You have to stop wandering alone at night. You must stay put for your own sake, do you understand?"

"I understand. Thank you very much," he murmured. "I understand. I understand what you are saying. I understand, thank you."

"Moishy, it's important. It's important for you, it's important for *shem tov* – for your good name. It would be a *chillul Hashem* if someone mistook you for the attacker. We cannot let the goyim think we're a bunch of hoodlums."

"That's right. That's correct. *Shem tov* is very important. It is very important to have a good name. Rav Hillel says it's very important. He was a *gadol*, Rav Hillel. It's very important."

The conversation was breaking her heart. She remembered him and Yitzchak, the sparks in their eyes as they learned, the animation, the excitement. Now one was dead, the other a zombie. For a second she felt overwhelmingly angry at *Hashem*. Yitzchak was bad enough, but how could He abandon Moshe so cruelly? But her ire was quickly quelled by the immediate guilt that followed whenever she doubted her faith.

"Please, Moshele. Stay out of the brush at night. Please."

"Yes I will. Thank you very much. I will. Thank you very much. I will."

She got up and left, leaving him to flounder in his own world.

Rina greeted them at the threshold of her door.

"They won!" Sammy shouted excitedly.

"I know," Rina said, smiling. "I tuned in the game on the radio."

To Decker's surprise, she stepped outside and closed the door behind her.

"Boys," she said, "why don't you take Detective Decker, Cindy, and Eric into the backyard and show them our orange tree?"

"Huh?" Sammy asked quizzically.

"Go on," she said sweetly, prodding them in the right direction.

"*Ma at osah, Eema?*" asked Sammy.

"*Shmuel Dov, lechu kulchem hachutza achshav!*" she said forcefully, then quickly smiled at the others. "It's a beautiful tree. Excuse me for a moment." She went inside the house, leaving them marooned on her doorstep.

Sammy frowned. "Wanna see a tree?" he asked.

"Sure, let's see the tree," replied Decker.

He wondered what the hell was going on and was resentful that Rina hadn't pulled him aside to explain herself.

"C'mon," said Jake.

Cindy giggled. "Is this a rare Orthodox custom, Dad? After baseball games, one pays homage to the holy orange tree?"

"That's a snide and rude remark, Cynthia," Decker snapped.

Cindy's gaiety vanished, and she looked downward. Decker sighed and put his arm around his daughter.

"I don't understand this place either, Cindy."

133

"I was just making a joke."

"I know. I'm feeling a little put upon now. Sorry."

"Well, here's the tree," Jake announced. It was a fifteen-foot mandarin orange loaded with fruit.

"Bitchin," said Eric flatly.

Sammy picked an orange, peeled it, mumbled a prayer, and popped a section into his mouth.

"They're real sweet." He handed the rest to Decker, who gave it to the teenagers.

"You can pick some if you want," offered Jake. "Eema won't mind."

"Sure. Why not?" Eric said, plucking a few oranges. "Nothing better to do."

As the kids busied themselves with harvesting, Decker walked over to the side of the house and stared at Rina's front door. He felt like pounding the shit out of it. He despised being left in the dark. It was one of the reasons he obsessed on his cases; he needed a sense of closure. He hated vacuums and was angry at Rina for creating one.

A minute later, the door opened. Rina and a young woman emerged, linked arm-in-arm. They spoke briefly, and Rina leaned over and kissed the woman's cheek. Decker squinted as he studied her profile, and a second later he recognized the face.

It was Sarah Libba Adler. She looked so different from the last time he had seen her. Much younger and not as frail. Her posture was erect and her dress was stylish. The blond wig she wore fell gracefully to her shoulders, framing a delicate face no longer cut and bruised. No one would ever suspect that she had been an assault victim. The scars that remained were internal.

Rina watched Sarah walk away, then rejoined the others in the backyard.

"I'm sorry," she apologized. "I'll get you kids a sack. Take as many as you want."

She noticed immediately that Peter and Cindy had changed their clothes. Cindy had put on a short-sleeve

134

shirt and a lightweight cotton skirt. Peter was wearing a polo shirt and a pair of designer jeans that looked brand new. Although the clothing hugged his body, showing off his muscular build, he appeared odd in it – like a kid dressed up for a birthday party. She left for the house; then, returning a moment later with the sack, a stack of cups, and a pitcher of iced tea, she began to play hostess.

"It was a close game," she said to Sammy.

"It was a *good* game," he said emphatically between slurps of tea. "But you know what else happened?"

"We heard a robbery on the police radio, Eema," Jake said, his eyes gleaming.

She looked at Peter. "What?"

"An armed robbery happened a couple of blocks from the stadium," he explained. "We heard the whole thing over the radio. The kids thought it was pretty neat."

"I wanted to go see it, but Peter wouldn't let us," Sammy complained, handing Rina his empty cup.

"Detective Decker," Rina corrected. "And he showed good judgment."

"They caught the guy," Cindy added. "They had to tear gas the place to get him out."

"You know what else we heard, Eema? A disturbing the peace call, a disorderly conduct, another robbery, a purse snatching, and something else . . ."

"A battery victim," Eric answered.

"There's no shortage of crime in this city," Peter said and shrugged.

"It was so neat!" Sammy exclaimed, pounding his fist into the glove with excitement.

"It sounds like Detective Decker's police radio was as big a hit as the game."

"The game was great," Sammy said. "Can I have some more tea please?"

"Sure." She poured him another cup and refilled the others.

"We stopped off at Peter's ranch," Jake said. "He has horses. Can we go ride them today?"

"*Detective Decker*," she scolded. "Where are your manners?"

"He *told* us to call him Peter," Sammy said, irritatedly.

"Can we go ride the horses?" Jake asked again.

Rina hesitated.

"It's fine with me," Decker said.

"Not today. It's getting late."

"I'm not tired," Sammy protested.

"Not today, Shmuel." She tousled his hair. "Some other time, okay?"

"Yeah, sure."

"Sammy, I promised you a ball game, you got your ball game. I keep my word. If I say some other time, it will be some other time, all right?"

He nodded.

"You boys thank Peter for taking you."

"Thank you," Sammy said glumly.

Peter held out his hand. When Sammy gave him his own, Decker flipped him into the air, caught him, and placed him on the ground. Then he did the same series of acrobatics with Jake. The giggling boys charged him, but Decker threw them up as quickly as they pounced.

The whole day had left Rina feeling inadequate. The useless conversation with Moshe. Being put on the defensive by her friends. But mostly it was Peter. Why did she trust this strange goy as if he were a lifelong friend? And why did he have to be *so* good with the children? As much as she tried, she couldn't be both a father and a mother to her boys. They required roughhousing that was just too physically demanding for her. They needed a constant male figure. The boys at the yeshiva were nice, but didn't provide consistency. She had tried a Jewish Big Brother once, but it hadn't worked out. It was nearly impossible to get someone who had an understanding of her religious views.

She let them horse around for a minute, then said:

"Boys, that's enough."

136

"It's okay," Decker said holding Jake upside down. "I can use the workout."

"They're a little overexcited, Peter. Time to quiet it down."

He recognized the tone of voice. Like Jan. *You're working her up, Peter.* He reminded himself that these weren't his kids, he had no say-so in their rearing. He stopped wrestling.

"You two want to go out to dinner?" Decker asked the teenagers.

"Uh, we sort of made some plans with our friends, Dad."

"Fine," Decker said, then raised his eyebrows to Rina. "They hit the teens and they're gone."

"Dad?"

"What?"

"Can we borrow the Plymouth?"

Peter laughed. "No, you can't borrow the Plymouth."

"Just for about a half hour? We'll be real careful."

"Cynthia, that's outrageous. You can't borrow a police car to go cruising with your friends. Give me a break, honey."

"Just asking." She shrugged. "We'll wait for you back at the car."

"Fine."

"Nice meeting you again," she said to Rina.

Rina said good-bye and handed them the bag of oranges.

Eric dragged Cindy out of the backyard, and the two of them exploded into laughter as soon as they were out of sight.

Decker looked puzzled.

"I must have missed some private joke."

"Don't worry about it. You'll miss many more in your day." She turned to her sons. "Boys, go inside. I want to talk to Peter alone for a moment."

"Do we have to?" Sammy asked.

137

"Yes, you have to. Now." After they had left, Rina said, "I'm sorry for shooing you away like that."

"It's all right. You had your reasons."

"Sarah Libba was over when you came back from the ballgame. We were talking and lost track of time. She couldn't bear to see you face-to-face."

"I certainly don't remind her of good times."

"That, and she's embarrassed. But she does appreciate what you're doing."

"I'm glad," he said. "How's she holding up psychologically?"

"Better."

"That's good."

"You changed your clothes," Rina commented.

"You're an open book, Mrs Lazarus. Disapproval was painted all over your face."

"It's the yeshiva, Peter. The people here have standards . . ."

Decker said nothing.

"And it's me, also," she admitted. "I should be more tolerant, I guess."

"Don't worry about it."

They stared at each other for a moment.

"The kids are waiting," Decker said.

"Thank you for everything."

"Sure. Take care, Rina. And don't ever hesitate to call me if you need something, even just to say hello."

"I won't."

It was close to eleven o'clock, and she thought she heard something outside. It wasn't loud or clear enough to alarm her, but it alerted her to her own vulnerability.

She thought of calling Peter, but changed her mind. She was beginning to wonder if she heard the noises at all. Was she just using them as an excuse to talk to him?

That was ridiculous. Why should a grown woman need an excuse to talk to another adult? If she wanted to call him, she should call him. After all, he'd said to phone anytime.

She picked up the receiver.

What would she say?

She thought a moment. She'd thank him again for taking the boys. Sort of a polite follow-up call.

But it was eleven at night.

He'd be up. She couldn't picture the man as an early-to-bed-early-to-rise type.

She dialed and felt her heart beating in anticipation. On the third ring, a throaty woman answered. Quickly, she apologized for the wrong number and tried again.

When the same woman answered, she placed the receiver quietly back in its cradle.

She was positive she had dialed correctly.

15

Florence should have been back a half hour ago. It was taking too long, and Rina began to worry. She put down her stack of papers, got up from the chair, and pressed her ear against the door. All she heard were crickets and a mockingbird going through its repertoire. Drawing the curtains back, she peeked out the window. The moon was full, the night starlit, but she saw no one.

She stared at the phone.

She had spoken to Peter a few days ago when he'd offered to take the boys to his ranch this Sunday. She'd thanked him and said she'd think about it, but her tone had been very cool. He'd noticed the frost in her voice and had asked if anything was wrong.

Nothing was wrong.

Except that woman.

Rina couldn't erase the thought of him and *her*, whoever she was. That voice. That soft, husky, *sexy* voice. It stuck in her craw like a fishbone. She knew Peter was a regular man, not a priest, and she hadn't given him an inch with which to work. It was absurd for the woman to bother her. But jealousy had seeped into her marrow like a chilly London fog. She'd shied away from calling him in case *she* answered.

But now her fear for Florence's safety overrode her petty resentment.

She dialed his number at home, and no one answered. Please let him be at the station, she thought. She tried his work extension and felt immediate relief when he picked up the call.

"Peter, I'm worried."

"What's wrong, Rina?"

"I think something's happened to Florence. She left the mikvah to walk Shayna Silver home and should have been back a good half hour ago. She may be out patrolling, but I'm too nervous to open the door to find out."

"*Don't* open the door," he said. "I'll be right over."

"Thank you."

She paced mindlessly, like a palace guard, back and forth for ten minutes straight. This was solving nothing, she thought. Better to do something. Better to take your mind off being alone. She started straightening out the supply cabinet. They were low on shampoo. She took out a pen and wrote down "shampoo" on a list tacked onto the cork bulletin board. Her handwriting was lopsided and spastic.

Get hold of yourself. Peter should be here any minute.

The door rattled. Her eyes fixed on the handle as she watched it twist and turn, fighting against the dead bolt. Gripped with fear, her heart took off on a sprint, her body was seized with the shakes. The rattling grew violent and was followed by hard thumping against the door.

Do something!

She staggered over to the phone, picked up the receiver, but dropped it.

The pounding shook the floor like a tremor.

She retrieved the phone and placed it to her ear. No dial tone. Frantically, she clicked the switch to get a connection, but the line was dead.

Sudden silence.

Her body was too heavy for her wobbly legs. Her knees buckled, and she slid to the floor.

She lay on the cold tile, desperately sucking air into her parched throat, hearing only her own shallow breaths.

Then a crash! Something flying toward her! Sharp slivers of light raining down on her! She shielded her face, but her arms and legs were stung and began to leak droplets of red. A gush of warm air. A human arm

141

through the window curtain, groping, dancing like a hand puppet. Then it was gone. Receding footsteps. Approaching footsteps. A loud banging at the door.

She screamed.

"Rina!" Decker boomed.

She tried to call out to him, but only a faint moan escaped from her throat.

He began to bang furiously. She heard two quick blasts, and the door caved in.

Decker rushed over and scooped her up in his arms. He sat down on the chair and hugged her tightly.

"Thank God," he whispered.

"I'm okay," she whispered between rapid breaths.

"What about Florence?"

"Nothing."

She sat nestled in his arms for a moment, then climbed off his lap.

Decker looked around. The window was shattered, the floor sprayed with broken glass. He reloaded his .38 special and picked up the phone.

"The line's dead," Rina said.

"Bastard must have cut it."

He unhitched the portable radio from his belt.

"This is unit number 16-552 requesting immediate back-up at Yeshivat Ohavei Torah, 344 Deep Canyon Thoroughfare in Deep Canyon. Send units to the north-east corner in front of the mikvah. *Mikvah* – Mary-Ida-King-Victor-Adam-Henry. See the woman."

He switched off the radio and absently kicked some shards of glass.

"I have to go look for Florence, Rina. I can't wait here in good conscience for back-up while she's alone out there."

"I understand. Let's go."

Decker hesitated while thoughts ran at fast-forward through his brain.

"No," he said. "It would be better if you waited here. The guy had a gun last time and knew how to use it. I

142

can't adequately protect you in the dark, and you could easily get hit by cross fire. Besides, he'll have seen my car. I doubt if he'll come back."

Rina was paralyzed with fright at the idea of being alone but said nothing. At this point, Florence was more important.

Decker paused, then pulled out a small gun from a belt holster and offered it to her.

"I brought an extra with me. Sometimes guns have been known to jam, and I didn't want to take any chances. It's all set, so be careful. You probably won't need it, but just in case, aim for the body, Rina, not the head. You're more likely to hit that way. If the guy comes at you, *don't* hesitate! Pull the trigger and blow the fucker away."

She nodded and took the gun.

"Send me up some help just as soon as it comes." He turned on his high-power flashlight and was off.

The brush was dry and crisp under his feet, the bugs out in full force. He worked methodically, sweeping the light over an area before stepping forward, constantly checking for cover in case the bastard started to shoot. Midway up the hill, a sickeningly sweet smell wafted its way toward his nostrils. Decker scrunched up his nose, then, like a hound dog, used the stink to locate the source. Thirty feet away there was a deep pit next to an oak grove. He walked over.

The big, black woman who'd pounded his back had been left to rot like a beached whale. Her body was twisted and savaged – a leg angled perpendicular to the hipbone, her left foot dangling from a tendon at the ankle, an arm half-ripped from its socket. Her face was a death mask frozen with shock and terror. The slash across her throat was wide and deep, swarming with flies and gnats. Her bowels had emptied, and up close the stench was overpowering. Decker fought back a wave of nausea and made his way back to the mikvah.

Rina saw Peter coming out of the forest. He had been gone too short a time. She knew it had to be bad.

The back-up officers arrived. Rina recognized the patrolmen as the two who'd been there the first time – the Latino and the muscleman.

Decker waved them over.

"What's up?" Ramirez asked.

"A one-eighty-seven about two hundred fifty feet up and over to the left. See where those oaks are?"

Ramirez shined a light into the hills and nodded.

"If you've got a rope, I can start to mark off the area," Decker said.

"Got one in the trunk," Hunter answered.

"Might as well get on with it. Lab boys should be here soon. I called them right away."

"How did the stiff bite it?" Ramirez asked.

Rina cringed, and Decker caught it. He took Ramirez aside.

"Someone bisected her neck."

"Jesus," Ramirez hissed. "I hate slashers."

"Scum of the earth," Decker agreed.

"Looks like we've got company."

A few of the yeshiva boys were ambling over to the area.

"Damn!" said Decker "There'll be more of them – the sirens and the lights will bring them over. Keep everyone out of the woods and bathhouse, Luis. I don't want any gawkers lousing up the evidence."

Hunter handed Decker a rope while the two uniforms began to contain the crowd that was gathering.

Rina felt a heavy hand on her shoulder and jumped.

"How are you holding out?" Decker asked.

"I don't know . . ." She gave him back his gun.

"This isn't routine for me," he said softly, tucking the gun into his belt. "It must be a nightmare for you."

She nodded weakly.

"I'd better cordon off the area."

"Was it bad?"

He looked at her, hating what he had to say.

"Yeah. It was bad."

"Oh my God," Rina muttered, tears rolling down her cheek. "She was a wonderful person, Peter. You met her."

"It's a shitty deal, Rina."

"My God, why her?" Her voice cracked. "Why us?"

"I don't know, honey. But I swear to you, I'll find out." He loosened his tie. "Can you stand being alone while I'm up there, or do you want me to wait with you? There's certainly no emergency."

"I'm okay," she said in a cracked voice. "Go do your job."

"Sure?"

She nodded.

"All right. I'll be back in a minute. When the others come, direct them to the flares."

They descended in droves. Marge, Hollander, a dozen policemen, techs from the crime lab, an ambulance, a detective who looked like a linebacker. The place was crawling with humanity, figures buzzing over the hillside like drones around a hive. Rina's eyes blurred, her throat tightened, and she began to sob helplessly.

She felt arms around her waist, a chest to lean on, heard a familiar heartbeat. She clung to Peter tightly, fearful of letting go lest she fall off her psychic precipice.

She was brought out of her trance by a firm tug on her shirt sleeve. Chana Marcus took her arm and pulled her out of the embrace. Embarrassed, Rina took a step backward and wiped her tears on a tissue the unsmiling woman offered her.

"I'll walk you home, Rina," Chana said, making it sound like an order.

Rina looked at Peter. He was impassive.

"Do I have to stick around?" she asked him.

"Absolutely. I'll need you to clarify a few things."

"I'll wait over there, then."

145

"Suit yourself."

Rina walked away with Chana.

Meddling bitch, thought Decker.

Ed Fordebrand wiped the sweat off his forehead and bull neck, and began to itch. It was a peculiar psychosomatic reaction. Every time he saw a stiff, his skin felt afire. His enormous biceps began to swell with red hives, and the bulbous nose turned red and puffy. He took off his glasses and rubbed his eyes.

"I can't understand it," he said to Decker, scratching the newly formed lumps. "The fuckin' doctors say it's all in the head. I ask you, Deck, if it's in the head, why the hell does it show up on the body?"

"Ever think of switching out of Homicide to Vice, Ed?" Decker offered him a cigarette then took one for himself. "Think how that would swell your body."

"I'd miss out on all the beautiful scenery," Fordebrand answered, pointing to the corpse. "Ah, I've been doing this too long, Deck. I'm a stubborn old shit and refuse to admit it's getting to me."

"Well, it's gotten to me." Decker grimaced. "It's goddam ugly. Let's talk down below."

He led the beefy man away from the corpse, walking toward the foot of the mountains.

"You've gone soft since you left Homicide, Deck."

"I met the woman once, Ed. I liked her. To see her ripped apart, left out like carrion by some demented animal . . ."

"The pits, buddy. No question about it." Fordebrand rubbed his crimson bumps. 'What's your impression? Think it's related to the rape?"

"Yup."

"I'll take the case as a formality if you need a dick from Homicide, but if you want this stiff, it's yours, Deck."

Decker shook his head.

"I don't know. I'm getting a little overinvolved in this one, Ed."

146

"The pretty lady with the black hair?"

"You've got it."

"Darling little thing – and young. Nice way to ward off a mid-life crisis."

"Hell, she's bringing one on. Anyway, I don't want to fuck up this case by getting tunnel vision. That's why I called you down here."

"So what do we got"? Fordebrand asked.

"We've got a rape that happened six weeks ago – "

"The Foothill asshole?"

"Don't know. Inconsistencies in the M.O., but I never really got a good fix on how the woman was actually raped. Main thing that doesn't jibe is the shoes. The lady was wearing sandals, not sexy little pumps. My gut feeling is no."

"Okay, one rape." Fordebrand grimaced, clawing at his neck. "Now a one-eighty-seven at the same locale – a weird locale. Pretty big coincidence. What else connects the two?"

"The mikvah – the vandalized building. It's a Jewish ritual bathhouse. Someone tried to break in tonight, smashed the window. Luckily, I showed up and scared him away. But if he's brazen enough to break in after ripping off the guard, he's going to try again."

"You think he's after *her?*"

"Yes." His voice was serious. "I think he is. So far, he's attempted to get her here. Hasn't tried her house. That could mean he's fixated on the place and not her, or maybe he just hasn't gotten up the gumption. She's got two small boys, Ed. He breaks into her place, she's finished."

"Where are the kids now?"

"At a neighbor's. The guard used to walk her there, she'd pick them up, and then they'd all walk home together. But that still leaves the rest of the night for them to be alone. It's fucking scary."

"You like the little babe. This must be giving you some sleepless nights."

147

"A few." Decker inhaled his smoke.

"Can she get away for a while?"

"I'm sure as hell going to suggest it."

"Any candidates for the perp?"

"Couple of weirdos. I'm going to check them both out."

"Spurned lovers?"

Decker smiled. "I wouldn't call them lovers. Maybe would-be's that never made it past the first date."

Fordebrand slapped him on the shoulder.

"I got a heavy case load, Deck. Biker warfare going down. Five d.b.s that look like ground round. You don't need me. You're thinking straight, and you're motivated. It'll be your collar. If your head gets muddy, give me a call."

"All right. I'll send you a copy of the report. If the M.O. sounds remotely familiar to anything Homicide has on file, let me know."

"No problem."

"Take care of those welts, okay, big buddy?"

"They always shrink down a couple of days later." Fordebrand blew his nose and looked to one side. "I think the Chosen People are trying to get your attention."

The Rosh Yeshiva was waving. Decker excused himself and walked over to him.

"Mrs Lazarus said it was Florence Marley, the security guard. Is this true?"

He looked over and saw Rina surrounded by a group of women.

Damn it. They were pumping her. He had to get her away from them before the whole case blew up.

"I'm not at liberty to say, Rabbi, until the next of kin have been notified – "

"Detective, parents entrust their boys in my care. I am responsible for every life that resides here. Please, you must tell me."

Decker looked at the old man. His eyes were full of rage and fear.

"Don't say anything to the others, but yes, it was Mrs Marley."

"Such a fine woman . . ." The old man shook his head. "I interviewed her. She has young children, four of them. Her husband works two jobs so between the two of them they can afford to send them to private school . . . I can't believe this! What in the name of *Hashem* is happening here?"

"That's what we're trying to find out."

"Why are they doing this to us?"

"Rabbi – "

"*Do* something!"

There was nothing Decker could say to him. He placed his hand on the rabbi's shoulder.

Marge walked over.

"Nothing so far, Pete. The hills are empty."

"Marge, do me a favor and get Rina Lazarus over here. She's talking."

"Sure."

"We have a right to know what's going on," broke in the Rosh Yeshiva.

"She may inadvertently say something she shouldn't," Decker answered.

"We feel the burden of this horrendous crime, Detective. Hiring Florence Marley was our doing. Her death is our responsibility."

Decker understood the old man's concern, but had to do his job.

"Rabbi Schulman, I suspect the incidents have little to do with the yeshiva, but a lot to do with Rina. If she leaks something she shouldn't have, she could be putting herself in danger."

"No one here would hurt her."

"We can't be positive of anything right now, Rabbi."

"Do you possess information to which I'm not privy?"

"Rabbi, right now I'm not sure of anything."

"Are you holding back, Detective Decker?"

Decker was silent.

Marge brought Rina over.

"What's wrong?" she asked.

"Rina, you shouldn't be talking to anyone."

"They just wanted to know who it was – "

"I don't care. If they want to know something, tell them to ask me."

"They're scared."

"Rina, you've got to keep your mouth shut, plain and simple."

She looked to the Rosh Yeshiva for advice.

"Rina Miriam, I think the good detective suspects one of the *bochrim* as a *rasha*. Does he have reason?"

Decker was furious. He didn't know what a *rasha* was, but he knew it wasn't a compliment.

"Don't say anything."

"Rina Miriam – "

"I mean it."

Rina's eyes darted back and forth between the two men.

"Rina, you once told me that saving a life takes precedence over everything in Judaism," said Decker. "By talking, you'd be endangering your life."

The old man's lips turned upward in the hint of a smile.

"It's a strange world when a gentile enlists *halacha* for the purpose of persuasion. I give you credit, Detective."

The rabbi pulled out his cigarette case and offered hand-rolled cigarettes, first to Decker, then to Marge.

"I will break this impasse and make it easy on you, Detective, as well as on you, Rina Miriam. You told him about Shlomo Stein, am I correct?"

Rina said nothing. The Rosh Yeshiva turned to Decker.

"You'll be pleased to know that Shlomo Stein was learning in the *bais hamidrash* the entire evening. His *chavrusa* can confirm this. A *chavrusa* is – "

"I know. A learning partner."

The old man looked at Rina.

She turned red.

"The *chavrusa*'s name is Shraga Mendelsohn. Feel free

to interview both him and Mr Stein, Detective. I can guarantee you they have nothing to hide."

Schulman focused in on Rina.

"I agree with the detective, Rina Miriam. You need to learn the virtue of silence."

"TV people are here, Pete," said Marge.

"Well, I think this is one time when we all can agree on silence," Decker said.

"Absolutely." Schulman nodded and puffed on his cigarette. "Newspeople. Human vultures."

"You'll get no argument from me." Decker looked at Marge. "You want to handle it?"

"I think they want you, Pete."

"They want blood," Decker said under his breath. "Marge, take Rina home. I don't want her face on the news – "

"Oh, no!" Rina exclaimed.

Two patrolmen were leading Moshe Feldman out of the forest. The cameras zoomed in on the emaciated man who was mumbling incoherently and followed his pilgrimage down to Decker.

"We found him wandering around, Detective – "

Decker cut the officer short. "Read him his rights?"

"Yes, sir."

"Take him down to the station."

"Peter, please – " Rina tried.

"Take him in," Decker said, louder.

"Detective Decker, you don't understand about Moshe – "

"I do understand, Rabbi. There's nothing more to say. Marge, get Rina the hell out of here. They're coming this way."

Decker stomped away, but Rabbi Schulman caught up with him and grabbed his arm. The old man had a vise grip and kept up with Decker's brisk pace without a wheeze.

"Detective, Moshe has lived here seven years and spent the last two wandering around in the hills. Every man,

151

woman, and child knows he's out there, and no one has ever been worried or perturbed by his peculiar habits. There have never been any rapes or murders before all of this. Orthodox people don't rape and murder. That includes Moshe. He's harmless. He baby-sits children in the *shul* – "

"People can snap, Rabbi."

"Moshe snapped a long time ago, but he never was and never will be violent. He couldn't do something like this."

"You had your chance, Rabbi. He was released into Mr Adler's custody – damn, here they come."

A bright-eyed Asian woman spoke up first, wielding her microphone like a weapon:

"Detective Decker, who's the man being led out of the woods? Is he a suspect in the murder?"

"Detective, does this killing have any connection with the Foothill rapes that have been plaguing this area?"

"Detective, how was the victim murdered?"

"Was it someone from the yeshiva?" (Mispronounced yesh-eye-va.)

"There've been reports the victim was a woman. Was she raped?"

"Do you suspect the Foothill rapist?"

"Rabbi, do you have any information about the suspect now in custody?"

"Rabbi, is the victim one of your students?"

Decker turned around and faced them.

"I have no comment at this time, and we are withholding identification of the murder victim pending notification of kin. Thank you."

He squeezed into an unmarked, pulled the old man in with him, and took off.

"I thank you kindly, Detective."

"I wouldn't throw my worst enemy to those wolves. Where's a safe place to drop you off?"

The rabbi ignored the question and continued debating. The man was relentless.

"If it's Moshe, Detective, where is your evidence? Was

152

there a weapon? The last time you were here someone shot at you. Moshe wouldn't know how to shoot a gun. He'd blow his toes off. You saw Moshe. Does he look like a man who could tackle a two-hundred-pound security guard? Does he look like a man who had just finished murdering – winded and exhausted or full of scratches and blood from a struggle?"

"His clothes were torn."

"He wears torn clothing. Check his room. All of his clothes are worn, all of his clothes are old."

Schulman's eyes were bright and active. It was pointless to continue, thought Decker.

"Where can I drop you off, Rabbi Schulman?" he repeated.

"I'm coming down to the station with you."

"I'm afraid that's impossible, Rabbi."

"If you would give me time, I could convince you that Moshe is harmless – "

"Someone very convincing swayed me the first time. Now a woman is dead, and I want some answers. I pray to God it's not Feldman, because if it is, I'm responsible for her death."

"I insist Moshe has harmed no one. Arrest me instead."

"Rabbi, this is the twentieth century. If the cup was found on Benjamin, Benjamin is going to be tried for theft. And try as he may, Judah can't do a damn thing about it."

The old man looked perturbed.

"Rina has been teaching you Torah?"

"I learned that in Bible school. That's the Christian equivalent to your place."

"*Lehavdil.*" The rabbi cranked open the window.

"Now where can I take you?" Decker tried again.

"To Moshe! I am a lawyer! I will act as his counsel!"

"Are you licensed to practice in the State of California?" Decker asked.

The rabbi paused and readjusted his hat.

"No," he admitted softly.

"Then you cannot act as his counsel – "

"The man is incompetent. Incompetents are entitled to have their parents present during questioning."

"You're obviously not Feldman's father. Are you his legal conservator?" Decker asked.

"Not technically. But I am his spiritual leader and can promise you this, my good friend: Anything you will obtain from him in my absence will be inadmissible in court."

Decker suspected the old man might be right. He made an abrupt U-turn and headed toward the station.

16

Decker waited for the right opportunity to talk to the sobbing black man. He stood in the corner of the tiny living room, now packed with people, and tried to be invisible, but his oversized frame and complexion made him sorely conspicuous. Besides, he knew he reeked of cop. He'd received several sidelong glances since arriving, but no one dared to make eye contact with the stranger.

He scanned the crowd. The neighbors had brought baskets and platters of food, enough to make the card tables sag, but his stomach was in knots, and eight o'clock was too early for him to eat. Besides, he knew the spread was for friends only. The news had traveled fast, and people must have risen at dawn to cook and bake. Florence's preacher must have called and told them.

A little boy plowed into him, smiled, and scooted off. Being dressed in their Sunday best didn't stop the kids from romping around and chasing each other. Their mothers scolded them intermittently for their frisky behaviour, but seconds later they were off and running. A few of the shyer ones stayed close to their parents while gorging themselves on sweets.

Decker saw an opening and walked over to Florence's husband, Joe. He had made hundreds of condolence calls, but they still pained him. Joe was a big man, but he looked withered from exhaustion, overwhelmed by grief.

"Mr Marley?" Decker said.

The man regarded him.

"You must be the detective."

155

His voice was barely above a whisper, as if it was an exertion to speak.

"I'm Detective Peter Decker. I've been assigned to your wife's case. I had an opportunity to meet her before this all happened. She was a fine woman. I'm so sorry."

The man nodded graciously, then said:

"Florence didn't have any enemies, if that's what you were going to ask. Everyone loved her. Look at all the people here. They were all her friends. Nobody here would want to hurt her."

"I know they wouldn't"

The man let out a hollow laugh, followed by a trail of tears down his cheek.

"She wanted to be a cop, Detective. That's what she always wanted to be from the time I met her. I told her it was dangerous to be a cop. Besides, you saw Florence. The woman liked to eat. So she trained to be a security guard, and that suited me fine. Not too much danger in security work, right, Detective?"

"This was very unusual, Mr Marley."

"But it doesn't make her any less dead, does it? It's a freak situation, but she's still dead."

Marley grabbed Decker's arm.

"Who did this?"

"I don't know, Mr Marley."

"I heard you arrested somebody."

"He was released."

"Released?"

"He wasn't the right man. Besides, there was insufficient evidence to charge him with the murder – "

"Insufficient evidence," he hissed, then spat on the floor. "That's what I think of your insufficient evidence!"

Decker waited for more. Marley was looking for a scapegoat on whom to vent his frustrations, and at the moment, the detective didn't mind supplying the poor guy with one. But Marley stopped.

"Why did you come here?" he asked quietly.

"To tell you I was sorry. And to let you know I'm doing everything possible to find your wife's killer."

Joe lowered his head and nodded.

"Mr Marley, when you get a chance, when your head clears a little, maybe you can remember something unusual that Florence might have said about the mikvah – "

"The whole culture was strange to her, but she liked the place. Liked the women. They liked her. They gave her a present on her birthday . . ."

The man heaved a big sob.

"Did she mention seeing anyone hanging around there?"

"Not that I can recall."

"Well, don't concern yourself with it right now. But if something comes to you, give me a call."

Decker gave him his card.

"Thank you for coming, Detective Decker," Marley said, looking at the small stiff rectangle.

"Feel free to call me anytime."

Decker left the bereaved man, stepped outside, and noticed the day had turned hot already. He had walked halfway to his car when he was stopped by the preacher, a slight, mocha-colored young man with cornrowed hair, dressed in a clerical collar, black shirt and matching pants.

"Excuse me, sir. I couldn't help noticing you."

Decker smiled to himself. "What can I do for you, Reverend?"

"You're the policeman in charge of the case?"

Decker nodded.

"Are you making any progress?"

"Unfortunately, these things take time."

"In other words, nothing."

Decker remained impassive.

"Perhaps you'd like to do more. We're setting up a memorial fund for Florence Marley. We'd like to build a new classroom in the church in her honor. Perhaps you'd like to contribute?"

Decker sighed, took out a wallet, and pressed a twenty and a ten in the man's hand. It cleaned him out.

"That's most generous, Detective."

"Yeah, well, we all do what we can."

Decker left the Marley house just in time to get caught in rush-hour traffic on the Harbor Freeway north. He was heading toward the downtown interchange and knew he was going to be stuck for a while. He considered playing cop and pulling out the light to sidestep it all, but he wasn't particularly eager to get to work. He eased the Plymouth into the left lane, cutting in front of a Datsun which gave him an angry honk. Decker ignored it, but the driver wasn't satisfied with just a simple reprimand. When they were both at a standstill, he thrust his head out of the window, let go with a tirade of verbal abuse, and flipped him off.

At the first opportunity, Decker swung his car next to the Datsun. He took the red light off the dashboard and reached out to place it on the roof of the unmarked. The 280 ZX pulled onto the freeway shoulder.

Decker parked the Plymouth, got out, approached the Datsun, and looked through the rear window. Nothing suspicious. He regarded the man. Mr Junior Executive. Fancy jacket, silk tie, prissy mustache. Probably lived in a condo and coked his head on the weekends. Now he looked as if he was going to piss in his pants.

"May I see your license, sir?" Decker asked.

"Officer, I'm sorry about the outburst – "

'Your license, sir?'

"Oh sure." The man fumbled around, finally locating the ID, then handed it to him through the open window.

Decker looked it over.

Ronald Elward. Five eight, 160. Blue eyes, brown hair. Twenty-eight years old. A little prick.

"Mr Elward, you need to learn about freeway manners."

"I'm sorry – "

"I could arrest you as a public nuisance."

The man blanched.

"This is a warning. Consider yourself lucky."

"Yes, sir."

Decker pulled the car out and edged back into the traffic. He was still crawling, but he felt a little better.

It had been a long night – the murder, four hours of interrogation, and a mound of paperwork.

Moshe Feldman had been an impossible suspect to grill because the usual techniques of interviewing didn't work on a schizophrenic. He seemed oblivous to the fact that he was a suspected murderer. The possibility of incarceration left him apathetic. The man was in outer space. He spoke freely and uninhibitedly, talking even when advised to remain silent, but most of what he said was gibberish – not all of it in English. Decker asked the rabbi to translate the Hebrew (actually Aramaic, the detective learned), and the old man said he was quoting from the *Gemara Sukkot*.

Feldman's counsel was equally difficult. The rabbi had brought in some mouthpiece from Beverly Hills – a contentious bastard if ever Decker had seen one – but sharp. The attorney objected to every question he posed, so the detective had spent at least half his time trying to rephrase himself.

Hours of interviewing had led nowhere.

The search of Feldman's living quarters had proved equally fruitless. The wandering scarecrow lived meagerly, out of choice, in a potting shed covered with sheets of tarpaper to keep the rain out. The shack was bereft of basics such as bed or bathroom, but loaded with mowers, hoes, shovels, claws, clippers, stakes, wire, fertilizer, potting soil, seeds, and plant food. Against the rotted wooden planks was a makeshift closet of stapled boxes full of old clothes of varying sizes. Most of the garments were soiled white shirts, stale-smelling black pants, old black hats, and fringed dickies, but in the corner hung a white robe embellished with gold thread, lace, and

159

embroidery, and a prayer shawl trimmed with a collar of silver. These were set aside from the rest of his wardrobe, encased in a plastic cleaners' bag. Rabbi Schulman told Decker that Moshe slept on the floor and ate only fresh fruits and raw vegetables that he grew in a small garden patch behind the lean-to. For the Sabbath, he indulged in challah, wine, and a pot of soup and boiled chicken that the Rosh Yeshiva's wife cooked for him.

The oddest thing about the place was the room's centerpiece – a bookcase fashioned of dark, oiled walnut and windowed with leaded beveled glass. It was an antique and, judging from the amount of marquetry and carving, obviously worth money. Inside were prayer books in Hebrew and phylacteries.

Some potentially incriminating evidence had been found at the scene of the murder. A shred of material from Feldman's jacket was hanging on an adjacent oak branch, and nearby were fresh footprints that matched the shoes he was wearing. But it was nothing to make a charge of murder stick. The man was a compulsive hiker. The jacket could have been ripped a long time ago, and he could have left his tracks before the murder took place. Most important, there was no concrete evidence in the preliminary lab reports to link him directly to the murder – no bloody clothes, no weapon, no fingerprints, no microfibers of his clothes or hairs found on the deceased or vice versa.

Moshe was released, a free man – of sorts.

Decker pulled the car into the precinct lot, walked into the squad room, poured himself a cup of coffee, then summoned Hollander and Marge into an empty interview room for a powwow.

"Who wants to go first?" Decker asked.

"Feldman walked, huh?" said Hollander.

"We don't have anything on him except that he was in the wrong place at the wrong time. Not enough to sock him with a robust Murder One."

"Do you think he did it?" Marge asked Decker.

"No. What do you think?"

"I don't think he did it, either. Mike?"

"I'll make it unanimous."

"I don't think he did it," said Decker, "not because he's not crazy enough, but because he's not strong enough."

He paused, gulped some coffee, and continued:

"The woman outweighed him by seventy pounds and was taller by five inches. More important, Florence had confidence. She was a pro."

"Unless he was on PCP," said Marge.

"According to the serum and urine analyses, he was clean," Decker said.

"So who are we dealing with?" Hollander asked, yawning and rubbing his eyes.

"Someone big and strong," Marge said. "Like your size, Pete."

Decker nodded. "I could have restrained her. I've got four inches on the woman and know what I'm doing, but let me tell you guys, it would have been a struggle. To subdue a big woman like that who'd be lashing out would require beef – real muscle."

"Remember, about fifteen years back, a sweetheart named Edward Kemper from Santa Cruz? A real psycho," Marge said, slumping in the folding chair. "Blasted his grandparents and mother. A necrophile. Cut up a slew of coeds, screwed 'em, and traveled around with their dismembered hands."

"Reach out and touch someone, huh?" said Hollander.

Marge ignored him. "The darling was six nine, two-eighty."

"Yeah, we could be dealing with someone like him," Decker said. "Or someone even a little smaller but with a lot of bulk – like Fordebrand."

"The anonymous linebacker," Marge thought out loud.

"Yup. So how about we do this?" Decker said. "We'll

run a check on all the bad boys around town with large builds – six feet, two hundred pounds minimum."

"Gonna come up with a healthy list," Hollander grunted.

"Yeah, but we won't know shit unless we try. Any other possibilities besides Feldman and football players?"

"Weight lifters?" Hollander said.

"They'll show up on the list, Mike," said Decker.

"How about someone who knows karate?" Marge suggested.

"Then why would he bother with a knife?" Hollander responded.

"Maybe he gets a thrill out of slicing?"

"It's a possibility," said Decker. "Low on the list, but a possibility. The Bruce Lee killer. Who else?"

"How about the Foothill prick?" Hollander asked, lighting up his pipe. The room became blanketed with a thick haze. "He knows how to manhandle women."

"Florence wasn't raped," Marge reminded him.

"So maybe he crossed the border and decided to kill," Hollander said.

"I wouldn't be a bit surprised if the bastard eventually does kill," said Decker. "He's getting increasingly more violent, and we all know that rape and murder are on one big continuum. But rapists who start killing usually mix the violence with sex. Florence wasn't sexually assaulted in any way."

"Let's back it up," Marge said, finishing her coffee. "Maybe the killer wasn't Mr Muscles. Maybe Florence just freaked at the sight of an attacker and froze with fear."

"Not that woman," Decker shook his head. "She once stopped me on the way to the mikvah. She was tough and loud."

"Did the preliminary autopsy show any head injuries?" Marge asked.

"No," Hollander answered.

"So she wasn't knocked out beforehand," Marge said.

162

"Also, her facial expression was pure terror," Decker said. "I think the poor woman was wide awake and knew what was going to happen to her."

The three of them sat for a moment in silence and digested it all.

Hollander broke the silence.

"I'm gonna get another cup of coffee. Anyone besides me want some swill?"

They handed him their mugs.

"How's tricks, Pete?" Marge asked after he left.

"Been better. I need some sleep." Decker yawned as if to illustrate the point. "Hey, I got the invitation to the recital."

Marge smiled.

"Ernst and I have some lovely duets picked out. Going to be quite a crowd. I'm a little nervous."

"You'll pull it off."

"Hey, I'll be among friends, right?"

"I'm a friend. I promise not to laugh too loud."

"Mike's bringing Mary. Bring someone."

Hollander reentered, carrying a tray of coffee cups, a pint of milk, and a few packets of sugar.

"Great service, Michael," Marge said. "I'll leave you a big tip."

"I'll take anything you'll give me, Marjorie."

Decker took a sip, then said:

"I've got another scenario for the murder. The killer wasn't alone."

"I like that," Marge agreed.

"They ambushed her," Decker continued. "One held her down while the other slashed."

"Sounds as reasonable as a Goliath," Hollander said. "Any candidates for the dynamic duo?"

"Stein and Mendelsohn," Marge said. "Mike and I did some poking around at the yeshiva last night. Rabbi Schulman told me Stein was studying, but it turns out it wasn't in a group. Seems the only one who could attest to Stein's whereabouts was his friend Mendelsohn. They were studying together in a deserted classroom, and no one remembers seeing them. They could have slipped away without being noticed."

"Mendelsohn have a record?" Hollander asked.

"No, but that doesn't mean anything," Marge said. "All weirdos start out clean."

"What would be the motive?" Hollander asked.

"Let me run this by you," said Decker. "We know weirdos sometimes find each other and pool their pathology, right? Let's suppose that both Stein and Mendelsohn are psychos. And they find each other at the yeshiva and become friends. They talk, and bizarre ideas pop into their head – rape, murder."

"Like Bianchi and Buono," Hollander said.

"Exactly," Decker said. "I'll check them out. I'll also poke around the yeshiva for anyone else who looks interesting. Mike, how about you picking up Cory Schmidt and friends? They're also possibilities. He admitted vandalizing the yeshiva, so we know he's been there before. Maybe he saw women coming out of the mikvah and came back one night to take advantage."

"But we're right back to where we started, Pete," Marge said. "How could Cory have overtaken Florence?"

"Maybe he did the rape alone the first time and brought his friends back for a gang bang. What if he wasn't alone the first time? Had his friends along keeping watch. When Rina called out, it scared them all away, and the others didn't get their turn with Mrs Adler."

"But how would the boys know about the Marley woman?" Hollander asked. "She wasn't there at the time of the Adler rape."

"They might have come back another time and seen her patrolling," Decker suggested. "Next time they came prepared. They got her out of the way and tried to break into the mikvah to get to what they were really after."

"So they had to know that Rina was there," Marge said.

Decker tensed. "Or at least know someone was in there. Maybe not Rina."

"Or maybe they came back to seek revenge on Rina *specifically*, for the rousting we gave them last week," said Hollander. "Cory may have felt it was all her fault."

"The possibilities are numerous," Marge said. "It could be the linebacker psychopath, but personally I like the boys for the bad guys. First, there's a bunch of them. They could really get a grip on the woman. Second, boys of their ilk tend to ingest a lot of illicit chemicals. The murder smacks of drug-frenzied adolescence. The dismembered arm and leg, the slit throat. Spaced-out teenage boys who love gore and have low impulse control."

"Okay," Hollander said. "I'll look into Schmidt and his buddies."

"Then that leaves me to check out the list of giants," Marge said, then looked at Decker. "Someone should talk to Rina. Find out if she can tell us a little bit more about the break-in at the mikvah."

Decker nodded.

"You know, Pete," Marge continued, "if she's the target, maybe she should split for a few days."

"Exactly my thought." Decker felt a rush of anxiety and changed the subject quickly. "What do you two make of Feldman's clothes and shoe prints at the scene?"

"Maybe he's the original wandering Jew and was hanging around the area before the whole thing took place," Hollander said through a cloud of blue smoke.

"Let me run *this* by you," Decker said. "Guy is roaming in the woods, sees something unusual, and goes over to investigate. He spots Florence lying there dead and mutilated. It freaks him out, but he's too psychologically incapacitated to tell us about it. Or . . ."

"He could have witnessed something," Marge said.

"Exactly," Decker said. "How are we going to penetrate that warped mind?"

"See the rabbi," Hollander said.

"I already have," said Decker. "I laid out the same

165

scene for him. The rabbi admits that Feldman was exceptionally incoherent last night and agrees it might be because he saw the murder take place. The old man knows a shrink who may be able to pull something out of him."

"I hope he's better than the last doctor of theirs that we used," Marge said. "She really fucked up."

"True," Decker agreed. "But this guy – Dr Marder – sounds very well qualified. I checked him out with Behavioral Sciences, and he's considered an expert in hypnosis. Most important, he was Feldman's original shrink, treated the guy when he first started to decompensate."

"Wasn't too successful," Hollander said.

"No, but he does have a rapport with him."

The door to the interview room opened, and Fordebrand popped his head inside.

"Phone call, Pete."

"Thanks, Ed." Decker stood up. "Anything else?"

"I'm fine," Hollander said.

"Ditto," answered Marge.

"Okay. Meeting adjourned." Decker walked over to his desk and punched the flashing white button.

"Decker."

A familiar background noise. Jesus, everything all at once. It was her. Keep her on the line. The longer the better.

"Hello?" he asked.

"Hi."

He coughed.

"Excuse me, Miss." He checked his watch, then let go with a series of hacking coughs. Don't overdo it, he warned himself.

"Pardon my coughing. I've got this cold that just won't quit. Tried everything, but . . . Anyway, what can I do for you, Miss?"

"I was wondering . . . That sounds like a nasty cough."

Decker coughed again.

"It is. I've had the darn thing for a week. Can't seem to shake it. Just when I think it's abating – "

"Yeah, anyway, I was wondering about the Foothill rapist."

"Well, I'm the man to talk to. Excuse me." He coughed again, took a sip of water, and got back on the phone. "How can I help you?"

"That description of the man that the nurse gave the police. They showed it on TV, on the news. Do you have a copy of it?"

"The composite drawing?"

"Yeah."

"I have a copy of it." He cleared his throat and took a deep breath. "I'd be glad to send it to you if you'll just give me your name and address."

Just a whir on the other end.

"Hello, Miss?"

The line disconnected.

Shit! But at least the tap was hooked up. Hopefully, he'd stalled her long enough. He dialed the police operator immediately. She told him that someone would get back to him right away. Five minutes later the phone rang.

"Decker."

"It's Arnie, Pete. Got some specific boundaries for you."

"Shoot."

"The call is in the Sylmar vicinity, north of Glenoaks, south of San Fernando Road, eastern border is Astonia, western is Roxford, inclusive."

"Well, that narrows it down."

"A little more time and I could have gotten even more specific."

"Rub it in, why don't you?" Decker said. "Pay phone?"

"Naturally. Hope this helps, Pete."

"It should. Thanks."

"Bye."

Decker got up and went over to the squad room's

receptionist. Shirly was an overweight, big-busted brunette in her early forties. Her best feature was an infectious smile.

"Hello, Shirley."

"What do you want, Decker?"

"The yellow pages for Sylmar."

She opened up a drawer and handed him a canary-colored directory.

"If it's the massage parlors you want, ask MacPherson."

"I'll look on my own. I don't trust his taste."

She winked and flashed him a grin that he had to return.

Decker took the phonebook to his desk and looked up laundromats, laundries, and dry cleaners. An hour later he had narrowed the list down to two dry cleaners, two laundries, and three laundromats in the area. His watch told him it was half past ten. First he'd talk to Rina.

17

The aftermath of last night's horror had left Rina drained
and riddled with anxiety. She was short-tempered with
her boys and more than happy to send them off to camp.
But once they were gone, depression overtook her. She
berated herself for failing as a parent, for being an
uncaring human being, for talking too much to the goy,
for her shortcomings as a Jew. She sank into a corner and
cried. When the tears stopped, her mood changed
abruptly, and she began to pace with nervous energy.
She'd been wanting to clean out the closets, and today
was as good a day as any. She tried to concentrate on the
task single-mindedly, but her nerves were frazzled, and
midway through the overhaul she left piles of unsorted
clothes on the floor, fell down on the sofa, and sobbed.

She had just about finished her second bout of hysteria
when the doorbell rang. She didn't want to answer it
looking terrible and in a mood to match, but running
away never solved a damn thing. Getting up from the
sofa, she peered through the peephole and opened the
door.

Peter looked just as haggard as she. His clothes were
wrinkled, his eyes were red and swollen, and the normal
ruddiness of his cheeks had turned to paste.

"Can I come in?" he asked.

"No."

"I have to talk to you."

"So talk."

Decker looked around.

"Rina, please. Unfortunately, this isn't a social call. If

you won't let me in, meet me down at the station. That way we can make the whole thing nice and official, and you won't have to be so afraid of what the neighbors might think."

"How long do you think it will take?"

"I don't know, but you're wasting time right now."

She let him in.

Decker looked at the heaps of clothes strewn about the room.

"Are you planning to go somewhere?"

"Just cleaning out my closets."

She saw he was weary. Felt his fatigue. She shouldn't be sniping at him. Ultimately, they were on the same side.

"Have a seat, Peter," she said quietly. "Would you like some coffee?"

He smiled. "Thank you, I would."

"How do you take it?"

"Black . . . and strong."

She busied herself in the kitchen and came back with two steaming cups and a basket of fruit.

She sat down and tucked her bare feet under smooth, silky legs. Decker glanced at them, then averted his gaze and closed his eyes altogether, imagining her caressing his body. He could sure use a soft touch right now.

"You didn't get much sleep, did you?" she asked.

Decker opened his eyes, took a sip of coffee, then set the cup down on an end table.

"Not really, I saw Florence's family this morning. They're good people, Rina. It hurt."

"I know what they're going through." Her eyes began to mist. "At least Yitzchak died among loved ones and at peace. She went so horribly."

She lowered her head and looked the other way.

He wanted to hold her, but resisted. Though he had only comfort on his mind, she was distraught enough to misinterpret his intentions. Instead he nodded sympathetically.

170

"I still can't believe it," Rina said wiping her eyes.

"I'm sorry. This must be so rough on you."

She didn't say anything.

Her eyes were dull and sunken, her hands trembled. She hesitated when she talked. It ate at him to see her in such misery.

"I've got one piece of news that'll cheer you up. We released Moshe."

A spark ignited in her.

"Of course he's inncoent. You shouldn't have arrested him in the first place."

Decker sipped his coffee and said, "Rina, I want you to promise me that you'll keep what I tell you between the two of us."

She nodded.

He related the incidents of last night, and his theories. When he was finished, he said:

"Rina, we're going to have to face facts. Whoever it was who killed Florence, didn't rape her. He wanted her out of the way to get to who he was really after."

Rina swallowed hard.

"I think it would be a good idea if you visited your parents for a couple of weeks."

"I'm not going to run away – "

"Just listen to me. I'm not talking forever. I'm talking until we can get a handle on this thing. We'll pull Cory in for questioning, interview Stein and Mendelsohn, look around for something odd. Maybe we'll get lucky. In the meantime, I'd like to know that you're safe and sound, hidden somewhere out of reach."

She smiled. "Do you worry about me?"

"Of course I worry about you. I worry about your boys, too. I'd invite you to stay with me, but I know what the answer would be."

He looked at her hopefully, but she shook her head.

"So I think the safest and most logical thing to do is to have you conveniently disappear for a couple of weeks."

"What if you pull Cory in and find nothing? What if

171

nothing happens while I'm away? What am I going to do? Live in permanent exile until something happens? If I'm the target, the monster or monsters are going to follow me. I'm not going to run away. *Hashem* will look after us. He always has."

Decker frowned.

"Rina, be practical. Doesn't God help those who help themselves?"

"Sometimes one just has to have faith."

He wasn't about to get into a theological argument with her. He tried a different approach.

"What about your boys?"

"What about them? They haven't been bothered."

"You're going to wait for them to be attacked?"

She clenched her hands to keep them from shaking.

"Peter, why are you *scaring* me like this?"

"Because I want you out of here and safe."

"And if he follows me? You won't be around, and I'll have no one to turn to. No. I refuse to go. I'm not going to run away. If need be, I'll fight the S.O.B. on my own turf! I'll learn self-defense! I'll buy a gun!"

"And in the meantime?"

"I'll start today. I'll enroll in a karate program."

"It takes a while to learn these things, Rina. Do you think you're going to get a black belt overnight? Besides, the man had a gun – "

"I'll buy a gun and take shooting lessons."

"Proficiency isn't developed in a few short lessons. I've seen how this guy handles a gun. He's a goddam marksman."

She said nothing for a moment, blinked, then tears spilled over her cheeks.

"My boys are going to get hurt, and it'll be my fault."

Decker sighed. "Honey, no one is going to get – "

"First Yitzchak, now this." She looked at him. "God must be punishing me. I must be doing something wrong."

"No one is punishing you. It isn't – "

"My husband, my children . . ."

172

"No one is after your kids specifically – "

"It's all my fault. *Hashem* has His reasons for putting me through this."

What a crock of bullshit, Decker thought. He felt guilty. Initially, she'd reacted with anger, which was healthy, and he'd quelled her fire. Now, she was internalizing the bad hand she'd been dealt.

"Rina, *none* of this is your fault. And no one is after your kids. If they're out of the way, they'll be safe."

She was silent.

"Compromise, Rina. It's summertime. I know the high school boys here go to school year round, but your kids don't. If you have it in your mind to stay, then stay. But at least send the boys to your parents for a week."

"They're on vacation," she said weakly. "They'll be back Monday."

"Okay, do this. Over the weekend take the boys and move in with Sarah Adler. Tell her and Zvi what's going on, and I'm sure they'll understand."

She nodded.

"Go about your Sabbath as usual, and on Sunday spend the day with me at the ranch. You were thinking of letting the boys come over and ride the horses anyway. This'll be a perfect excuse. On Monday take the boys to your parents."

"All right," she said weakly.

She broke into tears.

"Come here," he said extending his arms. She fell onto his chest and sobbed on his shoulder. He hugged her tightly. "We're going to get the bastards, honey. I swear to you, we will."

"What do I tell my parents?" she sniffed. "I certainly can't tell them the truth."

"How good a liar are you?"

"Not very."

"Then keep your excuse simple."

She sighed.

"I guess I could tell them the boys have been asking to visit. It's not really true, but the kids do like to see them."

"How much do the boys know?"

"I haven't said anything and I try to be reassuring, but they know something's wrong. They're scared, Peter. I was like this when Yitzchak was dying. Maybe they think I'm going to die." She sighed heavily. "I'll talk to them, try to make it clear that this is only temporary. They're trustworthy. If I tell them not to mention anything to their grandparents, they won't."

"Good." He stroked her hair. "I'd feel a lot better if you went with them."

She shook her head.

"No. If anything happens next week, at least it will only happen to me."

"All right. Just promise me you'll keep in constant touch. Try not to be alone or at least have someone nearby. And call me if you leave the grounds."

She nodded.

"Even if it's just a quick errand."

"Okay."

"Promise?"

"Yes, yes. You're as bad as my parents."

"I know I'm a nag. Cindy tells me the same thing."

Rina snuggled in closer, and they sat embracing in silence. To his surprise, even in his current state of exhaustion, he was becoming aroused. Goddam it, he thought, enjoying the feeling and not knowing what to do with it. He felt awkward breaking away from her when they had fitted together so nicely, but knew he couldn't go any farther. Back to business.

"Are you up to telling me about the mikvah break-in? If you're not, just say so."

"I'm okay. Anything I can do to help find this *mamzer*, I'll do." She gently slid out of his arms and sat next to him. "Unfortunately, there's nothing much to tell. First, he tried to get in the door. When that didn't work, he

174

threw that boulder through the window. He stuck his arm in – "

"His arm?"

"Yes. One arm."

"Was it gloved?"

"No. It was an arm sticking out of a shirt sleeve."

"What color was the skin?"

"White."

"A Caucasian," he muttered to himself. "Do you remember the color of the shirt sleeve?"

"Dark. Navy blue or black."

"Do you recall if the arm was scratched from the window?"

"No. I was too busy protecting my eyes from the flying glass."

"You did right, Rina. You handled it perfectly." He took a peach and bit out a chunk. "The lab boys went over the mikvah thoroughly. The prints they lifted from the door handle are useless – incomplete and smudged. They didn't bother with the window. I'll send a crime tech back and see if he can't come up with some blood scraping or prints from the casement."

"He can come anytime. The mikvah's shut down anyway."

"Do the women get some dispensation from their mikvah obligation?"

"It doesn't work that way. But, *Baruch Hashem*, there are other mikvot in Los Angeles. They're using the nearest one from here, which is an hour's car ride away."

"I'm sorry. But it's probably for the best."

It wasn't for the best, she thought. But how could she begin to explain the importance of the ritual bath – how integral it was to all of Judaism? The rainwater pool was the symbolic essence of *Taharat Hamishpacha* – family purity. Its waters were used to cleanse the dead spiritually, and immersion in it was essential before a non-Jew could be converted. Even cooking and eating utensils made of metal were dunked to render them clean. Mikvah was a mainstay of Jewish life – as much a part of Orthodoxy as dietary laws, circumcision, or the Sabbath.

She didn't try to educate Peter. She was much too weary, and he probably wouldn't understand. No one would except another of her own kind.

She shrugged.

"Is there anything I can do for you now?" he asked.

"No. Nothing. But thanks for offering."

"Okay," Decker said, finishing the last bite of peach. "Rina, we've pretty much ruled out Moshe, but it wouldn't hurt to let people think he's still under suspicion. Might make the real killer get careless and do something stupid."

She nodded and patted his hand maternally. "Take care, Peter. Get some sleep."

"Later," he said.

After I do my laundry, he thought.

18

Dry cleaner number one was owned by a Korean couple surnamed Park. They barely spoke English and didn't seem to understand a word Decker was saying. The only other person who worked for them was a black woman of fifty named Lilly. Decker spoke to her. The voice didn't match. He scratched the place off his list.

Number two was owned jointly by two white couples in their mid-thirties. They worked alone, and neither of the women's voices matched the anonymous girl on the phone. Onward.

At the Ti-Dee-Rite Launderette he got lucky.

The place was in a small, shabby shopping center with a 7-Eleven on one side and a donut shop on the other. He parked the unmarked between a souped up '58 Chevy and a Ford flatbed, and took out a sack of dirty laundry. If nothing else panned out, at least he'd have clean undershirts.

The laundromat was large. The central floor space was taken up by sixty Speed Queen machines. On the rear wall were a coin-operated soap dispenser, a laundry bag dispenser, and a bill changer. Directly in front of the machines were three free-standing tables for sorting and folding. The left wall had twenty built-in industrial dryers; the right held ten more dryers, four extra-large washers for bedspreads and rugs, and a pay phone. A couple of women sat on orange plastic chairs and waited for the wash cycle to finish, biding their time by thumbing through out-of-date magazines. A young man with a harelip loaded wet clothes into a dryer. A few other

177

people were busy at the machines. In a corner sat a woman in her mid-twenties. Her face was round, almost pleasant, but marred by tight, thin lips. Her arms looked abnormally short, almost dwarf-like. She was wearing a name tag. Decker couldn't read the name but could make out the word MANAGER written underneath in bold black letters.

He walked over to an empty washer and loaded the clothes. Closing the lid, he placed some coins into a slot and fed them into the machine. When the washer didn't kick in, he started banging it furiously. Immediately, the manager got up and came over.

"Take it easy, mister!" she scolded.

Decker grinned inside.

"Stop hammering the thing to death. What's the problem?"

Her name tag said Rayana Beth Mathers. *Hello, Rayana.*

"The thing's broken. It ate my money."

Slowly, Rayana eased back the slot.

"You put in two quarters and a nickel. You need two quarters and a dime."

She pronounced "quarters" as "quatters."

"You're from Boston?" Decker asked, smiling.

She smiled back.

"You got a good ear for accents, huh?"

He nodded and stared at her. She lowered her head coquettishly, then looked up at him. Her face suddenly blanched, and she tried to take off. Decker grabbed her arm.

"What's wrong?" he asked.

"Leave me alone. I want a lawyer."

"Why on earth do you need a lawyer, Rayana? I just want to talk to you."

"I've got nothing to say."

"Well, then just listen."

"Take your hands off me!"

178

A few patrons turned around, curious looks on their faces.

"You're attracting attention," Decker whispered.

She stopped struggling in his grip.

"That's better," Decker said, not releasing her arm. "Now, how'd you know I was a cop?"

"You look like one."

"Then how come you didn't make me for one right away? What was it? Did you suddenly recognize my face? My voice?"

"Maybe."

"Let's sit down, Rayana."

"Just let go of my arm, okay?"

He complied, and again she tried to run off. He latched onto her other arm.

"What the hell are you trying to do?" he said softly.

"I don't know anything."

"Know anything about what?"

"Know anything about anything. Leave me alone."

"Let's just talk about the phone calls."

"What phone calls?"

"The phone calls you made to me."

"I didn't call you up."

"I've got some voice prints that say you did."

"Bully for you."

"Come on," Decker said, leading her to a plastic chair. He sat her down and pulled up another chair. "Rayana, you called me because you were concerned about something. You know something, and you're too scared to tell anyone. Come down to the station with me. I'll get you a lawyer, and we'll make a deal. I guarantee we'll deal with you. You turn state's evidence, and you'll not only walk out a free bird, you'll be looked upon as a hero, Rayana."

She thought about it for a moment.

"I don't know what you're talking about," she said finally.

"Rayana, we're very close to catching this guy. If we do

and you're implicated in any way, you're going to be in deep shit, honey."

"I honestly don't know anything."

"C'mon. I've got your voice prints. Let's cut the crap."

"Okay, okay," she sighed. "I called you a couple times, okay? Maybe I was curious about something, okay? That doesn't prove I did anything wrong. Or prove I know something."

"How'd you know about the shoes, Rayana?"

"Maybe I knew this guy once who liked shoes."

"What's his name?"

"I forgot."

"Come on!"

"I don't know anything about any *rapes*. I don't know anything! Wanna arrest me? Arrest me. I don't know anything. I called you and asked you about shoes, and that's all I did, and so far as I know, that ain't a crime."

"Harboring felons is a crime. Withholding material evidence is a crime."

"I'm not withholding or harboring anybody."

"Who's the guy you know that likes the shoes?"

"What guy?"

He was losing her, damn it!

"Take a look at these, Rayana." He pulled out some snapshots. "Take a good look."

She gave a tentative glance to the first one, then pulled her head away.

"No, come on. Stare at these for a while. I want you to see what you're protecting."

She flipped through the photographs, and a look of nausea passed over her face.

"One woman was raped and sodomized so harshly that the membrane between her vagina and anus ruptured. She came down with a massive cross-infection and had to have a hysterectomy. The woman was twenty-one, Rayana."

"That's too bad." She handed the photos back to Decker. "But I don't know anything."

"I'm going to have to pull you in for questioning."

"Go ahead."

Tenacious little bitch.

"Let's go."

"Is it gonna take a long time?"

"Probably."

"I'd better phone the owner and tell her."

"Go ahead."

She made a quick call.

"She should be here in a few minutes." Rayana sighed dejectedly. "Man, she was pissed. I think I woke her from her nap."

Decker flipped his wrist and checked the time. "She'd better be speedy."

"Let's just go."

"You don't want to wait for her?"

"Hell no! You think I want her to see me being led outta here by a cop. Let's just get it over with."

Decker escorted her out to the unmarked. He forgot his laundry.

"They let her go?" Fordebrand asked.

"Yeah. Nothing to hold her on. Not a goddam thing. Usually someone who'd bother to call would be aching to confess, but she closed up." Decker thought for a moment. "Maybe she was afraid of implicating herself and didn't believe it when we offered her immunity. Hell, maybe she's involved."

"You have reason to suspect her?"

"Nothing concrete, damn it. She was a loss."

"She'll be back," Fordebrand said. "She'll just have to get pissed or worried enough. Then, like a homing pigeon, she'll be back."

"Yeah. But in the meantime the asshole rapes someone else. Hollander is tailing her, trying to find out who her companions are. Maybe she'll be stupid and lead us to someone."

"You want to grab a steak somewhere, buddy?"

"Sure, just let me check for messages."

He walked over to his desk and found a manila envelope sitting atop a pile of mail. The name and address were typed on a separate piece of paper and taped to the front side of the parcel. "Detective" was misspelled.

"When did this come in?" Decker said out loud to no one in particular.

"I don't know," Fordebrand said.

"Around noon," MacPherson answered. He was a black robbery detective – a ladies' man who quoted Shakespeare and Bacon. "While you were playing Eliot Ness with the cleaning maiden. It's already gone through bomb squad. You're safe."

"What the fuck . . . ? There's no postage on it. Did it come through the mail?"

"Why don't you open it up, Peter?" MacPherson said.

Decker gingerly broke the seal and gently dumped the contents onto his desktop. Out fell a plastic sandwich bag with something wrapped inside and a typed note. It read:

Check this out in the killing of the fat black bitch at Jewtown.

Decker didn't even bother to unwrap the contents. He picked up the phone and called the crime lab.

He had a steak, fries, salad, and a beer with Fordebrand, then went home and slept for a couple of hours with Ginger curled at his feet. When he woke up it was nearly six P.M. He'd made an appointment earlier to speak with Stein and Mendelsohn. It was getting late, and he'd have to move it. Before he left the ranch he fed the animals and phoned the station.

The bag had contained a bloody, unwashed buck knife. The handle was bone with a metal ID tag insert. The name on the tag was Cory Schmidt. Preliminary blood typing and fiber analysis showed Marley's blood on the knife and beige threads from her uniform. Marge had already requested a search warrant for Schmidt's house and an arrest warrant for Schmidt, but so far they'd been

182

unable to locate Cory or his friends. They were still looking. Decker left a message that he was going to do his interviews and to beep him if he was needed.

Well, golly! How convenient! Who the hell would want to set up Cory? His friends? The real murderer? But how would the real murderer know about Cory as a suspect? Unless he was an insider in the yeshiva and knew that Cory had pulled a knife on Rina. The interviews suddenly seemed more pressing.

Shlomo Stein sat hunched over a volume of Talmud. He'd been sitting that way since Decker started the interview a half hour before. His eyes remained fixed on the text in front of him, but the fidgeting of his hands and the shaking of his leg were giveaways; his mind was decidedly elsewhere. His beard was black and heavy and trimmed to a Van Dyke point a couple of inches below his chin. He wore a white shirt with sleeves rolled up to the elbows, a pair of black slacks, and a large black velvet yarmulke.

Why the hell was he being so uncooperative, Decker wondered? What did he have to gain by being so outwardly contemptuous? Decker looked over the notes he'd taken, then said:

"I want to go over this again with you."

"What's the point?"

"Why don't you let me be the judge of that?"

"You're not a judge. You're a cop. I have only one judge, and He's the one I'll ultimately answer to."

"Well, right now why don't you bear with me and answer my questions?"

Stein said nothing.

"You were studying the entire time with your partner when Florence Marley was killed?"

"Yes."

"The entire night?"

"Yes."

"And you didn't leave the classroom?"

"No."

"To get a breath of fresh air?"

"No."

"To get something to eat? To go to the bathroom?"

"No."

"You put all your body functions on hold for twelve hours, Mr Stein?"

"The learning of Torah liberates one to the point that one forgets such banalities as body functions. The words of Hashem envelop and whisk one out of the corporeal and into the spiritual. I was trying to soar above my meager earthly existence and grow close to *Hakodosh Boruch Hu*. Of course, you couldn't understand that."

"What I do understand, Mr Stein, is that while you were spreading your heavenly wings in holy ascent, Florence Marley was hacked up by some psycho. It caused quite a commotion out there – all the people and noise. You didn't hear a thing?"

"I was learning."

That was supposed to explain it all.

Decker tapped his pencil against his note pad. He ached to break through the man's holier-than-thou attitude. The hell with it.

"How'd you go from pimping to praying, Scotty Stevens?"

Stein burned with a rage that glowed on his face.

"Why don't you crawl back into your anti-Semitic sewer, Detective, instead of raking innocent Jews over the coals? I know what you're doing. You're trying to be a big *sheygets* hero to impress a woman who is unattainable to you. You're a goy, Decker. She'd rather be raped by a scum-of-the-earth Jew than let you touch her. Ask her. Ask her what's halachically correct."

"Why? Are you the scum-of-the-earth Jew who tried to rape her?"

"Crawl back into your gutter," Stein mumbled, then returned his eyes to his book.

"So no one can attest to your whereabouts except Shraga Mendelsohn – your partner."

184

"Yes."

"Did Mr Mendelsohn ever leave you alone to attend to his bodily needs, or was he also imbued with the holy spirit?"

"I don't remember. Why don't you ask him?"

"I will, Mr Stein. And if there are any inconsistencies, you'll hear from me again."

"I don't doubt it," Stein growled. "Amalek always has a way of rearing its ugly head."

Decker scribbled down "Amalek" in his note pad, then stuffed it in his breast pocket. He'd ask Rina what the word meant. He hated insults he didn't understand.

"I don't know what I can tell you that Shlomi hasn't already said. We were together the entire night."

"Just a few questions, Mr Mendelsohn."

"Well, let's get going. It's almost time for *mincha*"

Mendelsohn rocked back and forth, avoiding Decker's eyes, and bit into an already chewed-up left thumbnail. Behind a full blond beard was a youthful, handsome face. Smooth complexion, light blue eyes, straight thin features that were almost too delicate. His black hat covered most of his hair, but a few blond strands managed to peek out from under the rim.

"Did you ever leave Mr Stein alone?"

"Alone? No."

"Not to get something to eat or to go to the bathroom?"

"I might have gone to the bathroom. Oh, I called my wife to tell her I wasn't coming home."

"When?"

"I don't remember the exact time. Early, around eight I guess."

Mendelsohn chomped on the cuticle of his thumb. A tiny red rivulet began to ooze out. He sucked up the blood and moved onto his index finger.

"How long did it take you to make the phone call?"

"I used the pay phone in the main lobby. Maybe I was

gone five minutes. Not long enough for Shlomi to disappear, murder, and return. And I wasn't gone long enough to murder and return. I don't know why you're bothering us like this."

He screwed up his face and clenched his hands.

"I do know. It's because of Shlomi's record. Well, he can't make his past go away. But I'll be damned if you're going to use it against him in the future. I don't care what Rina told you about him, he's changed. She had no right to say anything to you. To talk to a . . . an *outsider*."

Decker ignored him.

"You were studying with him the entire time?"

"Yes."

"Do you two ever do anything else together besides study?"

Mendelsohn looked blank.

"Like what?"

"Hobbies. Fish, for instance. Do you two ever talk to each other about secular things?"

"There is nothing else besides Torah. All other things are *nahrishkeit*."

"Well, what about your family, your wives?"

Mendelsohn's face registered confusion.

"What about them?"

"Are they *nahrishkeit*?"

"Of course not! They're part of Torah!"

"Do you talk to your wife about Torah?"

"No. Well, yes. As it pertains to the household, to the raising of the children. But we don't learn together."

"Why not?"

Mendelsohn giggled to himself.

"You don't learn Gemara with your wife, Detective." He shook his head. "*Ayzeh goyishe kop*."

"So your wife knew you were learning all night."

"Yes."

"And it didn't bother her to be left alone?"

"Of course not! She supports it. Why else would I be in

186

a *kollel* if she didn't approve? My Torah learning is her salvation also."

"And you called her around eight?"

"What are you trying to prove? That I murdered a black woman that I've never met and used the phone call to my wife as an alibi? Detective, Jews don't murder, Jews don't rape. Your people murder and rape, not mine."

"Do you believe in the Ten Commandments?" Decker asked.

"Of course."

"That they are God-given laws?"

"Yes."

"And God gave them to the Jews?"

"Yes."

"And the Jews He gave them to were considered righteous men and women?"

"What are you getting at?" Mendelsohn asked, gnawing at his right thumbnail.

"Simply this. If God was so sure that righteous Jewish men and women wouldn't murder, why did He bother with the sixth commandment?"

The thumb began to bleed.

Decker's ranch was four acres of scrub oak and fruit trees
set into parched terrain. It was located midway between
Deep Canyon and the police station, in a pocket of land
that once had been used for commercial grazing. Devel-
opers had harbored lofty plans for the acreage during the
real estate boom of the late seventies, but when interest
rates shot up suddenly, the ground went fallow. Decker
bought the parcel cheap and went about sinking roots.
He'd needed something tangible – something to call his
own – after his divorce.

He drove Rina and the boys along a narrow, rutted
road past rolling hills, empty stretches, and an occasional
barn, house, or grove of fruit trees. After a long, bumpy
ride, the unmarked finally pulled onto a large strip of
blacktop, next to a jeep. Also parked in the driveway, in
front of the garage door, was an old, wheelless red
Porsche with the hood up. Adjacent to the asphalt were
groves of citrus, heavy with oranges, lemons, and grape-
fruits, breathing their fragrance into the hot summer air.
The ground beneath them was newly watered and speckled with rotting fruit, glistening in the sunlight.

They piled out of the car, and the boys took off
immediately into the trees to play a game of tag. Rina
stepped out, stretched, and looked around.

Decker's home was a modest one-story dwelling, fashioned after a barn. The exterior wood, painted a deep
red, was sided with white cross-thatched beams and
decorated with rectangular planter boxes full of geraniums
and impatiens set beneath the picture windows. He'd put

care into the place, she thought. Decker unlocked the front door. Rina called out to the boys, and they went inside.

They walked into a small living room, sparely furnished but flooded with sunlight. She liked what she saw. The floor was wood planks of unfinished fir partially covered by a Navajo rug, and the ceiling was peaked and beamed. The room had an overstuffed sofa, two buckskin chairs, a free-form driftwood coffee table, and a recliner parked next to the front window with a view of the grove. Across from the sofa was a large fireplace, trimmed with brick and flanked by twin copper cauldrons.

Decker led them through the living room, a small dining area, and out a side door between it and the kitchen. The backyard contained a barn, a stable, a holding pen, and a corral. Bales of hay stacked five high leaned against the barn, and to the rear, a mesa of flatland led to the mountains.

He excused himself to change, went into the barn, and came back out in jeans, boots, and a T-shirt. At his heels was a brilliant copper-colored Irish setter. From the wag of its tail, the dog was overjoyed at Decker's presence but contained itself. Decker told the dog to sit, and it obeyed instantly. Without hesitation, Jake walked over to the setter and petted it, but Sammy waited until Rina approached it, then followed.

"He's *beautiful!*" Rina said, stroking the gleaming fur. "And so well-behaved."

"He's a she." Decker noticed Sammy's reticence. "Come here, Sammy. Ginger's very friendly. Too friendly. She's a terrible watchdog."

The boy gave the dog a cautious pet and smiled. Jacob was already trying to entice her into a game of tag.

"She looks like you, Peter," Rina said, smiling.

"That's what Cindy said when she gave her to me."

"Birthday present?"

"Divorce present. She figured I might be lonely." Decker let out a small laugh. "At the time, all I wanted

189

was solitude. Anyway, Ginger's going with us on our ride. She'll be our guide. C'mon, girl."

The setter followed Decker back into the stable, and ten minutes later he came out with a saddled Appaloosa filly named Annie. Patiently he explained to the boys the do's and don'ts of riding, put them on the horse – Jake in front, Sammy behind him – and led them around the corral. When they were acclimated, he took Jake down, gave the reins to Sammy and let go. Then he saddled up another filly and hoisted Jake upward. Within an hour the boys were riding the horses on their own, squealing with uninhibited joy. The dog jumped at the horses' hooves, barking playfully.

Decker watched them closely, shouting out appropriate instructions when necessary. Rina stood in the background and clicked a camera, as excited as they were. She was glad they'd come. It was a day the boys would remember.

Decker took a brown stallion from the stable, mounted it, and rode to her.

"I want to take them for a short ride in the hills."

"Fine."

"Help yourself to anything you want."

"Okay. Take your time."

"You know, you could come with us. I've got a couple more horses in the stable that can use some exercise."

She shook her head.

"Sure?"

"Positive."

He turned around and led the boys out of the corral. They rode off, unbothered by the heat and glare, unaware of anything else except the open land that beckoned to them.

Rina went inside the house. The sun had cooked her scalp, and her head began to throb. The boys would probably be hungry after their ride, so she might as well set up for dinner. She took a stack of paper goods and

190

some plastic utensils out of a bag she'd brought from home, having explained to Peter that his dishes and flatware weren't kosher even though they'd been sterilized in a dishwasher. She could tell he didn't understand the logic, but he was nice enough not to debate the issue.

His dining area contained a round cherrywood table, four matching chairs, and a six-shelf mahogany bookcase. Having forgotten place mats, she unfolded several napkins and covered the table surface. She set out chicken left over from Shabbos lunch, potato chips, and juice. Not exactly well balanced, but at least the kids would eat it.

When she was done, she walked over to the bookcase and studied its contents. The top two shelves held a set of law books, police manuals, and police academy texts – books on law enforcement, criminology, search and seizure policy, forensics, ballistics, firearms, and evidence. Below them was a row of sociological and criminological studies: *History of Homicide in America, Criminal Statistics in Los Angeles, The Challenge of Child Abuse, The Juvenile Offender, Detective Work: A Study in Criminal Investigation*. The lower half of the bookcase was devoted to fiction; his taste leaned toward best-sellers and spy novels. She noticed a total absence of detective fiction.

She found a *Natural History* magazine wedged between two textbooks and pulled it out. The lead article was on the African tree frog. Settling down on the living room couch, she skimmed it quickly, looking at the pictures, too jittery to really concentrate on the text. Finally, she gave up and tried to stop thinking about the murder and rape. Forcing herself to take advantage of the peace and quiet, she sat back and closed her eyes.

An hour later there were hoofbeats in the backyard. The three of them stomped in with Ginger, the boys sweaty and excited.

"Boy, am I tired!" said Sammy, happily plopping on the couch.

"I'm starved," Jake moaned.

191

"I'm going to take a shower," Decker said, setting out a bowl of water for the dog. "Be back in a few minutes. You can feed them in the meantime."

He disappeared.

"You kids can go ahead and wash up in the kitchen sink," she said, piling their plates with chicken and potato chips. "You don't have to make *Al netilas yadaiyim* because I didn't bring any bread."

The boys washed, then sat down at the table.

"Did you have fun?" she asked.

"Yeah, but my legs are sore," Jake said.

"My butt is sore," Sammy added. "This chair is like a rock. Can I have something to drink?"

Rina pulled out individual cartons of apple juice, poked straws in the openings, and gave them each one.

"I can't cut with a plastic knife, Eema," Jake said.

"Eat it with your hands. Did you guys see anything interesting in the woods?"

"Just some jackrabbits and squirrels," Sammy said. "Nothing weird, but it was real neat. I felt like a cowboy. I wonder if the yeshiva will ever get horses."

"Maybe one day," Rina said.

"Can we have a dog?" asked Jacob.

"No. The house is way too small."

"A little dog?"

"No."

"It was real quiet out there, Eema," recalled Sammy, dreamily.

"It was hot," Jake complained, sipping the last drops of juice through his straw. "Can I have some more?"

Rina handed him another carton.

"Can we come here again?" Jake asked.

"I don't think so," Rina answered quietly.

"Why not?" Sammy asked. "Peter said it would be okay."

"It's not right to impose."

But she knew that was an excuse. It was she, not Peter, who didn't want them to return.

"Besides, school's starting soon, and you have *shiur* on Sunday – "

"Not all day Sunday," Sammy protested.

"There's Maccabee soccer league, computer club, and piano lessons. You're going to be swamped with activities."

Sammy sighed and pushed his plate away.

"What's wrong, Shmuel?" Rina asked.

"Nothing," the boy sulked.

They ate in silence for a while. Ginger walked around the kitchen, then began to beg at the table.

"Can I give Ginger some chicken?" Jacob asked.

"Don't do anything until you've asked Peter."

Jake looked at the mournful dog. "Sorry," he told her. She whimpered.

Rina stroked Sammy's arm.

"I've been trying to find another Jewish Big Brother for you guys – "

"I don't want a Big Brother," Sammy snapped.

"Why not?" she asked.

"Shmueli says they're all perverts." Jake said.

"They're not perverts," she said.

"They're weird," said Sammy. "The last one that took us to the movies was weird."

"So we'll find a good one," Rina said. "In the meantime, the yeshiva boys are always happy to play ball with you – "

"Not really. They do me a *big* favor sometimes and let me play deep center. Just forget it, Eema."

"You do understand why Peter can't be a Big Brother?" Rina asked him.

"Yes. Just forget it!"

Sammy was holding back tears. Rina brushed the hair out of his eyes and repinned his *kipah*.

"It's just not fair," he said in a cracked voice.

"No, it isn't," she agreed. "Listen, maybe we can work something out with another organization who'd – "

193

Decker walked in, hair wet and slicked back, carrying a big box.

"Why the long faces?" he asked.

Rina waved her hand in the air, and he didn't press it.

"Don't beg, Ginger." Decker placed the carton on an empty chair, then poured out a bowl of dry dog food.

"Can I give Ginger some chicken?" Jacob asked.

"The grease isn't good for her, Jake."

"What've you got in the box?" asked Sammy.

"These are some Jewish books and articles that my ex-wife's grandfather brought over from Europe. When he died, no one in the family wanted them, so I took 'em. I've been meaning to take them to the yeshiva."

Decker ripped open the sealed top and held up a leather-bound book with pages edged in gilt.

"Does this mean anything to you?" he asked.

"Wait a minute," Rina said. "My hands are dirty."

She and the boys washed their hands, and Decker took the carton of books into the living room.

Jake picked up the book that Decker had been holding. "That's a *machzor*," he said.

"A what?"

Sammy took it and opened it carefully. "It's a prayer book for the New Year. This side is Hebrew, but I don't know what language this is."

He handed the book to Rina.

"It's German," she said. "Was her grandfather from Germany?"

"I don't know," said Decker.

"Look at all these beautiful *sepharim*," Rina said, pulling out another volume. It was bound in dark green leather, the cover lettering stenciled in gold. She looked at the date of publication – 1798.

"A lot of *sepharim* were destroyed during World War Two. These may be very valuable, Peter."

"Look at this, Eema," said Sammy, holding up an elaborately filigreed, foot-long scroll case.

"Yeah, what is that?" Decker asked. "See, you pull this

194

tab over here, and the text comes out of this slit. It's illustrated with all this beautiful artwork – "

"This is unbelievable!" Rina said, pulling on the tab gingerly.

"*Megillas Esther*," Sammy said.

"Fantastic." Rina was awestruck. "Look how clear the lettering is."

"Can you read it?" Decker asked her.

"It's easy," Jake said, rattling off the first line.

"You know what it means?" the detective asked.

"Yeah, it's talking about this king, Ahashverus, and his kingdom," Sammy said. "*Hodu v'od Kush?* What are those countries again?"

"India and Ethiopia," said Rina.

"Amazing," Decker said.

"The kids are bilingual," Rina explained. "Yitzchak only spoke Hebrew to them."

"What do you do with this?" Decker asked.

"You read it on Purim, of course," Jake said.

"Of course," Decker repeated.

"It's my favorite holiday," Jake explained. "You get to dress up in a costume, and the shul has a big Purim party after they read the megilla. All the older boys get drunk and throw up. It's so gross, but it's real funny. The next day you get to stuff your face with cookies and candies that your friends bring you."

"You're allowed to get drunk?" Decker asked.

"You're supposed to get drunk," Sammy said.

"You're not supposed to get drunk," Rina said. "Tipsy maybe."

"You're supposed to drink until you can't tell the difference between cheering Mordechai and booing Haman, pooh, pooh, pooh. That's *drunk*, Eema."

"I can't picture the yeshiva letting loose like that," said Decker.

"It's real exciting," Sammy said animatedly. "The older kids juggle bottles or balance them on top of their heads – "

"Drunk?" Decker asked.

"There's a lot of broken glass," explained Jake. He started to giggle. "Last year one of the rabbis dressed up as Haman, pooh, pooh, pooh, and we all got to throw rotten tomatoes at him."

"Haman's a bad guy, huh?" Decker asked.

'Yeah," Sammy said. "He was one of Hitler's ancestors."

"Really?" Decker asked Rina.

"Some say. If they weren't bretheren by blood, they were spiritually. They're all Amalek."

Decker's eyes darkened. "What's that?"

"Originally, a tribe at the time of Israel's liberation from Egypt. They were purposefully mean and spiteful to the Jews as they left. Now the term is used for any person or group bent on the total destruction of the Jews. I consider Yassir Arafat – *y'mach shmo* – Amalek, for example."

Decker said nothing.

"Anything wrong, Peter?"

"Nothing," he said quickly, then peered into the box and brought out another book.

"This is *Bava Metzia*," Sammy said taking the text from Decker. "I'm going to learn it this next year."

"Somebody in your wife's family was a scholar," Rina said. "This is Talmud; it's what is studied in the yeshiva."

"I've got a whole set of these books upstairs in another trunk, and they all have this strange layout of the text. You've got a big block of Hebrew here. Then all these columns of Hebrew surrounding the block. What is this?"

"The big block, which is written in Aramaic, is the legal question that's being discussed. This particular book starts out with the laws of lost and found."

"This isn't a Bible?"

"No. It's a treatise on Jewish criminal and civil law."

"So what are these columns all about?"

"Rashi, tosafot – " She stopped herself. "Commentaries – different interpretations of the legal question."

"Do you follow these laws?"

"Oh yes!" she exclaimed. "That's what being a Torah Jew is all about."

"How'd this all come about?"

"The primary laws were given to Moses by Hashem on Mount Sinai – some were written, some were passed along orally. Later on, the oral laws were written down and interpreted by the Amoraim – a group of prominent rabbis. The final laws were decided by rabbinic vote between the third and sixth centuries."

Decker was silent. She knew what he was thinking.

"There are allowances for today's problems. Like electricity. The question of whether we could use electricity on the Sabbath didn't pop up in the Talmud."

"And who decided whether you could or couldn't?"

"The scholars of the day."

"Can you?" he asked.

"No. It's considered kindling a fire, which is prohibited on the Sabbath. That isn't to say we sit in the dark Friday night. We leave the lights on before the sun goes down, or some of us put the lights on a time clock. We just can't flick the switch on or off."

"I can see where this gets very complicated," Decker said.

"That's why there are yeshivot. It takes a lifetime to learn all of it."

"I'm bored," Jake said. "Can I watch TV?"

"Why don't you go outside and play with Ginger?" Peter suggested. "She looks bored, too."

Jacob looked at Rina.

"Fine with me."

Jacob ran outside with the dog.

Decker looked at Sammy, who was immersed in a book. "You want to go outside with your brother?" he asked.

"Huh?"

"He likes to read," Rina said. "Sammy, why don't you

sit in the big chair? It's more comfortable, and there's better light."

The boy didn't answer.

"He doesn't hear me when he's concentrating," she explained. "Shmueli, honey." She gently tugged on his shirt sleeve. The boy stood up, and she led him over to a chair on the far side of the living room, then walked back to Decker, who was in the dining area clearing the table.

"Sammy's a real little rabbi," he said, dumping the plates in the garbage.

"Like his father," she said, pitching in.

"Or his mother. You seem to know what you're talking about."

"No, he's like his father – extremely intense. Jakey is much more like me. Believe it or not, I'm really an easygoing person."

"I can believe it. You've handled yourself very well under all the stress."

Decker pulled out a chair.

"Why don't you sit down? I can clean this up. You're a guest."

She sighed heavily, sat down at the table, and rested her chin in the palm of her hand. "I don't know. I'm so nervous all the time, always on edge."

"Don't you think you deserve a night out on the town?" he said quietly, not wanting the boy to hear.

She turned away from him.

"Those *sepharim* are beautiful. I can't imagine your in-laws not wanting any of them. They're works of art."

"They were about as Jewish as I was. We celebrated Christmas and Hanukkah. We ate ham on Easter. We even joined a Unitarian church when Cynthia was school-age. My ex-wife was adamant about letting her choose her own religion, even though I had no objections to Cindy being raised Jewish. You can't get much more assimilated than that."

"True."

"By the way, you nicely sidestepped my question."

She glanced at Sammy.

"Peter," she whispered, "as much as I enjoy your company, I can't go out with you."

"I'm not talking about a date. Something platonic. Marge Dunn is giving a recital with her boyfriend, and I'm invited. I wouldn't mind a little company."

"What does Marge play?"

"Flute."

"Is she good?"

"She's terrible. But we all love her and tell her she's terrific. Anyway, all her boyfriends have been musicians, and her latest is a violinist. The two of them are planning to butcher Haydn. I need someone to go with."

She said nothing.

"It'll be really a harmless get-together. I just don't want to be stuck there alone."

"Won't there be other detectives that you know?"

"They'll all have dates. If I show up alone, I'll be conspicuous. Then, someone'll start trying to set me up, and I'm not interested in being set up. You'd be doing me a big favor."

"I'm sure you know *other* women," she said waspishly, then regretted saying it.

"What's *that* supposed to mean?"

She blushed.

"Oh, nothing really. I'm sure you have no shortage of women, that's all."

"They're beating down my doorstep," he laughed, touched by the tinge of jealousy in her voice. "Can't you hear?"

"Now I know what all the loud thumping noises were."

She grew serious.

"If feelings were everything, I would have gone out with you a long time ago. I like you. This is very hard for me, Peter. Please try to understand. My religion is my life."

"Let me ask you something. If I were Jewish, but the same person, would you go out with me?"

"Certainly, if you were religious."

"Plain Jewish – like my daughter – isn't good enough?"

She hesitated a moment, then said:

"It's not a matter of good or bad, Peter. Your daughter is a *fine* person regardless of her religion. It's an individual choice. I don't feel any more comfortable with assimilated Jews like your in-laws than with non-Jews. How could they have given away beautiful treasures like these books? It takes a lot more to be a Torah Jew than just an accident of birth."

Well, that ends that, Decker thought.

He walked over to the refrigerator and pulled out a six-pack of Dos Equis.

"Okay. I give up."

"Please don't be angry."

"Nah, I'm not angry." he opened up a green bottle and took a gulp. "I don't understand your reasoning, but at least it's nothing personal."

"Believe me, it's not."

"I honestly thought you could be worn down, but you're tough."

He took a few more swigs, finished off the bottle, and tossed it in the garbage.

"It's damn frustrating, though."

Decker stared across the room, then returned his eyes to Rina.

"Anyone else ever chase you like this?"

His tone of voice had become abruptly neutral, and his eyes were hard. She didn't know what to think.

"Not really," she said softly. "I met Yitzchak at seventeen and married him six months later. I was out of circulation very young."

"How about recently? Anyone ever ask you out and you refused?"

"A couple of the *bochrim* I dated – like Shlomo. When they asked me out a second time, I said no. Except for Shlomo, they've all left the yeshiva."

"Who else?"

"It doesn't matter."

"It matters to me."

She stared at him, then asked:

"What are you getting at?"

"Nothing really," he said mildly. "Just grasping at straws."

But he had taken on a cop's demeanor. She found herself relieved that the conversation had turned more businesslike.

"No one outside of the yeshiva men ever asked you out?" he asked.

"Well, after Yitzhak died I went back to UCLA to finish my BA. A couple of grad students and a professor asked me for a date. They didn't seem broken up by my refusal."

"How long ago was this?"

"A year, year and a half ago."

"Do you remember their names?"

"The professor's name was Dooley. Frank or Fred. I don't even think he's in LA anymore."

"And the students?"

"Blanks."

"Anyone else?"

She paused.

"Matt Hawthorne asked me out ages ago. But Matt's harmless."

"Matt's the teacher who's been guarding the place on Friday night?"

"Yes, he and Steve Gilbert. In a pinch they've even walked me home at night, so if either had wanted to do something, he'd have had ample opportunity."

"Not really. Not if he didn't want you to know his identity."

"You *are* grasping at straws."

"What'd Matt say when you said no?"

"He made a joke out of it. Said he was only teasing, that he'd wanted to take me to a nudie show and watch me blush. But if you knew Matt, you'd know that's the

201

way he is. A little crude at times, but he doesn't mean anything by it."

"How long have you known him."

"About five years. Both he and Steve had been working at the yeshiva when Yitzchak and I arrived."

"How about Gilbert?"

"What do you mean?"

"He never asked you out?"

She paused for a long time.

"Actually we went out for a drink once. But," she quickly clarified, "it wasn't a date. He's been engaged to the same girl on and off for five years, and this was one of his in-between periods. It was also a year after Yitzchak died, and I was so lonely. But we concentrated on him. He was feeling very low, and I gave him a shoulder to cry on."

"Never asked you out again?"

"No. As I said, it wasn't a date. He knows as well as Matt that I only date Jewish men. Besides, Steve loves his fiancee. I've met her, and she's a very nice girl. Both of them have trouble making decisions; they keep setting dates and breaking them. He's due to get married in about six weeks, and it looks like this time it's going to go through."

"What's he like?"

"Quiet, but not unusually so for a physics type. I was a math-physics major in college, and I knew lots of guys like him."

"What about your students, Rina? Any of them seem a little off?"

"They're *boys*, Peter!"

"They're the same age as Cory Schmidt."

"*Lehavdil*. In answer to your question, no. The kids I teach are terrific."

"And you know every single one?"

"There are a hundred boys in the yeshiva's high school. I know close to every single one. They're fine, normal boys."

He threw his arms upward, stretched, then opened another bottle of beer.

"You're probably right."

But she sensed he wouldn't leave it at that.

"We'd better be getting back, Peter. I can't wait until you take the books over to the Rosh Yeshiva. He could tell you a lot more about them than I could, as far as value. Rav Aaron is often asked by galleries to appraise works of Judaica. His study is like a museum."

"I'd like to see it."

"He'd show it to you. He's very proud of his collection."

"Rina, I want to ask you an off-the-wall question."

"Okay."

"In Moshe's closet was a beautiful white robe that was protected by a cleaners' bag, completely out of character with the rest of his wardrobe. Does it have any religious significance?"

"Yes. It's a *kittel*. A man wears it when he marries, when he prays on the High Holy Days, and when he's buried." She paused. "Why do you ask?"

"Curiosity. My box contained a similar garment. I took it out and had it wrapped in plastic to prevent it from yellowing."

Rina became pensive.

"God knows why Moshe kept his," she said. "It must be a painful remembrance for a man whose marriage went sour."

Decker smiled sadly.

"True enough," he said.

20

Decker walked down a flight of steps and into the basement chemistry lab. He was surprised at how modern it was. The room was spacious, bright, and well ventilated. There were thirty hooded stations, each equipped with standard lab paraphernalia – bunsen burners, beakers, titrating cylinders and hoses, stirring rods, and an assortment of measuring devices. At the back wall sat Gilbert at a long bench table that held ten personal computers. He was busy typing on a keyboard and didn't turn around until Decker was halfway across the room. Then he stood up and offered the detective a chair.

"Have a seat."

"Thanks." Decker glanced at the computers – six IBM PCs, four Apple MacIntoshes. "Looks like some money has been spent here."

"The parents are getting more particular. They want their sons graduating with something more marketable than theology."

"Does that cause any problems with the rabbis?"

"A few, like Rabbi Marcus, seem to find the twentieth century objectionable. However, Rabbi Schulman is a very practical man. He knows on which side his proverbial bread is buttered."

Gilbert took off his glasses, pulled a tissue out of his shirt pocket, and began to wipe his glasses. He continued: "The computers were donated by a couple of rich families. The lab was built at cost three years ago. The construction company's president had a boy who was going here. Schulman is a great fund-raiser."

"Do you like teaching here?"

"It's a job. I need the extra income."

"Rina says the boys here are really bright."

"Very bright, very spoiled."

"Are they a challenge to teach?"

He put his glasses back on.

"At times. Most of the challenge is appeasing the parents when their precious babies aren't performing up to snuff." Gilbert stared at Decker. "What's on your mind, Detective?"

"Just a few questions." Decker took out a note pad.

"I didn't rape anyone."

Decker said nothing. An odd reaction. It was unusual for anyone to start off with a flat denial of guilt.

"Anything else?" Gilbert asked in a bored tone of voice.

"You were in Nam," Decker stated.

"Yes."

"What unit?"

"I'm sure you know."

"You tell me."

"I was a clerk in Saigon," Gilbert said. "I was never in heavy action."

"Records say you were a sniper."

"For a week."

"What happened?"

"I was transferred. Maybe they were impressed with my typing."

"Weren't you frustrated? All that skill – "

"I came home with my balls intact. That's more than I can say for a lot of others. Were you over there?"

"Yes," Decker answered.

"Doing?"

"I was a medic."

"Oooh." Gilbert gave a half smile. "Very messy."

"How long have you known Mrs Lazarus?"

"I've known Rina about five years."

"Did you know her husband?"

205

"I'd met him. I didn't know him."

"Did he and Rina seem well matched?"

"I think she could have done better, if that's what you're asking."

"Ever think of asking her out after her husband passed away?"

"She's inaccessible to me. I'm not Jewish." The half smile reappeared on his lips. "She's inaccessible to you too, Detective."

Decker ignored him and continued.

"Where were you the night of Florence Marley's murder?"

"With my fiancee's parents. Phone number 675–6638. I'm there every Wednesday night. Check it out."

"What's their name?"

"MacLaughlin."

"Where were you the night of the Adler rape?"

"What day of the week was the rape?"

"Thursday."

"Teaching the computer club."

"What time is the club over?"

"Around ten."

"The rape was around ten."

"So?"

"That puts you in the area at the time of the rape."

"You know, Detective, Rina's sons are in the computer club. It was my idea to bring them in; I thought they'd have a good time fooling around with the machines. Rina would pick them up at the club after her mikvah job, and I'd walk them all home. But they haven't come around lately, and when I asked Rina why, she was evasive. You have her distrusting everyone in pants except you and maybe Zvi Adler and Rabbi Schulman. I don't like being held up to scrutiny because I know her and have a dick."

"Why are you wearing long sleeves? It's hot as hell outside."

"Dress code."

"I've seen many students with their sleeves rolled up."

206

"I'm not a student. I'm a teacher."

"Do you mind if I see your arms?"

Gilbert paused.

"Yes."

"Why's that?"

"I don't like you."

"I'd like to see your forearms, Mr Gilbert."

He hesitated, then rolled up his sleeves. They were both free of scratches.

"Satisfied?" Gilbert said, rebuttoning the cuffs.

Decker stuck the note pad in his pocket and stood up.

"Thank you for your time."

"He was Joe Cool," Decker told Marge. "Unflappable."

"No scratches?" Marge asked.

"No. But he hesitated before showing me. Maybe he wasn't so sure if there were or weren't."

"When do you talk to the other one?"

"Six-thirty. After work, at his apartment."

"Then what?"

Decker shrugged.

"Do you suspect Gilbert?"

"I suspect everyone I've talked to. Unfortunately, I don't have any evidence."

"Except Cory Schmidt," Marge corrected.

"Yeah, Cory is tied to the murder. I don't know about the rape." Decker sipped coffee, then put the cup on his desk. "What about Professor Fred Dooley?"

"He's been on sabbatical in Greece for the last six months."

The phone rang.

"Decker."

"It's Mike."

"How're you doing with Rayana?"

"Diddlysquat," said Hollander. "But I got some good news for you."

"What?"

"I found Cory Schmidt."

"Where?"

"At a head shop in Sun Valley. I nosed around and found out one of his friends used to work there. Sure enough, the little shit was in the back room toking on some homegrown weed dipped in dust. Sucker's as high as a kite. I've got him cuffed. Right now I'm waiting for transport."

"Good going, Mike. Bring him in."

The kid was full of spit and fire and had to be physically restrained by an officer. Decker closed the door to the interview room and stood across from him with his hands folded across his chest. Schmidt was wearing a Black Sabbath midriff T-shirt and a pair of black leather pants. His hair was dirty and hung limply to his shoulders.

"I wanna lawyer, pig," he spat.

"You'll get one," Decker said. "It'll be by the book, Cory. It's too big to lose on a technicality. But let me tell you this, son. You're fucked."

"I ain't your son."

"We've got evidence. We've got lots and lots of evidence."

"Bullshit!"

"Do you want to confess?"

"Fuck you."

"Sure, now?"

"Fuck you, asshole."

"Get him out of here."

Moshe Feldman's shrink, Dr Marder, had phoned while he was with Cory. Decker returned the call and thanked him for being so prompt.

"No problem, Detective. I've just dropped the report in the mail. If you have any questions about it, feel free to call me. I can't disclose any of our other previous therapy sessions because, of course, those were confidential. This evaluation is different because it was court ordered."

"Can you summarize the report for me now?"

"Sure. It is my professional opinion that Moshe Feldman witnessed something traumatic and brutal that night. Whether he actually saw a murder, a rape, or a beating, I don't know. I don't think he knows. Whatever he saw or heard involved more than one person. Moshe remembers seeing four people. That's about it."

"Do you trust this guy, Doctor?"

"I don't think he was fantasizing."

"What is he? A psycho?"

"No. He's not psychotic or psychopathic in any classic sense. No hallucinations, no voices telling him to kill or rape, so far as I know. He has a conscience – an overly developed one at that. The guy is crippled by guilt. If I had to put a label on him, I'd say he was schizoid with an affective disorder. He's oriented – he knows who he is and where he is – but his emotions are inappropriate or flat."

"Do you think he could be dangerous?"

"I can't predict that. Any psychiatric professional who says he can predict future behavior based on past performance is full of horseshit. Do I think he would kill or rape? No. Would I stake my professional reputation on it? No."

"So he could be violent?"

"At this time, I've no indication that he's violent. But I'm not saying he could never be violent."

"And you think he saw something brutal being carried out by at least four people."

"Yes."

"And you believe him?"

"Yes."

"Thank you very much, Doctor."

"I hope I've been helpful. I like Moshe. I have a great deal of respect for Rabbi Schulman. I used to learn under him. The man is brilliant. I'd like to see the yeshiva free and clear of this mess."

"So would I," said Decker.

* * *

"Okay," Marge said, handing Decker the report. "Some of the shoe prints matched Schmidt's. But a lot didn't. The report says seven different prints were lifted."

"One of them was Feldman's."

Marge thought.

"Yeah, one of them was Feldman's, one of them was Marley's. I figure it like this: Schmidt and friends makes five; Feldman makes six; Marley makes seven."

"You think there were five of them who attacked Florence?"

"Yeah."

Decker skimmed the pages of the document, then said, "I just spoke to Feldman's shrink. He says Feldman remembers seeing only four people. But his accuracy is up for grabs."

"How many guys were involved with Rina that day at the supermarket parking lot?" Marge asked.

"Four. Cory and three of his cohorts."

"So if it was the same guys who attacked Marley, Feldman should have seen five people – Cory and his friends and Marley."

"Unless Marley was down by the time he witnessed the scene," Decker said. "In either case, it still doesn't add up to five people who attacked Marley."

"So maybe Cory brought along an extra?"

"Could be." Decker plopped the papers onto his desk. "It would be nice if we could round up all the shoes of every suspect we have in this case and check them for matching prints."

"And maybe collect a couple of pairs of loafers while you're at it."

Decker looked down at his weather-beaten oxfords.

"No joke. Where's Cory now?"

"In a holding pen. He's due to be arraigned this afternoon. Hollander is going down to court. Prosecutor's going for top bail and thinks he'll have no trouble getting it. Schmidt's his own worst enemy."

"Who's been assigned to the case?"

"George Birdwell."

"He's good." Decker leaned back and rubbed his eyes. "Anything new with Rayana?"

Marge shook her head.

"Mike says same old shit. Hasn't discovered anyone new. Rayana goes to work, comes home, and surfaces only to walk her dog. It wears a doggy sweater all the time – even in this heat. God forbid Poochy should catch cold.".

"Shit."

Early evening. The air was still scorching, thick, and smoggy. Decker pulled the Plymouth into a red zone and put an LAPD sticker on the dashboard.

Matthew Hawthorne lived in an apartment district in Sun Valley. The area was full of multiple dwellings boasting exotic names like *South Pacific* and *Blue Hawaii*. None of them lived up to their tropical labels. The exteriors were gray stucco, and the landscaping had withered in the heat. The majority of them had pools, but the water, instead of iridescent blue, was algae green. Hawthorne lived at number 12, on the second floor of *Bali Hai*. Decker knocked, and the door flew open.

"I've got my alibi all pat." The teacher laughed nervously.

What a weirdo, Decker thought. He stepped inside. The flat was a single. A brown tweed sofa stood against one wall, a composition board coffee table in front of it. Two brown vinyl side chairs faced the sofa. Decker could see the kitchen off to his right and a door that probably led to the john. The wall behind the chairs was covered with bookshelves.

Decker sat down on the couch and pulled out his pad.

"How long have you known Mrs Lazarus?" he asked, skipping the small talk.

Hawthorne's left eye twitched.

"About five years. I was already teaching when she and her husband came to the yeshiva."

211

"What'd you think of her husband?"

He didn't answer immediately.

"Mr Hawthorne?"

"Well, he seemed like a typical yeshiva man." He stopped talking and appeared to be thinking. "I never thought she belonged there altogether."

"Why's that?"

"I don't know. I realize she's very religious, but she also has a good sense of humor, and she isn't afraid of men, you know? I mean some of the women are really androphobes. I try to talk to them, and they're so nervous, they make me nervous. Rina used to be very relaxed. Now, of course, she's a wreck. But I can't blame her for that. I mean if I were in her position, I'd be very tense also."

"Did you like her husband?"

"I don't think I ever said more than hello to him. Either he was quiet, or he didn't like me. I don't think he was wild about Steve and me working with his wife. But he never said anything rude to me."

"Did you ever think of asking Mrs Lazarus out after he died?"

Again, Hawthorne paused.

"No. She only dates Jews – religious Jews – if she dates at all. Her oldest boy, Sammy, sometimes talks to me. He says she doesn't go out."

"Sammy volunteered that information to you?"

Again the tic.

"I asked him about her once. I was interested in her welfare."

"But you never asked Mrs Lazarus out?"

"No."

"She seems to recall that you did."

"Really?"

"Really."

"Not that I remember. Hey, maybe I joked about it, but I didn't think she took me seriously."

"Did you ask her out jokingly?"

212

"Sure. All the time. I still do. I told you, I never thought she took it seriously."

"Where were you the night of the Adler rape?"

"The Adler rape?" Twitch. "I thought you were going to ask about the Marley woman."

"Where were you both nights?"

"The night of Mrs Marley's murder I was out with a friend named Jack Oates. I can give you his phone number, and he'll verify it. We saw a movie at the Capitol in Glendale – a documentary on street life in Cleveland called *Street Smarts*. Very good flick."

"What time was the movie over?"

"Around ten."

Decker didn't push it. He'd get the exact time from the movie theater.

"How about the night of the Adler rape?"

"I don't remember."

"It was on a Thursday night."

"I don't know. I was probably home reading. I read a lot."

"You watch a lot of TV?"

"Not a lot. Maybe the news."

"You don't regularly watch any Thursday night TV?"

He thought.

"No. Nothing regular comes to mind. Maybe I did see something that Thursday, though, I'll recheck the schedule."

If you have to do that it won't mean anything, Decker thought.

"What time do you get off work?" Decker asked.

"Usually around six, sometimes six-thirty."

"Ever have any extracurricular activities with the boys?"

"Not in a formal sense, like the computer club. The boys aren't as interested in literature as they are in science and religion. Sometimes I shoot the shit with the kids about sports. But I'm usually gone by seven. I don't like

213

to hang around more than I have to. 'Course, for Rina, I'm happy to help out by patrolling."

"You like her?"

"Sure. Don't you?"

Decker didn't answer. Instead he looked at Hawthorne's forearms. They, too, were clear.

"I think that about does it."

"Well, that was painless. I expected a lot worse."

"Such as?"

"I don't know . . . Maybe tarring and feathering."

Decker didn't smile.

"I'll need the phone number of your friend Mr Oates."

"Certainly." He wrote it on a piece of paper. "Take care of Rina. I care about that little gal."

He sounded earnest, as if he meant it.

21

Marge Dunn showed up as a green blip dancing on the grid of the Plymouth's computer screen. The dot moved slowly to the left, stopped, then reversed back to the right. Decker stared at the monitor while sipping black coffee from a large styrofoam cup, and readjusted his legs. His muscles were beginning to cramp. Three hours and nothing.

Hollander had his nose buried in a *New York Times Book of Crossword Puzzles*. Occasionally his eyes would glance at the screen, but why bother watching if Decker was there? It was hot as blazes in the car, and he couldn't understand how Pete could drink that swill. Hollander slurped the last of his Coke and tossed the paper cup onto the backseat.

"Anything?" he asked Decker.

"Same old shit."

"Maybe we should check in with her?" Hollander suggested.

"No," Decker replied. "I don't want to catch her at the wrong time. If she's with a suspect, he'll get scared away as soon as he hears us buzz in. If it's anything, she'll check in with us."

"What's a five letter word for a raccoon?" Hollander asked.

"C-o-a-t-i."

"Yeah, it fits. Thanks."

Decker's expression soured. He hated crosswords because they reminded him of loneliness. He'd gone through a slew of them after his divorce. A few minutes later Hollander asked:

"How long are we going to keep this up?"

"Let's wait until we hear from Marge."

"How reliable do you think this Rayana is?"

"Well," Decker said, eyes still fixed on the screen, "from what she described, Macko sounds like our man. Now, whether she had second thoughts and warned him off is another story."

"She was pretty pissed at him."

"Goddam fucking people," Decker muttered. "Stupid bitch. She looks the other way while he's out raping and beating up other women, but he kicks her precious poodle, and all of a sudden she decides he's a menace to society."

"No way to get her as an accomplice?"

"Nah, she really didn't do anything."

"She withheld evidence," said Hollander.

"We gave her complete immunity to get her to talk," Decker reminded him. "All part of the game. But at least she talked. Man, did she talk. You couldn't shut her up once she got going."

"She was worried we'd pin something on her. She wanted to clear the air."

"I think so. I think that was the main reason for her coming forward. She thought we were close to finding Macko and didn't want to drown in his shit. The dog was just the catalyst."

The radio buzzed, and Marge's voice came through the speaker.

"Nothing," she said.

"Getting plenty of fresh air?" Hollander asked.

"My arches are killing me," she said.

"Hang in there, sweetheart."

He passed the microphone to Decker.

"Hey, Margie."

"You know where I'm located?"

"Right in the back alley of Sid's Pizza and Beer Stop. This new gadget is wonderful."

"I'll never eat pepperoni again. The smell has permeated my clothes."

"How's the lighting, Margie?"

"Backlighting from the street lamp, plus a bulb over the rear door of the restaurant. I'm beginning to wonder about Rayana's credibility."

"She never said definitely. You want to call it quits?"

"No. I've still got about an hour's worth left in me."

Hollander groaned, and Marge heard it.

"What the fuck is he bitching about? I'm the one who's walking my ass off."

"He does it to keep in practice," Decker answered.

"I'm signing off. I see someone."

The dot was still. Decker and Hollander watched the monitor for a few tense moments, but soon the spot was marching along like the bouncing ball used in the old TV sing-alongs.

"What did you think of Margie's latest?" Hollander asked, putting aside the crossword book.

"Ernst? He seemed nice enough."

"Faggy, don't you think?"

"She likes 'em soft," Decker said.

"Macho Woman meets Superwimp, eh?"

"He's a good musician. That's a step up from her last."

"Yeah," Hollander agreed, "but how can he stand playing with her?"

"Guess love is deaf as well as blind."

"I can't picture the two of them in bed."

Decker shrugged.

"Bet she's always on top," snickered the fat detective.

"Hope not always. She'd crush him."

"Think he's Jewish?" Hollander asked.

Decker's eyes darted from the screen to Hollander, then back to the screen.

"If he is, Marge never mentioned it."

"I think he's a Jew. He looks Jewish. And with a last name like Katzenbach?"

"That could be German. Like the attorney general."

"He looks Jewish to me, Pete."

"You can't tell from looks," Decker said sharply.

"Take it easy. I'm not putting down your little honey."

Decker felt his ire rising.

"Why don't you go back to your puzzle?"

"Shit," Hollander said, tamping his pipe. "Stop gettin' so touchy. I can't even mention Jewto – the yeshiva – without you blowing up."

Decker pulled out a cigarette.

"Give me a light," he said.

Hollander pulled out a match book.

"You gotta admit, Deck, Jews, in general, look like Jews."

"Does Rina look Jewish?" Decker asked.

"She's dark."

"She's got a nose smaller than a button."

"Yeah," Hollander admitted, "and you've got a Jewish nose. But still, I can tell that she's Jewish and you're not."

"Fine, Michael. You're an anthropologist."

"'Course, maybe if you dressed her up in some normal clothes . . ." Hollander mused. "A low-cut blouse and a pair of jeans . . ."

There was a pause.

"Tight jeans," Decker added.

"Real tight jeans."

Both men laughed.

Marge buzzed through.

"As void as a black hole," she said.

"How poetic," said Hollander.

Decker picked up the portable radio.

"Are you getting tired?"

"The walking isn't so bad. It's these goddam pumps I have to wear."

"Macko's got a love affair with pumps," Decker said. "Look, if you want to call it a night . . ."

"Another fifteen minutes."

"Think you could adequately muscle an attacker?"

"To be honest, I have a few blisters. I couldn't give him much chase."

"We're coming to get you."

"Wait five minutes, Pete."

"Will do."

Decker clicked off the radio.

"Why don't we just go in and arrest the son of a bitch?" Hollander said, shifting his bulk in the seat.

"Because we don't exactly know where he is, Mike. He split from his former residence a week ago and hasn't been heard from since. Rayana just *thinks* he's around this area. He's been known to drink at Sid's."

"For whatever that's worth. What a flake!" Hollander lit his pipe and exhaled a cloud of acrid-smelling smoke. "What about a door-to-door?"

"And warn him we're onto his whereabouts? Might as well put a full-page ad in the *Times*."

Hollander checked his watch and grunted.

"It's not even midnight," Decker said. "Mary'll still be up by the time you come home."

"I dunno. She's going to bed earlier and earlier these days."

Marge's voice came through the radio.

"Someone is following me, guys."

Hollander started up the motor.

"Stay with it, baby," Decker said. "We're on our way!"

The attack came suddenly.

They could hear the fighting over the radio.

"Hold him!" Hollander yelled into the mike.

They got there just in time to see Marge lose her grip on the bastard. Hollander zoomed the Plymouth into the alley and caught sight of him running into the back entrance of Jose's Hacienda Mexican Restaurant. The car squealed to a stop, and Decker flew out after him.

Seeing the fleeing figure run out the front door, Decker tore through the restaurant shouting his location into his radio. The assailant dashed across the street, turned right, then ducked into an alley between a toy store and a Chinese take-out place. Decker followed, pivoted, and stopped. The alley dead-ended.

Barely winded but drenched with sweat, he scanned the layout. The walkway was deserted and stank of garbage but was well lit. Barrels, empty cartons, and dumpsters lined the narrow strip of uneven asphalt scarred with potholes. He heard hissing from the Chinese restaurant's kitchen fan, the distant rumble of a car's ignition kicking in, mosquitoes buzzing. Asshole could be anywhere or nowhere. Sight was deceptive, sound everything.

The alley was still, but not lifeless. Decker could *sense* the bastard's presence. Unhitching his revolver, he slowly began to walk forward, footsteps echoing against the pavement, eyes searching for the giveaway.

He peered into the first dumpster and a swarm of flies swirled across his face. Decker shooed them off and poked at the trash with the butt of his gun. Nothing but stench.

On to the next set of trash cans. The hissing grew louder.

Nothing.

The bin contained plastic bags full of rotten food. A few of them had ripped open, spilling out congealed chow mein vegetables and gray strips of foul-smelling meat. The maggots were having a feast. Aside from them, the bin was inert.

The hissing became rhythmic: a goddam percussion section. Decker finally identified it: not the fan, but labored breathing emanating from a clump of barrels and crates in back of the toy store. Empty boxes of GI Joe army toys. The same war scene was splashed across all the cartons: helicopters zooming over exploding bombs, machine guns bursting with fire, men in camouflage parachuting from jets.

Decker stepped toward the combat, toward the breathing.

Suddenly the boxes shot up, came flying at him; the army men had charged. A figure leaped up, popping out like a jack-in-the-box, wide-eyed, terrified. Too big for a toy . . .

"Police! Freeze!" Decker shouted, pointing his .38.

The figure took off, but Decker knew he had him. His long legs sprinted in huge strides, and he quickly overtook his quarry and wrestled him to the ground. The man kicked, bit, and managed to claw a deep gouge in Decker's forearm. The detective swore, flipped him on his stomach, twisted his arms, and tightly clamped on the cuffs behind his back.

"Hey, man, I wasn't doin' nothin'."

"You have the right to remain silent – "

"I wasn't doin' nothin'. I didn't do nothin'."

Decker groaned. Goddam same old shit. Same old excuses. *Not me. I didn't do nothin'. You've got the wrong man. She wanted it. She let me do it.* He finished reciting Miranda and radioed the car. As soon as the Plymouth pulled up, Decker brought him to his feet and studied the face. It was lean and young, the sallow skin pocked with acne pits and sprinkled with light stubble. The eyes were a muddy green, small and quivering convulsively. The mouth was two tight rims of pale flesh that drew back to expose brown protruding teeth.

Anthony Macko.

God bless the poodle.

"I tell you I wasn't doin' a fuckin' thing," Macko protested, spraying Decker with sour spittle.

"How'd you get your clothes all torn up, buddy?" Decker asked, pushing him toward the unmarked.

"Hey, I like torn clothes!"

"You like jumping a police officer?"

"I didn't know who you was."

"I said who I was."

221

"I didn't hear you good. I just saw some dude come chargin' at me. I thought you was a mugger."

Hollander and Marge stepped out. She looked at Macko.

"Yeah, it's him," she said.

"Hey, I never saw this broad in my life!"

"Sure. Your eyesight is very poor." Decker pushed Macko's body against the hood of the car, kicked his heels apart, and began to shake him down. Finding nothing, he shoved the punk into the backseat, then slid in next to him.

"I'm telling you, I don't know what the fuck you're talkin' about man!" Macko protested.

"What *are* we talking about, Macko?" Marge asked, flanking his other side.

"Hey, I'm not sayin' a fuckin' thing until I got a lawyer. I know my rights."

"Your rights won't save you now, Macko," Hollander said as he started the car. "You screwed up."

"Hey, man, I never saw this broad in my fuckin' life."

"Yeah, just like you never saw Brenda Crowthers," Marge said. "You remember her, the little blond nurse who worked at Mission Presbyterian Hospital?"

"Man, I didn't do nothin' to her."

"She tells it different, Macko," Marge said. "She spent three weeks in the hospital, and I bet you're the one who put her there."

"I ain't sayin' nothin' till I seen a lawyer."

"We got your girlfriend, Macko," Marge pushed.

"Lyin' little cunt! I ain't done nothin'!"

"What really happened with the nurse?" Decker prodded.

"I didn't do nothin'."

"You saw her one day after work, didn't you, Macko?" Marge said. "She was all alone, and her car didn't start. You offered to help, and she thought that was nice of you. But you got distracted. You forced her into the backseat of her car, locked the door – "

222

"You got the wrong guy!"

"Hey, Macko, you attacked me," Marge said, angrily. "I don't think I got the wrong guy."

"I ain't sayin' nothin'."

"Bitch turn you on?" Decker whispered.

Macko was silent.

"She had big knockers, didn't she?"

"I'm tellin' you, you got the wrong guy."

"And those fuckin' sexy little pumps, right?" Decker nodded eagerly. "Ooo. I love those little backless, fuck-me shoes."

Macko started to sweat. His eyelashes fluttered.

"In black, man," Decker continued. "Has to be black, right?"

"She let me do it, man," Macko said. "I'm telling you, she begged me to do it to her. She liked it rough, man. I didn't want to get rough, but she wanted it that way."

"Who else wanted it that way?" Decker asked.

The thin lips clamped shut.

"Ain't saying nothin' till I see my lawyer."

"You'll get a lawyer," Marge said, taking off one patent leather black pump and passing it to Decker across Macko's field of vision.

Decker stroked the shoe. "Who else wanted it rough, Macko?"

The rapist eyed the shiny leather and began to breathe audibly. He squirmed against the cuffs and his pants bulged.

"They all did."

"That little hostess from Benito's?" Marge asked.

"Yeah. I mean, no. I mean, I don't know what the fuck you're talking about."

Decker caressed Macko's cheek with the shoe.

"How 'bout the brunette from the library?" Decker asked.

"Don't know no brunette from no library."

"Funny, Rayana knew all about her," said Marge.

"I tol' you. Rayana's a lyin' cunt!"

"C'mon, Macko. You remember who we're talking about. She had on those spiked heels, and her shoes were two-toned with pointy toes. Oh, you liked those shoes, didn't you?"

A sick smile tightened the drawstring mouth.

"She was a bitch. They're all bitches. I'm telling you, they asked me to do it. They *begged* me."

"And the one from the bar at Canary's?" Marge kept at it. "She got a good look at you."

"Hey, she *loved* it rough. Thought it was kinky, and she loved kink. I'm telling you, she loved the kink. Hell, she invited me in her car, man. I'm telling you, she asked me in."

"How 'bout the girl from Jewtown?" Decker asked. "She beg for it also?"

"Jewtown?" For the first time, Macko looked honestly puzzled. "I don't know what the fuck you're talkin' about."

"The one with the nice black pumps?" Decker tried.

"Kikes!" Macko spit. "I wouldn't fuck those pieces of shit if they was the last bitches on earth."

Decker's eyes blurred for a split second. When they refocused, he realized his hand was on the butt of his .38.

Slowly, he let it drop onto his lap.

22

The Rosh Yeshiva greeted Decker with a warm smile and told him to place the two large boxes on his desk. It was an oversized slab of rich rosewood, the top protected by glass and completely clear of clutter – something that Decker found amazing. Gently, he lowered the cartons onto the area so as not to scratch the glass, then stretched. With Macko locked up, he could afford the luxury of the night off.

He looked around. The study exuded dignity and warmth. It was softly lit, carpeted in a rich brown wool pile, and furnished with a burnt brown leather sofa and two suede wing chairs. The rear and right walls were floor-to-ceiling bookcases overflowing with volumes of religious texts. Thrown in for contrast was one case devoted to secular philosophy and American jurisprudence. The front wall was a picture window that revealed a canyon view. The desk was placed advantageously, affording the rabbi a panorama of nature as he worked.

But it was the left wall – glassed-in cabinets filled with artifacts of silver and gold – that turned the room into a showpiece.

Lovingly, Schulman began to lecture about his treasures.

One shelf of menorahs: Several were German, seventeenth and eighteenth century, heavy and bold in their silver work; another was a delicate weave of silver filigree from Italy; still others were fashioned of bronze and Jerusalem stone from Bezalel, the art institute in Israel. One entire case was devoted to spice boxes – miniature silver replicas of towers from which hung parcel gilt bells and flags – from the best silversmiths of Europe. Each was stamped and dated. Along the top ledge of another case were special silver and carved wooden boxes used to hold something called an *etrog* – a citron in English – which Decker learned was a bumpy, aromatic fruit similar in taste to a lemon. The *etrog*, the rabbi explained, was used on the holiday of Sukkos.

There were two shelves of pointers, each in the shape of a hand with an extended forefinger. The Rosh Yeshivah put one into Decker's hand.

"What's this for?" the detective asked.

"In the synagogue, a reader – a *ba'al kriah* – incants out loud a weekly portion of the Torah," the rabbi explained. "Fingers aren't allowed to touch the holy scriptures. The *ba'al kriah* uses a pointer to keep his place."

Candlesticks, wine goblets, finials called *keterim* – crowns for the Torah scroll. The elaborate metalwork, the intricate carving, the splendor and sheer number of treasures. Decker was overwhelmed at the richness of a culture that had survived for over two thousand years.

"This is only a fraction of my collection," the Rosh Yeshiva said. "But it contains the choicest pieces."

"Truly incredible, Rabbi."

"Someday, when we both have more time, I will show you my Hebrew manuscripts. I can't keep them out in the open because overexposure to the elements will cause irreparable damage to the parchment."

"I'd like to see them when time permits," said Decker.

"Yes. Come and let us see what you've brought. The hour is late, and an old man's eyes are getting tired."

The rabbi glided over to his desk, opened the first carton, and pulled out a prayer book.

"I don't think I have anything really valuable. Not like these pieces."

"Nonsense, Detective. Quite the contrary. One *siddur* is priceless because it contains the name of *Hashem*."

226

He pulled out another book and leafed through it.

"These are in good to very good condition. If you were to put them up for auction, I would say they'd be worth fifty to two hundred dollars apiece. But they are worth much more to me personally. The thought of them sitting in an irreligious environment is very disconcerting. I will pay you a fair market value if you're thinking of selling them."

"I wasn't. But I'll tell you what. You may have them as long as I can visit them from time to time."

The Rosh Yeshiva smiled.

'Agreed."

"Do they have any historical significance?"

"Only to a Jew from the area. Most are from Germany." The rabbi unloaded the volumes onto his desk. "Rina Miriam told me these belonged to your ex-wife's grandfather. He must have been a German Jew."

"Look at this one here, Rabbi. The book is Hebrew, but the inscription is in another language, and it doesn't look like German."

The old man's eyes lit up.

"This is Polish." The Rosh Yeshiva shook his head. "I can't understand her family's complete disregard for their heritage."

"Some people are less sentimental than others," the detective said, picking up the megillah. "Isn't it beautiful?"

The rabbi took the scroll and studied it.

"It's of Polish origin also. This is worth a substantial amount of money: upward of three thousand dollars. The text is exceptionally clear and well preserved."

"How about if you display it in your collection? I'm not hard up for cash right now."

"You're a good man, Detective."

Decker shrugged and gave him a half smile.

The rabbi opened the next box and rummaged through newspaper.

"Rina told me those were Jewish law books," said Decker.

"Yes, my good friend, that is exactly what they are," the rabbi said, unwrapping a leather-bound text. "Jewish law books – a complete set. We can always use a set of *shass*. Thank you."

The old man turned away from the books and faced the detective.

"It's astounding what finds are tucked away in dusty old attics and basements. I will take good care of your valuables, Detective Decker."

"I know you will."

"Tell me something, Detective. When did the grandfather die?"

"Right before we filed for divorce. Must have been about five years ago."

"Interesting. And where was he living at the time of his death?"

Decker smelled more than just simple curiosity on the rabbi's part.

"Los Angeles. Why do you ask?"

"I'd like you to explain something to me, Detective. How is it that these books are wrapped in a *New York Times* that is dated just two years ago?"

What a cagey old man, Decker thought. He said nothing.

"I have extreme difficulty believing that your in-laws are complete and utter philistines. Would you care to amend your story regarding how these came into your possession? Or at least, make the fabrication consistent with the dates?"

Decker gazed out of the window.

"Why don't you sit down?" the rabbi offered.

The detective remained motionless.

"Where did you acquire these?" the old man asked softly.

"From my father," the detective said, still staring outward. "Not my real father, my biological father."

228

He locked eyes with the old man.

"I'm adopted."

"Your biological father was Jewish," the rabbi said.

"And so was my biological mother. And that makes me Jewish. But you see, I don't consider myself Jewish. I consider myself the product of my real parents – the ones who raised me. And I was raised Baptist, although I'm not really anything now. As Rina said to me the other day, it takes a lot more than just an accident of birth to make someone a Torah Jew."

"She said that?"

"Yep."

"Good for her. Then she knows about your origins?"

"No. I thought about telling her but decided against it. It would be too big a distraction at this point. We both have work to do. I need her to concentrate on a rapist, not on me. Besides, I could never spit in my parents' faces and suddenly declare myself a Jew, like my 'real' parents. It would upset them tremendously."

"So how did you come to have these books?"

"I was curious about my background. There were no open records when I started searching twenty years ago, but since I was a cop in the state where I was adopted, I was able to pull a few strings. To make a long and boring story short, I found out my mother was a religious girl from New York who was shipped down to Miami after getting herself into a little fix when she was fifteen. She's in her fifties now, with five kids and a load of grand-children. I'm not about to barge in on her and disrupt her life.

"The records also contained my father's name. He was a different story. Older. Never married, lived alone on the Lower East Side of New York in one of those projects. One day I got up enough nerve, flew to New York, and looked him up. We talked. He was a nice man, a retired diamond cutter, a big man like me, with big hands. I looked like him. It was a strange experience to resemble someone. Very strange. He kept trying to console me, as

229

if I were mad at him for some reason, telling me over and over that he and my mother weren't meant to be. He kept saying it wasn't *basheert*, repeating that word. I gave him my address and told him to keep in touch. I wrote. He never did. Finally I gave up.

"A couple of years ago, I received these books and a couple of other personal items of his – a prayer shawl, phylacteries, a *kittel*. No note. I called up the NYPD and asked them to check the obits. Sure enough, his name was there. It said he died of a stroke. What a bunch of baloney. The package was dated a week before he died. I know he killed himself. The M.E. was incompetent and didn't pick up on it."

"Or maybe, Detective, he knew he was about to die."

Decker smiled.

"That's a little romantic, Rabbi."

"You need to think a lot more like a Jew. *Hashem* can do anything, Detective."

"Maybe."

Decker sat down on a leather chair and lit a cigarette.

"I've never told a soul. I trust you'll keep this confidential."

The old man sighed heavily.

"Detective, your ex-wife didn't know you were Jewish?"

"I'm not really Jewish."

"I mean that you are Jewish biologically. I don't want to quibble with semantics."

"No."

"Were you married in a Jewish ceremony?"

"We had a combo wedding. A reform rabbi and a Unitarian minister. It was pretty unusual."

"Do you remember anything about the Jewish part of the ceremony?"

"I've tried to repress the whole thing." Decker smiled and thought. "I gave her a ring and said something about Moses. Oh, and I stepped on a glass. They gave my wife a wedding certificate that I signed. I don't know what happened to it. Why are you asking me this?"

"I'm trying to figure out if you're still legally married to your ex-wife. If there was a *kinyan*, a valid transaction."

"We've been divorced for five years."

"Civilly. But maybe not according to Jewish law. By any chance, has your ex-wife remarried?"

"Yes. About two years ago. She went all the way and married a real Jew this time."

The rabbi looked pained.

"*Vay is mere*. And do they have children?"

Decker looked at him.

"As a matter of fact, she just lost a premature baby. She was six months pregnant when she went into labor, but the baby didn't survive. She's okay physically, but my daughter tells me she's not doing too well emotionally."

"Now *that* was *besheert*," the rabbi said to himself. "Detective Decker, to be on the safe side, I'm going to prepare you a *get* – a Jewish divorce. A civil divorce is insignificant for religious purposes. Otherwise, your ex-wife's future children may be considered *mamzerim* – bastards – and be irrevocably stigmatized."

Decker's eyes grew cold.

"I'm stigmatized?"

"*You* are not a *mamzer*. Your parents were not married at the time of your birth, but you are still a full-fledged Jew. A *mamzer* is the product of an adulterous union between a married Jewish woman and a Jewish man, or of incest. According to Jewish law, it's possible that you're not legally divorced from your wife."

"She doesn't know I'm Jewish."

"But you knew you were Jewish at the time of your marriage?"

"Technically, yes."

"Do you have any objection to her finding out?"

"Not really."

"Then let me divorce you properly."

Decker smiled slightly.

"Let me ask you this, Rabbi. Had my ex-wife's baby lived, would it have been considered a bastard?"

"Debatable but possible. Every marriage is looked at individually because the consequences are so severe. Once decided, it is one of the few things in Jewish law that is completely irreversible. Why condemn your former wife's children to such a fate when the whole thing can be easily resolved? Let's divorce you according to halacha."

"What do I have to do?"

"Sign a document that I will prepare. And deliver it personally to your ex-wife."

"Fine."

"I'll need to know your ex-wife's Hebrew name, that of her father, and your father's. I'm assuming you don't have a Hebrew name."

"Not that I know of."

"All right. Your English name will be sufficient. I'll also need the date of your marriage."

"I can give that to you right now. The rest I'm going to have to find out."

"Write it all down for me tomorrow. Then I will come with you to your ex-wife's house and divorce you properly."

Decker smiled at him, still bemused.

"Okay."

The rabbi placed a hand on his shoulder.

"It was fate that led you here. It was *basheert*. Something pulled you to us."

A rape and a homicide, Decker thought. But he didn't answer.

"You were searching for something, Detective."

"So far as I know, Rabbi, I still am."

23

Cory Schmidt sat slumped in the interview room, head down, smoking a cigarette. His stringy blond hair was pulled back in a ponytail, and dark circles underlined his eyes. The prison denims he wore were wrinkled and too big for him. Taking a deep drag, he looked around, then turned his attention back to the tabletop in front of him. He had been stripped of his earrings, his wrist bracelets, and all of his bravado.

He fidgeted, growing increasingly jumpy in this piss-hole. Man, he felt alone. Someone had told his mother about the arrest a couple of days ago, but the lazy bitch hadn't bothered to show her face. She was probably glued to the boob tube – her fuckin' soaps. His old man didn't care, either. Too busy gettin' tanked somewhere. Shit! When you came right down to it, ain't a soul who gave a flying fuck about you. Not your parents, not your buddies, not your chicks. Nobody. He looked at the suit sitting next to him – some righteous fuck-off of a public defender named Ronson. Who was he trying to kid with his dipshitty beard and fako English accent? A first-class jiveass turkey fag. Dude didn't do a fucking thing except scribble notes, shuffle papers, and clear his throat, asking if there were any questions, talking to him like he was a retard. Man, there was nothing left to say. Cory finished the last hit of nicotine and wondered if he wasn't better off with a bullet in his head.

Decker stood outside the interview room waiting for Birdwell, the deputy D.A., to return from his phone call. The prosecutor was a young, good-looking, bespectacled black kid with a baby-smooth face and short kinky hair – a Berkeley grad, sharp, with a lot of spirit. He'd do well in the system. The detective wondered how he would have fared had he gone into public law. In retrospect, it had been a big mistake to join his father-in-law's practice. Estate planning and wills. Big bucks but mind-numbing.

Seeing Captain Morrison enter the squad room, Decker waved him over. David Morrison was in his early fifties, built wiry, with thin gray hair and flaccid cheeks. His tie was slightly askew, and he straightened it as he approached Decker.

"Where's Birdwell?" he asked.

"Taking a phone call."

The two men waited in silence until Birdwell returned.

"What do we have, George?" Morrison asked.

"He wants to trade," Birdwell said.

"What's the deal?" the captain asked.

"He'll cop a plea of assault to the Adler woman in exchange for the names of his cohorts on the Marley murder," the prosecutor answered.

Morrison turned to Decker.

"I thought Adler was a rape."

"The doctor screwed up the exam," said Decker. "While she noted semen in the vaginal and anal regions, she failed to note *any* penetration because it was so slight. So without the words *forced entry* in writing, technically, it's not a rape."

"And he wants Cory to be tried as a juvenile," Birdwell added.

"Well, he can forget about that," Morrison said. "So all we can get Cory on is assault?"

"No," Birdwell answered. "On the Marley case, he's a full-blooded Murder One. Right now I have more than enough for the prelim. If we want his buddies, we'll have to go down to an assault."

"No dice," Morrison said.

"Schmidt was set up," Birdwell said.

"Schmidt was at the scene of the murder," Morrison

234

said. "His shoe prints were lifted. So were tire tracks from his bike. I don't know who did the slicing, but Schmidt was there. No way a piece of shit like that is going to get away with a simple assault."

"Then we're letting his friends get away with murder," Decker said.

Morrison frowned.

"What do we have on his friends?" he asked.

"Right now, nothing," Decker said. "They claim that they were biding their time with their girlfriends. The young ladies verify their story."

"We know what that's worth," said the captain.

"Absolutely," the prosecutor said, scratching his head. "But with no hard evidence, it's their word against ours."

"And Cory's alibi for the night?" the captain asked.

"At first he claimed to be with them," Decker said. "But they denied it. So now he's without alibi and very amenable to making a deal. Schmidt's the way to get to them."

"Do we know that Schmidt didn't do the slicing?" asked Morrison.

"In the opinion of the M.E., the killing slash was done by a left-handed person," said Decker. "Schmidt is right-handed."

"That isn't conclusive, Pete."

"No," Decker admitted. "But the whole thing stinks, Captain. The evidence was dropped in our laps like manna from heaven. The knife was delivered to our doorstep, *unwashed*. Now, who the hell kills someone, with an identifiable weapon no less, and doesn't bother cleaning off prints and blood?"

"All right," Morrison said. "Let's concentrate on what we know. We know Schmidt was at the murder scene. We have a murder weapon that belongs to Schmidt. We also know that Schmidt wasn't alone. But we don't have anything on his buddies. Unless Schmidt turns state's evidence, we *won't* have anything on his buddies."

"That about sums it up," Decker says.

"Let's do it this way," said Morrison. "Let's not promise anything until the kid talks. Then we'll see about a deal."

"Ronson won't let him talk without a trade," said Birdwell.

"Then his client will be charged with Murder One," the captain said.

"What about his friends?" Birdwell asked.

"If the kid won't talk, we can't get his friends," Morrison said. "We'll go with what we have."

The three of them entered the interview room.

"Do we have a deal?" Ronson asked, fingering his vest.

Morrison looked at Decker and nodded for him to start.

"What happened the night of the murder, Cory?" Decker asked.

"Don't answer that," the P.D. responded. "Gentlemen, what's going on?"

"We'd like to hear Mr Schmidt relate the events that led up to the murder," Decker said.

"Mr Schmidt is not going to talk until we do some negotiating," said Ronson.

"Then we're charging your client with premeditated murder. You take over from here," Morrison said to Birdwell. "Meeting is adjourned."

He walked out of the room, followed by Ronson hot on his heels.

"Captain, this is absurd. You know the boy wasn't alone. You're willing to let murder accomplices go free?"

"I am if you are."

"You're willing to mark one to take the fall for three others?"

"There were three others, Counselor?"

Ronson swore to himself.

"Make me an offer, Captain. Give me something to work with."

"I won't give you a damn thing until I hear the kid's story. Suppose I hear it and decide I sold out for bullshit.

236

I'd feel awfully bad." Morrison stopped walking, faced Ronson, and smiled cryptically. "It's up to you, Counselor. Why don't you consult your client and let him decide?"

"Come on, Captain. Let's be reasonable about this."

Birdwell caught up with the two of them, smiling.

"Cory wants to sing."

"Oh shit!" Ronson exclaimed.

The P.D. rushed back into the interview room.

"Don't say anything," he ordered Cory.

"Fat fucking lot of good you did me, faggot," Cory spat. "I want another lawyer."

"Just keep your mouth *shut*."

"Hey, I'm the one being fucked over, not you." Cory looked at Decker. "Man, I didn't off her. I swear I didn't off her. You gotta help me out, Decker."

"Why don't you tell me what happened, and then maybe we can do something."

"Don't say a word – " shouted Ronson.

The boy ignored him.

"They're fucking me *over!*"

"Who's fucking you over, Cory?" Decker asked, soothingly.

"What are you gonna do for me if I tell you?" the boy asked.

"First, let's hear what you've got to say."

Morrison and Birdwell returned, shutting the door behind them.

"Mr Schmidt," the P.D. said loudly, "as your legal counsel, I am advising you not to speak until I've had a chance to confer with these gentlemen alone. I'm requesting you to go back to your – "

"And I'm requesting you to leave me the fuck alone!"

"They're bluffing, Cory," Ronson tried again. "Let me handle this."

"We're not bluffing," Morrison said. "And we're not promising you a goddam thing, Schmidt. But we've got ears, and we're willing to listen."

"I want to know what's in it for me," the kid said shakily.

"Nothing," Decker answered. "But look at it this way. You've got premeditated murder on the other side. And that's a capital offense. And you're over sixteen, buddy. That means you're going to be tried as a big boy, and you're going to pull some hard time."

Decker leaned in close and whispered.

"You're gonna get your ass reamed, Cory."

"Captain, I object to your detective's scare tactics and won't hesitate to cite them as grounds for appeal if you obtain a confession. I demand a moment alone with my client."

"The hell with you," Cory spat out. To Decker he said: "I wanna just say one thing. You gotta understand – I didn't kill no one. I'm innocent!"

"Look here, kid," Ronson said, snapping a pencil. "I don't need this shit. I'm trying to help you."

"Fuck you." Cory returned his attention to Decker. "I can talk, can't I?"

"Of course – "

"Do you understand that everything you say will be used *against* you, Cory?" Ronson said.

"Yeah, I understand. Man, let's just pretend it went this way. I'm not saying it did. Let's just pretend that it did, got it?"

"Cut the crap, Schmidt," Morrison barked. "And when you address me, you use *sir* or *captain*. If you can't get that straight, you're going back to your holding pen. Got it?"

"Okay, okay. I just want to make it clear that this is just pretend."

"Fine, Mr Schmidt," the captain said, checking the cassette recorder to make sure it was working properly. "It's all theoretical."

Ronson pulled out a pen and poised himself for writing. "You're sealing your death warrant, Mr Schmidt."

238

"Hey, I know what I'm doing. Like the captain says, it's thredical."

"Just get on with it, Cory," Decker pressed.

The boy placed both hands on the table and ran his tongue over his lips.

"Man, you gotta believe me when I say this. I didn't know what was gonna go down. It wasn't planned, man. I swear to you, I didn't know shit. Man, it was the *dust*. Never would have happened if we weren't flying on dust. I mean we weren't thinkin' too clear, man. I mean, I didn't know what the fuck was going down."

"What happened?" the captain said impatiently.

"*Maybe* we started off just sitting around, smoking joints dipped in dust, bullshitting about the kikes. Hey, man, nobody wanted 'em here. They just came, and nobody wanted 'em. Man, those kikes are weirdos. They ain't American. They're all spies for Israel, and they come here to bleed us of all our money and give it away. Man, we don't need any fuckin' foreigners telling us how to run *our* country, right? And that Jew bitch got us into trouble.

"Then *maybe* one of my friends said, 'Let's go down and kick some ass at Kiketown.' *He* said it. *Maybe* I didn't say anything. I swear I didn't say a word."

"Go on, Cory," Morrison said with exaggerated boredom.

"So, man, we was all flying and charged up. Man, we felt so good, 'cause *maybe* we did a few rocks of coke also. So we got on our bikes, and *maybe* we went down there. Hey, there's no law against looking the place over, right?

"So *maybe* we did a little more, like hopping over the fence, and one of my friends *maybe* asked me for my buck knife. Man, I swear I didn't think he was gonna do anything with it. Just maybe kick a little ass or maybe scare a little kike bitch into spreading her legs. I mean I didn't think he'd want to *waste* anybody.

"So I give him my knife, and we start to hunt for kike.

239

But then we saw this big fat nigger bitch with a mean-looking piece thinking she was Queen Shit. We see the nigger and, man, that was even *better* than a kike. So *maybe* we hid in the hills and made a little noise. Big fat coon comes up to see what's happening, and we knocked the gun out of her fat hands."

The boy began to pick his nose.

"Like I said, I thought we was just gonna kick some ass. Then *maybe* one of my buddies takes out my blade. Honest, I thought he just was gonna play around. You know a poke here, a poke there. But he wanted more, man. Fuck, he slashed her. Man, I was fucked-up blown away. I mean I was totally blown away. I've kicked ass, but I never wasted no one. I'm telling you, I was completely blown away. Shit, all this blood started pouring out in gushes, man, in fucking *gushes*. Freaked us all out, all this blood all over our hands, all over our clothes. The dude who did it completely freaked. Started laughing like some goddamn hyena, then began to hack away at her arm. The blood kept *coming*, man. The others stomped on her knee, and you could hear it break, you know? Man, you could hear the crack for a mile. Shit, it was weird, real weird."

"Who did the slashing?" Decker asked.

"It wasn't me, man. I didn't know he was gonna slash her. Man I didn't do nothing, just maybe stared while they ripped her apart. See, by then I was already coming down, but they were still flying, man. You know dust. It does weird things."

The P.D. groaned, scratched some notes, then lit a cigarette and gave one to Cory. All the others followed suit. The room became a cloud of tobacco haze.

"Then it all got kinda fuzzy," the boy continued, after filling his lungs with smoke. "I mean, I don't remember too much after the nigger bitch bit it. Just that it all got kind of fuzzy, and they were doing a number on her. Then, we heard noises like someone was coming, and we all took off. Man, I forgot to ask for my knife back in all

240

the mess. Or maybe it just got lost. I don't know where you got it. But I didn't use it on her, man."

"Who did?" asked Morrison.

Schmidt thought a moment, then said, "I don't think I should tell you that."

"Such discretion," muttered Ronson.

"You split after you heard the noise?" Decker asked.

"Man, we were *gone!*."

"Theoretically, Cory," Decker said, "what were the names of your friends?"

Ronson protested, but the boy ignored him.

"Maybe, just maybe, their first names were Clay, Dennis, and Brian. That's all I'm sayin' for now."

"Captain?" asked Decker.

"Yeah?"

"Can I talk to you for a moment?"

"Brief interlude, Counselor?" Morrison asked the P.D.

"Why the hell not?" snapped Ronson.

"Great," Birdwell said, adjusting his glasses. "I've got to make a couple of calls."

"I buy it," Morrison said to Decker when they were alone. "Do you?"

"Yup."

"The question is do you go for a sure thing and charge him with Murder One, or do you take a chance that a jury will believe him and try to get all four of them?"

Decker thought a moment.

"I don't feel comfortable letting him take the sole rap when there are three others involved. And I think it would be hard to convince a jury that Schmidt acted alone. Also, other shoe prints and tire tracks were found at the scene. Be interesting if they matched his friends'."

"If he turns state's evidence, then we can get warrants for his pals." Morrison tapped his foot. "Let's try for all four. Now how much do we give up in exchange? Letting him off with just an assault charge would be a travesty of justice."

"For more than one reason, Captain. I don't think he did the Adler rape."

Morrison knitted his brows.

"Why the hell not?"

"Someone tried to break into the ritual bath the night Florence Marley was killed. Cory didn't mention a thing about it. I think the perp who broke in that night was the same one who did the Adler rape. I made a tactical error by mentioning the rape the first time I questioned Cory after the supermarket thing, and the kid was somehow smart enough to use the information and plea bargain with it against the murder rap."

"Shit."

"You're telling me," Decker said. "I feel like a jackass."

Morrison paused.

"I'd like to have someone in custody before I dismiss the charges. He confessed, Pete."

"I just don't see it. Cory and his friends have had minor brushes with the law. And whenever there was a weapon involved, it was a knife. When we searched Schmidt's house, we found only one gun, and it belonged to his father. These kids are cutters. The Adler rapist had a gun. The night I first searched in the hills, someone shot at me. Someone who knew how to use a piece."

"Perps have been known to use different methods."

"Granted. But still, I'd like to delve a little further into the case before sticking it on Cory."

"I'm assuming you've questioned Macko about it?"

"Yes. It's not his baby."

"How's your caseload?"

"With the Marley murder and the Foothill thing out of the way, I've got a little more time on my hands."

"Any suspects?"

"A few."

"It would be handy if Schmidt knew he didn't have the Adler thing to bargain with. Let's say, we'll keep it quiet for forty-eight hours. See what you can do in two days."

242

"Thank you, sir."

Birdwell returned.

"Where do we go from here?"

Morrison briefed him.

"So what do you want to do with Schmidt?" the prosecutor asked, wiping his glasses. "Stall him?"

"Yeah, we stall him for two days," Morrison responded. "Tell him we're considering the trade."

The captain turned to Decker.

"Have Hollander or Dunn pick up his friends on suspicion of murder, while you search for the ritual bath rapist. I don't want them splitting on us when they get wind of the fact that Cory's in deep shit."

"What do we do if the Adler case comes up dry in two days?" Birdwell asked.

"Then we'll have to see about a deal." The captain turned to Decker. "Two days, Pete. Starting right now."

"Yes, sir."

Decker started to walk away.

"Pete," Morrison called out.

"Yes, Captain?"

"Good job on the Macko collar."

"Thank you, sir."

24

Rina waited for Decker in the park.

It had been two days since the capture of the Foothill rapist, a week since they had last talked. Though she would have loved to call him up – to congratulate him on a job well done – she didn't want to be a nuisance or give him the wrong idea. After all, she'd been so firm about not seeing him socially anymore.

But today he had called, saying he needed to talk to her, and they arranged to meet for lunch. Now she wondered if the rendezvous was wise. They could have spoken over the phone – there was no need to talk face-to-face – yet she had agreed and was excited about it. Being brutally honest, she asked herself whose needs were being satisfied.

He had occupied her thoughts since the first time she'd laid eyes on him. Feeling so vulnerable the night of Sarah's ordeal, she'd been attracted to his self-assurance and physical stature. And in all the time she'd known him, never once had he taken advantage of her momentary weakness. He was kind to her boys and respectful of her, never mocking her religious beliefs. And she loved when she dreamed about him, the images exhuming sensations in her body that had been buried for so long.

She felt happy when he was around; she missed him when they were apart. It was absurd. Theirs was a relationship that could never be. But she couldn't help her feelings.

The Plymouth pulled up, and Peter got out. She'd expected him to be overflowing with relief and joy at capturing a man who had plagued him for so many months. But his face was full of tension.

"Hi," he said, sitting down next to her.

"Congratulations," she said enthusiastically.

"For what?"

"For catching the Foothill rapist."

"Oh that." He took off his jacket and loosened his tie. "It's old news already."

Her eyes drifted to his shoulder holster, then stared at the ground.

"Must be a load off your mind."

"Oh yeah, no doubt about it. Nice to get the bastard behind bars. It's even nicer that it looks like he'll stay there for a while. We've got a couple of victims who picked him out of a lineup."

"That's wonderful," she said. "How'd you do it?"

"A little routine police work. But mainly, his girlfriend ratted on him after the son of a bitch got tough with her poodle."

"*Poodle?*"

"The guy kicked her dog. No telling what'll bring citizens to their senses."

A smile spread across his face.

"You're a sight for sore eyes," he said.

She let out a nervous laugh and smoothed out her silk dress.

"Why are you all dressed up?"

"I met my parents for breakfast. They like it when I dress up."

"I don't blame them. I like it too."

He thought for a moment, then said, "I thought you don't eat out in restaurants."

"This one was kosher."

"I remember a couple of kosher delis in Miami, but I didn't know there was anything like that here."

"There's a great deli in the Valley and a gourmet restaurant in Los Angeles. The one we went to this morning was a new dairy restaurant. We don't mix meat

245

and dairy products, so restaurants have to be one or the other."

"How was it?"

She smiled.

"Not bad. They have a few bugs to work out."

"But you felt comfortable eating there?"

"Yes. I happen to know the rabbi who supervises the place. He's very particular."

Peter's eyes twinkled, but he said nothing. Suddenly his head had begun to throb. He cupped his forehead between open palms.

"What's wrong, Peter?"

"Oh, it's only stress – "

"How long have you had these?" she asked with sudden urgency.

He looked at her.

"They're nothing new. Don't worry about it."

Reaching in his pocket, he pulled out a bottle of aspirin, tossed a couple of pills down his throat, and swallowed.

She knew she had overreacted because of Yitzchak. *Calm down. Not every headache is a brain tumor.*

"Would you like something to wash it down with?" she asked.

"Sure."

She handed him a can of coke. He took a swig, then winced.

"Your work is hazardous to your health."

"Speaking of hazards, I'm worried about *you*."

"The mikvah is closed," she said.

"But we don't have the rapist,"

"So Macko didn't do it," she said glumly.

"No. I would have called you immediately if he had. But I do have some other news. We've got Cory Schmidt in custody, charged with murdering Florence."

"Oh God! He *did* do it. That disgusting little piece of trash!"

"No argument from me there."

"When I think that he touched me, drew that knife . . ." She shuddered. "How'd you catch him?"

"He was set up."

"By whom?"

"I'm not sure. I suspect his friends. Either they were angry at him for ratting on them about the supermarket incident, or the kid who actually did the killing got scared, had Cory's knife, and found him a convenient scapegoat. That's not important. What is, is that the murder weapon appeared magically at the station. We obtained a search warrant, and Schmidt's shoes matched prints lifted from the murder scene. And his motorcycle tires match tracks found outside the yeshiva."

"*Mazel tov*. Did you tell Mr Marley?"

"I can't say anything until everyone is charged."

"When will that be?"

"We have to get a couple of things straightened out."

She was silent.

"Cory said he raped Mrs Adler, Rina."

Her eyes widened.

"Why didn't you *tell* me this?"

"Because I don't believe him. It just doesn't jibe."

"Then why on earth would he admit doing it?"

"He's trying to plea bargain. We're not sure at this point if it was Cory or one of his friends who actually murdered Florence. We think it was one of Cory's friends. Now Schmidt's willing to turn state's witness and rat on his friends if we lessen the charge to assault."

Rina's face went red with fury.

"Assault? He *raped* her!"

"The doctor screwed up – "

"He raped and murdered – "

"We're not sure he actually murdered, Rina. That's the problem."

"He's trying to get away with a lousy assault charge? The boy killed another human being. He pulled a knife on me, Peter! He deserves a firing squad!"

"If we can find the real rapist, he won't have the assault to plea bargain with."

She squeezed her hands together and clenched her jaw.

"The naked truth is we still have the mikvah rapist at large," Decker said.

Rina pounded her fist against an open palm.

"I know it's frustrating – "

"It's damn infuriating! How do you stand it?"

"Who says I stand it? These headaches don't come from nothing. But I try to ignore the garbage and do my job. The best revenge is to see the bastards behind bars. If I dwelled on the ones that got away from me, my work would suffer. We all have our methods of coping."

She looked at him. He seemed so tired. She gave his hand a light pat.

He smiled at her gesture and decided to shift gears.

"Kids come back home from the grandparents?"

"Yes. They had a good time but were more than happy to come home. My parents are overprotective – it's a hundred degrees outside, and they tell you to take a sweater, just in case."

"How long could the boys stand staying there without going nuts?"

"Why?"

"I'm just asking you a question."

"I know you too well by now. You never *just* ask a question. I'm not sending them away again."

"You may have to."

"Why?"

"Because the rape has to do with you."

"What makes you so sure?" she said struggling to hold her emotions in check. "Maybe Cory did do it? I mean, it's crazy otherwise, Peter. He and his friends murder Florence, then someone else tries to break into the mikvah to rape me?"

"It makes perfect sense if the guy happened to be hanging around, witnessed the murder, and took advantage of the fact that the guard was dead."

"Who'd be hanging around?" Rina's eyes widened. "Are we *back* on Moshe Feldman again?"

"I'm just looking at anyone who might – "

"*Gevalt.* He didn't do it, Peter. He no more raped Sarah Libba than he killed Florence Marley. How can you possibly consider him a suspect and brush off Cory so easily? It seems to me you're reaching. Why are you obsessing on Moshe?"

"I'm not obsessing. I'm trying to start from the beginning – "

"Are you afraid that this case will leave a blot on your perfect record?'

Decker lowered his head and gripped it hard.

"Oh Peter, I didn't mean that." She sighed. "I'm such a mess. And I'm taking out my frustrations on the person who's trying to help me the most. I'm sorry."

"It's all right. We're both a mess right now." He took another swallow of Coke. "Rina, someone tried to break into the mikvah that night. And that someone was after you. Just like the first time."

"Why do you say that? He could have gotten me if he wanted to. I would have come out a half hour later. All he had to do was wait."

"The point is he thought Sarah Adler was you. The first time I interviewed you, you told me that you ran late that evening. Sarah left the mikvah at the time you usually leave. Do you remember saying that?"

"No, I don't."

"Well, you did. I have it in my notes."

"Peter – "

"Listen. Sarah wore a black wig that could easily have been mistaken for your own hair. You told me she said the rapist went wild after he pulled off the wig. Of course he'd become unglued. At that point he realized that he had the wrong woman."

Rina said nothing. Tears started rolling down her cheeks. Memories flooded her head, dredging up past fears. Decker took her hand and brought it to his lips.

They felt warm and soft. She let the kiss linger for a moment, then she pulled her hand away.

"Rina, *think!* Who could be after you? Anyone else besides the people we've discussed?"

She shook her head.

"It had to be someone who was on the grounds that night," said Decker. "Someone who took advantage of Florence's murder."

He lit a cigarette.

"Which narrows the field of potential rapists down to all the men in the yeshiva," he muttered.

"It's not anyone from the yeshiva."

"Fine. Have it your way. The fact is there's still a rapist out to get you, and you're still here. You've got to get away – "

"No," she said defiantly. "We've already had this discussion."

"Just hear me out, all right? I've been working with sex crimes for three years now, and I don't say this to everyone. Sometimes rapes are random – the woman is in the wrong place at the wrong time – sometimes they're not. This is one of the cases where there's intentionality. The guy isn't out to pound out his hatred on the first woman he sees. He's out for you. You're symbolic of something to the son of a bitch."

"All the more reason I shouldn't run away. If he's out to get me, then he'll follow me."

"What about your kids?"

"Peter, where would I go? Back to my parents and involve them in this ordeal? In an apartment to live among anonymous strangers who don't give a damn about me? At least here people know what's going on. People look after me. You call me; Sarah calls me every night at eleven. Here people care. I can't run away. If you really think I'm in danger, then I'll learn how to protect myself."

She touched his shoulder holster.

"Teach me how to use it."

250

"Oh, that's a great solution. Play Annie Oakley, and you'll definitely wind up damaged."

"That's downright sexist."

"I'd say the same thing if you were a man, only I'd use Wyatt Earp."

She folded her arms across her chest.

"As I recall, you trusted me with your own weapon a while back."

"Florence might have still been alive. I had to look for her. I had no choice but to give you a gun."

"And I have a lot of choices now?"

"You have a good one. You can leave. You didn't have that option on the night of the Marley murder."

"Well, I don't think escaping is a viable option in this case."

"A gun is no good unless you know how to use it."

"So teach me."

"I mean use it *psychologically*. I know you could learn how to shoot. But when you point a firearm at an assailant, you'd better be damn sure you're willing to pull the trigger and blow the bastard away. Because if you don't, he's going to grab the gun and use it on you. Could you kill someone?"

"I kicked Cory when I had to."

"Could you *kill* someone?"

"If he was attacking my kids – "

"Could you draw a gun and kill someone if he was attacking you?"

"If I felt threatened, I think I could do it."

"You think?"

"*Yes*, then. Yes, I could."

"I don't believe it."

"You don't know me all that well."

"Maybe I've just seen too many nice people wind up in the morgue because they *thought* they could do it, also."

"I fought back with Cory, Peter. And it felt good. Not everybody fights back, either."

"It's not the same thing as pulling the trigger."

"You're the cop. You tell me you're worried about me. Then you tell me not to fight back."

"A gun is not the answer."

"Well, neither is escaping."

He touched his throbbing head, then took her hand again.

"I just don't want you to get hurt."

"I'm not reckless, Peter. I called you the minute I thought something was amiss. And I'll do the same thing if need be in the future. I'm not going to go after the rapist, but he's not going to drive the boys and me away, either. If I'm attacked, I want to be able to take care of my kids and myself. I just know I could do it."

She looked him in the eye.

"I could learn how to use a gun from someone else, you know."

"I know." Decker gave her a weak smile and looked inside the picnic bag. There was no sense pursuing the discussion.

25

The printer clicked rhythmically while spewing out a white stream of computer paper. When the machine finished its obbligato, Decker detached the printout from the remaining roll of blank paper and took the pile over to his desk.

He sat down, gulped lukewarm coffee, and stared at the columns in front of him, noticing that the print had become very light. It was the third ribbon he'd gone through in the last twenty-four hours. He squinted in an attempt to bring the words into sharper focus, but his eyes were too damn tired. Pushing aside stacks of papers, he rubbed them hard and stretched. His back and neck were stiff, his shoulders ached, and his head throbbed. Opening the desk drawer, he pulled out the aspirin bottle only to find it empty, and tossed it disgustedly in the trash.

Placing his hands behind his neck, he leaned back into the chair, propped his feet on the desk, and gazed upward, hoping that the ceiling would provide a burst of sudden insight. When nothing came, he figured it best to clear his mind and start over, get a fresh perspective. He rested a few more moments, enjoying the blank view, then sat back upright.

He studied the printout again. Hundreds of thousands of bytes of data had revealed nothing. He'd started with his original suspects and the MO of the crime. When nothing immediate panned out, he'd punched in the names of known local anti-Semites, then sex offenders now on parole, followed by yeshiva boys whom Rina had taught and men she'd gone to college with, throwing in people like a chef tossing in ingredients to revive a failed recipe. In the end he was no closer to the culprit. It boiled down to the same people. He picked up a pencil and scribbled the first name.

Shlomo Stein.

A son of a bitch. He fit his former image far better than his latter. The man had made no attempt to hide his contempt for the detective, and the police in general. Furthermore, he'd been preachy and condescending – nothing worse than a reformed felon. But his answers had been straightforward and on the level. Even more important was the fact that, on the night of the Adler rape, he'd been attending a Talmudic discourse with thirty other men.

Decker crossed his name off.

Shraga Mendelsohn.

Quieter than Stein, but still spooky. Spoke in a mumble. Inappropriate smiles and never made eye contact. If a case against Stein could have been made, Mendelsohn would have been great for the accomplice. But on his own, there was nothing. Besides, his alibi the night of the rape had been the same as Stein's. They were both at the lecture.

Scratch Mendelsohn.

Moshe Feldman.

Decker wrote a big question mark after his name.

Matt Hawthorne.

His alibi the night of the Marley murder had checked out. His friend had verified his presence at the movies. Furthermore, the candy counter girl remembered Hawthorne because he had made a weak attempt to flirt with her. The picture had ended at nine thirty-eight. It was possible time-wise that Hawthorne could have driven straight to the yeshiva, noticed Marley was dead, and attempted a break-in, but the scenario didn't make much sense. First, he'd have had to move very quickly and precisely to make the timing fit, and second, how would Hawthorne have known that Marley had been killed?

Hawthorne didn't have an alibi for his whereabouts the

night of the rape, claiming he was home alone, reading a book. But Decker figured the filled bookcase in his apartment was more than just a prop. Hawthorne was an English teacher and probably did read a lot. The bottom line was that he failed to arouse genuine suspicion. His agitation had seemed to result more from nerves than guilt.

Decker gave him a small question mark.

Steve Gilbert.

He was the most interesting. Not made a bit nervous by the presence of the police. Detached, almost amused by the whole thing. Not the spacey, schizoid physics major Decker had imagined. And he'd done a two-year hitch in the army, including ten months in Nam as a clerk. Unfortunately, the guy's personal records were sealed. Decker wondered why he hadn't been assigned to front-line combat. Maybe the army knew there was something kinky about him. Maybe he was trigger-happy. The asshole who shot at him had sure known how to use a piece.

Gilbert was on campus every Thursday with the Computer Club until ten P.M. The night of the rape had been a Thursday. The night that Decker was shot at had been a Thursday. Both incidents had happened around ten: Rina had placed the first call to the police at 10:08, and she had called him the second time at 10:15. That would have given Gilbert ample time to dismiss the club and perpetrate an attack.

But the night of the murder didn't fit. The time was off – Rina had called him at 10:45. More important, the Marley killing had taken place on a Wednesday, and on every Wednesday, Friday, and Sunday night for the last five years, Gilbert had eaten dinner with his fiancee's family thirty miles away, usually leaving around eleven. His presence had been confirmed by the prospective in-laws.

Decker walked over to the coffee pot, poured himself a refill and sat back down. He picked up a half-eaten corned

255

beef sandwich, the remnant of his dinner, and stared at the curly, pink strips of meat. The sandwich had laid heavily in his gut the first time, and after a couple of hours of sitting on his desk, what was left hadn't aged well. He tossed it in the garbage, sipped his coffee, and thought.

Dinner with your to-be in-laws three times a week for the last five years? No man who had anything in his crotch would put up with such shit. Dinner with the folks had been a constant sore spot between him and Jan. Once a month had been more than enough for him; Jan had preferred it closer to once a week. But even she would never have expected *three times a week*. Maybe Gilbert would get more assertive after the marriage – if the nuptials ever took place. That was strange, too. Who the hell stays engaged for five years unless there are *lots* of big problems? Maybe he was a wimp with women and was holding in a lot of rage toward them. Maybe he'd redirected his anger.

But how could he explain Gilbert as the mikvah rapist when, on the night of the Marley murder and mikvah break-in, he was having dinner thirty miles away?

Decker took another swig of coffee.

Unless . . . Unless, he happened to *not* be at his in-laws that night. If the dinners had been so codified, so routine, so frequent, the in-laws might have ignored occasional absences.

But Gilbert couldn't have known in advance that Florence was going to be killed. So what was he doing on campus?

Picking up a pencil, Decker tapped it against the desktop.

Maybe Computer Club couldn't meet that Thursday. Could be, the week of the murder, they had decided to meet on Wednesday.

A stab in the dark.

He picked up the phone and dialed Rina's number. Her

boys might remember if the club had had a change of schedule that week.

No one answered. Immediately, his sensors were up.

Where the hell would she be?

Maybe he dialed the wrong number. He tried again. Nothing.

"Shit," he said, slamming down the receiver. He'd told her to call him if she had to go out at night. She'd promised she would.

He decided to phone Sarah Libba Adler. Probably she'd know something. He dialed information and was told the number wasn't listed. Decker gave the operator his name and badge number and after a few minutes obtained the listing. She answered on the fourth ring. Children's laughter and horseplay could be heard in the background.

"This is Detective Decker, Mrs Adler. I don't mean to alarm you, but do you know where Mrs Lazarus is?"

A long pause.

"She's out."

"Where?"

Another long pause.

"Mrs Adler?" he asked.

"At the mikvah."

"The *mikvah?*."

"Something came up."

"I thought it was shut down."

"Not exactly. I tried to talk her out of it, but she can be very determined sometimes."

"That's certainly true," he mumbled. "Where are her boys?"

"I have them. She's due to pick them up at ten. If she's not back by then, she had instructed me to call you."

Swell!

"Anyone with her?" he asked, hoping it was Zvi.

"Matt Hawthorne."

Damn, he thought to himself.

"Detective, what's wrong?" Sarah asked, suddenly panicked.

"Nothing. Nothing at all. Look, Mrs Adler, I'm going to drive down there now just to ease my own peace of mind."

"I think that's a very good idea."

"You just take care of the boys."

"All right."

"Bye," he said. "Oh, call your husband and tell him to stop by there – "

The line had disconnected.

He called her back, but the line was busy.

He called the operator and placed an emergency interruption.

She reported that no one was on the line. The phone was out of order.

Accidentally, Sarah must not have put the receiver fully back on the hook.

He slammed down the phone and dialed the mikvah number.

The line was dead.

They'd never bothered restoring the service after the line was cut.

He tried the Rosh Yeshiva's office number and came up empty. He tried the rabbi's home number. No one was there. Then he called the yeshiva's answering service. The only numbers they had were office listings. No one answered any of them.

"Shit!" he bellowed. Grabbing his coat, he tapped Marge on the shoulder and stormed out of the building.

Marge picked up her purse and caught up with him in the parking lot. He threw himself into the driver's seat, gunned the ignition, and once she was inside, peeled rubber out to the street before she could close her door.

'Would you mind cluing me in?" Marge asked, placing a blinking red light on the roof of the car.

"Rina's at the mikvah."

"Why?"

"I don't know. I forgot to ask. Hawthorne is supposed to be protecting her." Decker slammed his fist against the dashboard. "Goddam! I can't believe she did that!"

Marge was confused.

"Did she call in and say she was in trouble?"

Decker shook his head grimly.

"I'm trying to get to her before something happens."

"Don't you think this is a little impetuous, Pete? After all, we really don't have a case against – "

"It was stupid for her to go there, Marge. She knew I hadn't written him off as a suspect." He pounded the wheel. "Fuck!"

"Take it easy, Pete," Marge said, thinking he was due for some vacation time. "He's walked her home safely before. There's no reason to think that this time is going to be any different."

"Yeah, yeah. Let me concentrate on my driving."

He was angry at himself. He should have told Sarah right away to send Zvi down to the mikvah, to wait there until he arrived. He shouldn't have left it as an afterthought. If only Sarah hadn't hung up. If only she hadn't left the phone off the hook. If only he could have gotten through to someone. He floored the accelerator until the car was pushing ninety-five, rattling like a diamondback. A bump on the freeway and they were hamburger. But Marge didn't say a thing.

Rina mopped up the last bit of water off the floor and turned off the heat. The mikvah had needed a good cleaning, and she was glad she'd decided to come.

Ruthie Zipperstein had begged her. The family car had been in the shop for a week, and she was three days past her mikvah date. Her husband, Yisroel, hadn't been able to scrounge up an auto to take her to the other mikvah, and they were going nuts. So Ruthie had asked if she couldn't surreptitiously help them out. Rina had agreed, provided that Yisroel would walk her home. But in the early afternoon he'd tripped and twisted his ankle. On doctor's orders, he was forced to keep off the foot for twenty-four hours.

Rina was about to call the whole thing off until it hit her. She was being terrorized by a ghoul who not only threatened her physical safety, but held her spiritually imprisoned. She was sick of it all – sick of looking over her shoulder, of compulsively and repeatedly checking the locks on her doors and bolts on her windows, of the paranoia that was crippling her daily existence. The invisible shackles of fear had to be broken.

But she had common sense, so she worked out a feasible compromise. She'd have Peter walk them home.

He wasn't in the first time she'd called, and she didn't leave a message, figuring she'd just call back later. Then she began to think: *Remember how it was when Yitzchak died? How dependent you were on him? How he always had taken care of everything? How you felt you'd never be able to function without him? Do you want to feel that way again? If you do, just keep running to Peter every time there's a crisis. He'll take care of you, too. And once again, you'll sink back into being a helpless Hannah – the way you were as a daughter, the way you were as a wife.*

Time to use your own resources.

She had called Steve Gilbert. He wasn't home, so she had left a message on his answering machine and then called Matt. He had been nice enough to agree.

She was proud of the way she'd taken care of her own business. It was important that she break her dependence on Peter. Now she was here without his help, and that was a psychological and spiritual victory. No longer would she allow the rapist to hold her hostage. There was only one *Hashem – Hakodosh Boruch Hu –* and He alone was omnipotent. She would put her trust in Him, where it always should have been, and let Ruthie perform the mitzvah of mikvah. After all, wasn't it perverse to deny a mitzvah when the very fate of one's existence was solely in the hands of the Almighty?

She rinsed out the mop and smiled. The routine was

coming back, returning order to her life. She checked her watch and flicked off the lights. Matt should be back from walking Ruthie home any minute.

She went into the reception area and dusted the table tops for the third time. Her cleaning was mindless, and she knew it. The place was as sterile as an operating room. Triumphantly, she put down the dust rag and sat down to wait for Matt.

But the silence had become eerie – palpable. She tried not to think about it. The room was sweltering because she hadn't bothered to turn on the air conditioner. Sudden anxiety flowed through her veins and nervous energy propelled her upright. Her hands had taken on a slight tremble, her legs felt weak.

She hoped Matt would be back soon.

Opening the linen closet, she began compulsively to rearrange the towels, then stopped. She had ten minutes to go before ten. At least she'd left Peter's number with Sarah. If worst came to worst, she'd just turn out the lights and wait for him in the dark.

Finally, there were footsteps and a gentle rap at the door.

"Who is it?" she asked.

"It's Matt, Rina."

She unbolted the lock and let him in.

"I was getting a little worried," she told him.

Hawthorne smiled.

"I ran into one of the kids on the way back here. You know these boys. Once they start talking sports, there's no stopping them. Sorry I'm late. Are you all done?"

"I'm waiting for the timer to go off in the dryer. Do you mind staying an extra minute?"

"No. Not at all." Hawthorne glanced around. "So this is the inner sanctum. I've always wanted to sneak inside a convent."

Rina smiled uneasily.

"I could see where this would be an easy target for a rapist," he said more to himself than to her.

The hell with the towels.

"Let's go," she said.

"What about the towels?"

"I just remembered that Sarah Adler is expecting me momentarily. If I don't get there soon, she's been instructed to call the police."

Hawthorne looked perturbed.

"That wasn't necessary."

"Just in case, Matt. It was for your protection as well as mine – "

"I don't need protection."

"I'm sure you don't – "

"You *do* trust me Rina, don't you?"

"Of course!" she exclaimed, too adamantly. "Why would I have called you if I didn't trust you implicitly?"

Hawthorne's eye began to spasm. He ran his hands through his mop of thick curls and looked at her.

"We'd better go," he said coldly.

She turned off the lights and locked the door behind them.

"I'm kind of offended," he said when they were outside.

"I didn't mean to offend you."

"Jesus. First, that redheaded giant gets on my case, and now you're giving me spooky looks. Do I look like a rapist?"

She stared at him, feeling suddenly light-headed.

"Matthew, please understand what I've been going through. I meant no offense to you at all."

The man's eye twitched again, then he lowered his head.

"It just burns me, Rina, that this creep has all the women here suspecting everything in pants. But I guess it's natural. It must be tough to be a woman, huh?"

She nodded and walked a couple of steps.

"Wait a second," Hawthorne said, bending over.

"What is it?" Rina asked nervously.

"I dropped my watch. Damn it, the wrist band keeps coming loose."

Hawthorne hunted around in the dark.

"Do you need help?" she asked.

"Nah, found it." He stood up, brushed specks of dirt from the digital face, and put the timepiece to his ear.

"It's still working."

"That's good," Rina answered, starting to get shaky. She walked a couple of more steps, then felt a firm tug on her arm. Instinctively, she yanked away.

"Take it easy, Rina," Matt said softly. "I didn't mean anything. I think I heard something."

Her heart was pounding, and she listened carefully.

"I don't hear anything," she whispered rapidly.

"Yeah, well I know I heard something," he said firmly.

"What do you want to do?" She forced out the words.

"I don't know . . . Uh, wait here. I'll see if I can't scare whatever it is off."

"Matt, I don't know."

"I don't want us walking into a trap."

"Why don't we just wait for the police. They'll be here if I don't show up at home soon."

Hawthorne's eyelid fluttered.

"I don't *need* the police," he said, emphatically. 'Just wait here, and I'll go by myself!"

"I don't want to wait alone."

"Then come with me."

She didn't want that, either.

"Why can't we make a mad dash across the grounds screaming like banshees?" she asked.

"I can take care of us, Rina." Hawthorne pulled out a knife that gleamed in the moonlight. "I wasn't taking any chances with this pervert."

She swallowed hard. "I'll wait inside the mikvah," she whispered.

"Good idea."

"Be careful, Matthew."

"Piece of cake, m'lady."

She watched him disappear into the brush. A moment later, she heard noises – the crunching and snapping of leaves and twigs. It was Matt searching, she told herself. The noises became louder, intensifying, echoing against the still of the night!

Sudden silence.

She wanted to call out to him, but was afraid of giving herself away. She walked back toward the mikvah, fumbled for the key, and with a trembling hand, managed to insert it in the lock.

That was as far as she got.

He pounced on her. A panther with a ski mask. Clothing black as midnight. Before she could scream, something soft and fuzzy was crammed down her throat. He threw her down onto the baked earth and fell upon her, pinning her hands and body, belly-down, against the ground. She felt something cold and metallic against her temple. He spoke. His voice was a gravelly whisper – unnatural – as if he were talking through a voice box. He said it was a gun and he'd use it if he had to. The faces of her boys flashed through her head.

She struggled in his grip, managed to free a hand, slid it under his shirt and clawed his ribs. He swore and smacked her cheek with the butt of the gun.

Her face went wet and numb, her vision blurred, and her head burst with pain. But she didn't stop. She went for his eyes, but he backed away and hit her again. She felt her energy ebbing. The cloth in her mouth was beginning to suffocate her. She felt her clothes being ripped, his bare hands on her flesh – her neck, her back, inside her underpants. His touch was slimy, evil. She went wild and, with renewed force, bucked upward. The sudden movement threw him off balance and knocked the gun from his hand. Pressure eased from her back.

Taking advantage of his loss of equilibrium, she yanked the gag from her throat and tried to scream, but it came out a dry croak. He tried to punch her, but she ducked aside and his fist hit the ground. Again she screamed, and this time her voice rang out like a diva's.

He covered her mouth with one hand and pushed her

stomach against the ground again, flattening her to the dirt. But she heard the noise, the rush through the bushes – she knew it had to be *him*. Sarah must have called.

She bit the thick flesh of the assailant's palm and felt his blood oozing into her mouth. He swore gutturally and pulled his hand away.

"Peter!" she screamed.

The attacker heard the footsteps, too. He sprung up and tried to run, but she was too quick. She grabbed his ankle, and he went down.

"Peter!" she screamed again.

The sound of running. Louder. It was approaching her.

"Peter!" she implored.

Where was he?

She saw the figure appear.

It was Moshe.

The assailant tried to free himself from Rina's grasp, flailing at her.

"Help me!" she screamed at the wisp of a man.

Finally, the rapist pulled free, but Moshe leaped and tackled him – his meager body an arrow shooting through the night – encircling the other man's waist and holding him tight. Together, they tumbled into a pile of eucalyptus leaves.

The attacker was taller and heavier, but Moshe was armed with an oversized volume of the Talmud. Raising it, he blinked several times and brought it crashing down on the man's head. The impact stunned him for a moment, but then he began to lash out at Moshe. Rina ran over and struck out at his face, trying to pull off the ski mask. He kicked her in the abdomen, she doubled over, and the man broke free.

"He's getting away, Moshe!" she gasped.

Moshe grabbed the back of a black shirt collar and pulled him down again.

Muttering the *Shema*, Moshe again used the heavy book to pummel his head. Rina crawled forward and bit

265

his ankle. The pain made him cry out and buckle, and she took another grab at the mask, missing.

"Hold him, Moshe!" she screamed.

Moshe's response was another slam to the attacker's head, while chanting allegiance to *Hashem*.

Rina searched for the gun. The moon was full, and she caught a glint of metal winking at her. Picking it up, she found it small and comfortable in her hand, almost toylike. In the distance she heard a siren.

Finally!

She slipped her index finger into the trigger.

The siren grew louder.

With a shaking hand, she cocked the gun and aimed.

The man was woozy but still struggling. She didn't dare shoot for fear of hitting Moshe.

She saw the lights of the police car.

The rapist swiveled and broke free. The gun in her hand spat fire. He slowed a split second, then took off.

But the delay was all that was needed. He ran toward the barrel of Decker's .38 special.

"Police! Freeze!"

The attacker turned toward the hills, but Marge and Decker leaped on him, pulling him to the ground. Decker slammed the butt of his revolver into his back, then pointed it at his head.

"One move and you're iced, fucker," Decker said, clamping on the cuffs.

"You got him?" Marge asked, gun drawn.

"Yeah."

"I'll go call in."

Decker lifted the man upright and pushed him onto the hood of the Plymouth.

"Just try anything, and you're dead meat, asshole," he said, slamming the masked face against the metal. "You're fucking dead meat."

"Take it easy, Pete," Marge said, trying to pull him off.

"You hear me, motherfucker?" Decker spat. "Just blink the wrong way, and you're dead meat!"

Rina watched as Decker, with one savage turn of his wrist, yanked off the mask.

It was Gilbert. His face was blanched, in stark contrast to the black clothing. His eyes were wild, puffy and glistening wet, his lips swollen from being bitten, oozing with blood.

Rina gasped and backed away. Then she thought of something.

"Oh my God!" she cried out. "Matt Hawthorne. He was walking me home. He heard something and went looking in the bushes."

"Where is he?" Decker pressed his knee into the small of Gilbert's back.

"Near the oaks," Gilbert mumbled. "Where those kids killed the black woman."

"Did you kill him?"

Decker saw that creepy half smile spread across his lips. A sudden burst of blood poured out of his nose down to his chin.

"If I did, it was unintentional," he said, giggling.

Decker smashed his face against the car.

Marge pulled Gilbert from Decker's grasp and shoved him to the ground. She bent down, cuffed his feet, turned him over onto his stomach, and pointed her gun at his head.

"Go look for Hawthorne," she told her partner.

Go cool off was the message.

Decker rubbed his hands over his face and looked at Rina. Her clothes were in shreds. The beautiful face was mangled, bruised, and scraped – her forehead, nose, lips and chin were bleeding, her left jaw already swollen to three times its normal size. Marge saw the look on his face, noticed his hand inch toward his holster.

"Don't even think about it, Pete," she said firmly. "Go look for Hawthorne."

He nodded and walked away.

"You are one lucky fucker," she said when Decker was

267

out of earshot. "He almost blew you away, and I almost didn't stop him."

Marge read him his rights and asked if he understood what she had said.

Gilbert laughed, then cried, then shoved his face into the dirt.

"From dust we came!" he cried out, spitting dirt. His mouth drooled a muddy trail.

"You don't understand. It was her fault!" he screamed suddenly, face purple with rage. The veins on his neck bulged and pulsated. "She did it to me. She had this power over me! She could have helped, but she didn't. She rejected me, just like all the rest of them. She said it was because I wasn't Jewish, but I knew the truth. She was laughing behind my back at me. I know she was. She *made* me unable to function. They all did. They all laughed at me."

He broke into tears.

"I'm so sorry, Rina. If you would have just given me a chance . . . If someone would have given me a chance. But the goddam bitches won't give an inch."

He struggled violently against the restraints.

"Do you understand that she has the *power!*" he screamed. "She could have used it for my benefit. A daughter of Judeah! The daughter of Zion! She is the magician and knows the art of healing, just as her ancestors before her. She is the daughter of Miriam, the great healer. Even her name is Miriam. But instead of helping me, she zapped me. She made me useless as a man. They all did. But I'd show her. If she wasn't going to give it to me, I was going to take it. If she hadn't laughed behind my back, telling me bull . . ." He began to stutter. "It's b-b-bullshit! She was *using* her Jewishness as an excuse. The truth was she was laughing at me. But I saw through it. The b-b-bitch. If she wouldn't have given me b-b-bullshit, I wouldn't have gotten mad. B-b-but she did. S-s-so I was going to get it. I was going to get it whether she liked it or not."

His face grew distorted, and he started to sob.

"Oh, God! Oh, my God, I'm so, so sorry!"

A wacko, Marge thought and turned away in disgust. She heard chanting, looked up, and saw Moshe fifteen feet away. The thin, ghostlike man had come through. Yet here he was, head buried in a book, chanting to himself while swaying back and forth, acting as if nothing had happened.

Another wacko, she thought.

The good wacko and the bad wacko.

A moment later a black-and-white pulled up. Folstrom and Walsh got out.

"Caught him in the act?" Walsh asked grimly.

"More or less," Marge answered. "You take over. I want to talk to the victim."

"Who's he?" Folstrom asked, pointing to Moshe.

"The hero."

"Should I get a statement?" Folstrom asked.

"You can try, but he's a little . . ." Marge made a circle with her index finger around the side of her head.

Rina was huddled under an elm tree. Her knees were drawn tightly to her chin, arms clasped around her shins, as if embracing herself.

Marge walked over and sat down beside her.

"I called an ambulance."

Rina nodded.

Marge placed her arm around her shoulder.

"It looks like it's over."

The tears began to fall down Rina's cheeks, stinging her wounds. When she spoke it was barely above a whisper.

"How can you work with someone day after day, for five years, and be so oblivious to what goes on in his head?"

"Don't blame yourself," Marge comforted. "A lot of crazies maintain. They hold jobs, have families, and slip by the police, the shrinks – all the so-called experts who should know better. I've had a couple of real foolers myself."

She shrugged, then patted Rina's shoulder.

"You did terrific, kiddo. I couldn't have done better myself."

Rina didn't respond.

Marge knew she was still in shock. She saw Decker walking down the hillside, helping a limping man. Another black-and-white pulled up, then a transport. They threw Gilbert into the back. The boys from the yeshiva began to drift over, and she saw she had a job to do. She excused herself politely and walked over to Decker and Hawthorne.

"Are you okay, sir?" she asked Hawthorne.

Matt glared at Gilbert in the backseat of the transport.

"I can't believe it," Hawthorne said. "I just can't believe it. There must be a logical explanation. There must be some mistake."

"There's no mistake," Marge said.

"Shit," Hawthorne muttered, rubbing his head. His forehead was raised and red, sporting a bluish lump. "Rina! Is she okay?"

"She'll live," said Marge.

Luis Ramirez pulled up and got out of his patrol car. Decker motioned him over.

"Mr Hawthorne, this is Officer Ramirez," he said. "If you're up to it, you can give him a statement while you're waiting for the ambulance to come."

Hawthorne nodded, still stunned.

"Why don't you come with me, sir?" said Ramirez. "You can sit down in the backseat of the patrol car. You'll be more comfortable."

Hawthorne acquiesced. A moment later the transport vehicle, with Gilbert inside, sped away.

Decker stared at the throng that had assembled.

"Where's Rina?" he asked Marge.

"Over there," she said pointing to the tree. "She's bruised, but she'll be okay. She's a tough lady, Pete."

270

He walked over and sat down beside her, but she didn't acknowledge him. He was suddenly tongue-tied, thinking only of how much he wanted to hold her, how he wanted to make it all go away.

Finally, she spoke:

"Help me up."

He lifted her in his arms and held her for a moment. Her face . . . what the bastard had done to her beautiful face . . .

He let her down on her feet as gently as he could.

"What should I do with this?" she asked, holding up the gun. "It belongs to *him*."

Decker pulled out a handkerchief, took the gun from her, emptied the barrel, and wrapped it up.

"I fired at him, so it's minus a bullet."

He nodded.

"I missed him."

"I'm surprised you did."

"So am I," she said.

Decker saw Zvi Adler approaching, looked at Rina, and realized suddenly that she was half naked. He slipped off his jacket and gave it to her.

She smiled weakly.

Zvi stopped ten feet in front of them. His face bore a painful look of déjà-vu.

"Oh, my God," he said softly, tears in his eyes.

"I'm okay."

He looked as if he wanted to say more.

"Can I do anything?" he asked her after a moment.

"My boys!" she gasped. "They can't see me like this!"

"We'll keep them for as long as it takes," Zvi said softly.

"Tell them the truth – that I had to go to the hospital for a check-up. I'll call as soon as I get there." She swallowed back tears. "They mustn't worry about me. They've gone through enough already."

"They won't, Rina. I promise you."

"Thank you."

"Are you sure I can't – "

"No. Nothing else. Just take care of my boys."

"Rina," he whispered gently. "Come over for Shabbos."

"Okay," she said, her voice breaking.

Zvi turned to Decker and offered him his hand.

"Thank you, Detective. How did you do it?"

"I didn't," Decker said. "It was Rina and Moshe – "

"*Moshe?*" said Zvi. "Moshe caught the *mamzer?*"

"Rina and Moshe," Decker corrected.

But Zvi was off. Running over to the rocking man, he embraced him warmly, hefted him onto his shoulders, and began to sing in a rich baritone. Soon others joined in and a circle formed around the two of them. The dance began, and within minutes the woods were filled with deep male voices and loud stomping.

"They seem to have forgotten about you," said Decker.

"It's okay." She was weeping and laughing at the same time. "It's easier for Zvi to deal with Moshe than me. My face must have frightened him off."

She tried to smile at him, but instead her lips quivered, turned downward, and her face fell. He took her in his arms and pulled her to his breast.

'It hurts," she sobbed. "My head feels as if it's going to explode."

"We're going to fix you up, honey," Decker said, embracing her. "You're going to be fine."

"I'll never be fine," she wailed.

"Yes, you will. I promise, Rina, you'll be fine."

"Oh, God!" she cried out in pain. She lifted her head and looked at him. "I'm going to miss you so!"

She sobbed on his chest while hugging him tightly.

"That hurts most of all," she wept in anguish.

Decker pushed her hair off her forehead.

"Hey, come on now," he whispered. "I'm not going anywhere."

She buried her head in his arms and clung to him tightly, finding security in his touch.

272

She felt a hand on her shoulder, looked up, and saw Chana.

"Come on, Rina," the woman said firmly. "The ambulance is here. I'll help you."

"In a minute," Rina said, wiping her tears on Decker's shirt.

"Mr Hawthorne is waiting – "

"I said in a minute," Rina snapped at the woman.

"*Ze lo yafeh*," Chana said.

"*Yafeh lo shayach po.*"

Chana threw up her hands and walked away.

Rina leaned her head on Peter's chest.

"She disapproves of my hugging you," she explained to him. "She said it wasn't *nice*."

"What did you tell her?"

"I told her *nice* wasn't important now." She brought his hand to her lips and kissed his fingers, one by one.

"I want to ride with you to the hospital," Decker said.

She shook her head.

"But I want to go."

"No," Rina answered. "I need to be alone. I need time to think. I just don't want to let go of you. Not just yet."

"As far as I'm concerned, you don't ever have to let go."

She said nothing.

Decker looked around. The crowd had become tumultuous – a mass of bodies singing and dancing. Men were on each others' shoulders. Others were spinning around in a circle, flying outward in centripetal motion. Never had he seen such unbridled jubilation. And in the center was Moshe, held high above the others, smiling, nodding, and mumbling to himself.

"Look," he said stroking her hair. "I'm taking a couple of days off to go camping in the mountains. God knows I can use a little peace and quiet. I know school starts in a week, so your kids are on their last leg of vacation. I'm not telling you what to do, and I'm going to go regardless of what you say, but, if you're willing, I wouldn't mind if the boys came along."

"I don't think so," she said, still hugging him.

He kissed her head.

"Okay. Whatever you say."

He touched her cheek and gently kissed her wounds. Closing her eyes, she ran her forefinger across his stubbled chin.

"You'll need kosher food for them," she whispered.

"So I'll buy kosher food."

"I don't know . . ."

Decker didn't push her. The last thing in the world she needed was to be talked into something. Besides, he knew that she, like he, would have to make her own decisions in her own time.

"I'll let you know, Peter," she said, breaking away reluctanctly. "One way or the other, I promise I'll call you."

"Do that."

She looked at the ambulance.

"I've got to go."

"Let me walk you – "

"No. I can make it on my own."

She cast a perfunctory glance over her shoulder, stood on her tiptoes, and kissed him lightly on the lips.

He watched her walk away and disappear inside the rear of the waiting ambulance. The doors slid shut, and she was gone. Decker sat down under the tree, pulled out a cigarette, and reached for a match, but found his pockets bare. So he stared at the crowd, holding an unlit cigarette between his thumb and middle finger.

A tall, thin figure materialized – the Rosh Yeshiva was coming his way, immaculately dressed as always and sure-footed. The old man took off his homburg, revealing thick white hair, readjusted the oversized black yarmulke that had been underneath the hat, and placed the hat back atop his head. Decker started to stand as he approached, but the rabbi motioned him back down and sat down next to him under the tree.

"Need a light, detective?" Schulman asked.

"If you don't mind."

The Rosh Yeshiva lit two of his hand-rolled cigarettes and gave one to Decker.

"Thank you," he said. "Some crowd, huh Rabbi?"

"We Jews have a penchant for the extremes of the emotional spectrum. We know how to mourn, we know how to rejoice. This is as much for Moshe as it is for the capture of Gilbert."

When he mentioned the teacher's name, the Rosh Yeshiva shook his head sadly.

"There was no way to know about Gilbert, Rabbi."

"True, my boy. Only *Hashem* is omniscient, and until He decides we're worthy of His communication via prophets or the Messiah, we mortals are forced to live in a state of ignorance. I've spent my whole life learning, Detective, acquiring knowledge not only from the scriptures of my belief, but from countless other sources – American law, philosphy, psychology, economics, political science: I have studied them all at great length. Yet, a madman can slip under my nose, and I realize I know nothing. I am still a meaningless speck of dust in the scheme of things. A most humbling experience."

"I know the feeling well," Decker said, smiling.

"It is good for the soul to be humbled," the old man said. "It forces one to take stock."

The detective nodded.

"Did you tell Rina Miriam about your background?" The Rosh Yeshiva asked.

"No."

Schulman sucked on his cigarette.

"Do you intend to tell her?"

"Not until I know how I feel. I can't call myself Jewish unless I know what that means. Otherwise, I'm not being honest with her – or myself."

"Are you interested in learning what it means?"

275

"I haven't been able to think about it until this guy was captured."

"And now?"

The big man shrugged.

"I think I'll take it a day at a time, Rabbi."

"Would you care to join the men in dance, Peter?"

"No thank you, Rabbi," he answered, self-consciously, "I'd probably step on my own toes."

"As long as you don't step on mine . . ."

The detective smiled.

"I still think I'll pass. But thank you for the invitation. I feel honored."

The men sat in silence and watched the crowd.

"Detective," the Rabbi said, nudging him in the ribs, "we've got company."

A hoard of television and newspaper reporters were about to converge upon them, lugging tripods, video cameras, Nikons, and microphones.

"You may do as you please," Rav Schulman said, standing up. "As for me, I'm going to dance."

Decker rose as they approached: pencils poised, microphones thrust forward – invading Huns, ready for battle. He brushed off his pants and turned to the old man.

"Okay, Rabbi. Show me what to do."

JEREMIAH HEALY

BLUNT DARTS

A kid had gone missing.

Run off? Maybe. Kidnapped? Possible. Still somewhere local or out of state? No telling – not when the trail is two weeks cold and there's no hard evidence of anything.

Not when his father, the Judge, doesn't even want an investigation. When there's no mother to worry since she'd died mysteriously a while back. And when the local police make it clear that private investigator John Cuddy is the sort of stranger they don't want in town.

Only the kid's grandmother and the kid's school teacher seemed to care – along with John Cuddy. Who was being well paid and who had already caught a whiff of a very nasty small town scandal . . .

'The plotting is impeccable, and everything comes together to make *Blunt Darts* one of the outstanding first mysteries of the year'

The New York Times

'A splendid debut performance'

Financial Times

HODDER AND STOUGHTON PAPERBACKS

IAN RANKIN

KNOTS AND CROSSES

It's frightening . . . And in Edinburgh of all places, I mean, you never think of that sort of thing happening in Edinburgh, do you?

Already two young girls have been abducted and killed. now a third is missing. Nothing in common between them: different areas, different circumstances. A random killer.

Polite, self-regarding Edinburgh is in a state of shock. All police leave is cancelled; the reporters gather like vultures.

Meanwhile Detective Sergeant John Rebus, smoking and drinking too much, his wife gone taking their own young daughter, has another, more personal puzzle on his hands. Someone is sending him taunting, anonymous letters with little pieces of knotted string and matchstick crosses.

Annoying but hardly very important. Not when a cold, methodical killer is stalking the frightened streets . . .

'Quite brilliant and enormously compelling.

Martyn Goff

'Highly recommended'

Literary Review

'Rebus is a fine creation'

H. R. F. Keating

HODDER AND STOUGHTON PAPERBACKS

B. M. GILL

DYING TO MEET YOU

Embittered ex-brilliant concert pianist Lowell Marshall feels strangely drawn to the rundown cottage that a surprise legacy has made him owner. His fascination is too strong to be explained away in ordinary terms.

He discovers a long forgotten sepia portrait of a young Victorian woman who once lived there and falls obsessively in love with her. When Rose, her contemporary real life double, walks in on him one day his sense of time begins to blur and his grip on reality weakens. Is she of the past or of the present? That the delightful, if bizarre, liaison with her might be dangerous doesn't occur to him. He has never been happier. All those violent impulses he once found hard to control have gone.
Or have they . . .?

'Dark toned, claustrophobic suspense'

The Guardian

'A chilling tale'

The Times

HODDER AND STOUGHTON PAPERBACKS

MORE TITLES AVAILABLE FROM HODDER AND STOUGHTON PAPERBACKS

	JEREMIAH HEALY	
☐ 43073 7	Blunt Darts	£2.50
	IAN RANKIN	
☐ 48766 6	Knots and Crosses	£2.50
	B. M. GILL	
☐ 48837 9	Dying to Meet You	£2.50

All these books are available at your local bookshop or newsagent, or can be ordered direct from the publisher. Just tick the titles you want and fill in the form below.

Prices and availability subject to change without notice.

HODDER AND STOUGHTON PAPERBACKS,
P.O. Box 11, Falmouth, Cornwall.

Please send cheque or postal order, and allow the following for postage and packing:

U.K. – 55p for one book, plus 22p for the second book, and 14p for each additional book ordered up to a £1.75 maximum.

B.F.P.O. and EIRE – 55p for the first book, plus 22p for the second book, and 14p per copy for the next 7 books, 8p per book thereafter.

OTHER OVERSEAS CUSTOMERS – £1.00 for the first book, plus 25p per copy for each additional book.

NAME ....

ADDRESS ....

PERTH & KINROSS DISTRICT LIBRARIES
....